OUR
LAST
NIGHT

An edge-of-your-seat ghost story thriller

TAYLOR ADAMS

JOFFE
BOOKS

aug 2023

Published 2016 by Joffe Books, London.

www.joffebooks.com

© Taylor Adams

ISBN- 978-1-911021-35-3

FOREWORD

I'm only including this foreword because the lawyer says I have to. I'm required to state that the bizarre and horrific events described herein are complete fiction, and that they definitely did not occur in Farwell, Idaho, over a twenty-four hour period between March 19 and March 20 of 2015.

Part I

READY TO FIRE

. . . As the winter of 1941 descended, the under-equipped and desperate German Wehrmacht often resorted to scavenging Soviet Red Army coats and weapons. In one skirmish near Demyansk, a squad-strength German force mysteriously abandoned a superior position — allowing the surprised Reds to take the hill without resistance. At the summit they found three Wehrmacht soldiers slain by self-inflicted gunshot wounds and a stolen Soviet rifle. The others had scrawled a message and tied it around the barrel: *Bitte, nehmen Sie es zuruck.* (Please, take it back)

Excerpt from "Cursed Objects of the New Century" (W. Louis), published by Haunted Inn Press in 2002.

Northern Idaho

March 19, 2015

The rifle was wrapped in plastic when he handed it to me. A rumpled, sock-like sleeve, opaque with smeared oil — the firearm equivalent of a body bag.

The old man looked at me. "You know what this is, right?"

I played dumb. "An M44?"

It was an M91/30 Mosin Nagant, over eighty years old and still ready to fire. These vintage battle rifles were once mass-produced in the millions, until the Soviet Union decommissioned them decades ago. A spike bayonet folds along the barrel, like a black coffin nail. The stock is birch wood. It's a bolt-action weapon, which means that after every shot, the user cranks a hand-powered mechanism to eject the spent cartridge and feed another. Even if the technology is antiquated, something about the Russian design is visually striking — even to non-gun enthusiasts like myself. It's clunky and stiff, but also strangely sleek. Strangely predatory.

"It's a blood gun," he said with knobby hands on the counter.

"What?"

"A blood gun."

"What's that?"

His eyes hardened. "It killed someone."

More than one, actually.

But I feigned surprise and set the rifle back on the counter, where it clanked uncomfortably on brittle glass. Joe's Guns was curiously empty this Friday morning, so nobody turned and looked. Talk radio murmured about Obamacare in the back office. This place catered to the *Call of Duty* crowd more than the traditional sportsman; the aisles were stocked with tactical (i.e. black) versions of everything, from range bags to socks, and the wall of rifles bristled with expensive optics, lasers, and a Vietnam-era grenade launcher that I suspected wasn't a replica.

The old clerk squinted at me. "Do I know you?"

"Nope."

"You look familiar."

I nodded at the Mosin. "Do you take debit?"

He laughed. I wasn't joking.

Resting between us, the antique rifle was looking more and more like a bagged corpse. Brown and earwax-yellow clotted the plastic in gooey bunches. I could smell the preserving agent Russian armory workers had bathed the parts in decades ago; a sweet petroleum odor, like hard candy soaked in motor oil. Cosmoline, I think it's called.

He looked at it, then at me. "Seriously?"

"Seriously."

"Why this one? Stock is carved up. Bore is pitted. Mosin Nagants are already the prawns of the gun world, but this one's uglier than a daytime hooker—"

"I'm not taking it to a beauty pageant."

"Yeah? If you're taking it out for whitetail, you'd be better off extending the bayonet and throwing it like a javelin—"

"I don't hunt."

"A target rifle, then? It might not even work."

I wondered if all firearm vendors were this abrasive. Then again, not all firearms had a body count. "I'd still like to buy it."

"Maybe you didn't hear me, son. This rifle *killed someone* last year. The previous owner stuck it in his mouth and blew his head off—"

"So it obviously works."

And it was under his chin. Not in his mouth.

For a long moment, we both stared at it in stalemate silence, and I half-expected the weapon to suddenly breathe and crinkle the bag. Then the old man deflated a bit. He didn't have a nametag, but I could discern from the trophy photos on the wall — he wasn't the eponymous Joe of Joe's Guns.

"The victim's family in Georgia is technically making the sale," Not Joe grunted. "Our store is just the middleman. The FFL-holder."

I was only half-listening. I knew all this already.

"I didn't know the victim," he said. "But I knew *of* him. Ben Dyson. He ran a semi-popular gun blog. His thing was obtaining crappy, century-old surplus rifles from the World Wars for dirt cheap. Mosins, Enfields, Arisakas. Then he'd clean 'em up — install scopes, cozy pistol grips, fancy synthetic furniture — and then he'd sell 'em for twice what he paid. Kind of like flipping houses."

I ran a hand over the bagged rifle. Wood and metal bones wrapped in a slimy, semi-transparent skin. As the legend went, this particular antique rifle didn't take kindly to being accessorized like a Barbie doll. Not that it had taken kindly to any of its past owners.

"I followed Dyson's blog." Not Joe chewed his lip. "So I saw his last post, the afternoon he shot himself."

"What did he write?"

"It was weird. Just one sentence—"

A bell dinged. Another customer entered behind me.

The old man looked up, then back at me, lowering his voice: "Look, I don't really want to talk about it. If you just *have* to know, I recommend trying this exciting new invention called Google."

Sarcasm. That was new on him.

"Are you buying the rifle or not?" he asked.

I touched the Mosin Nagant's twelve-inch spike bayonet through the milky plastic. It was folded along the barrel but the bladed, screwdriver-like tip was still honed to a vicious needlepoint. You could pierce a beer can with one good jab. And God only knows the species of foreign bacteria wriggling on its surface.

"Yes or no?"

"Yes."

The old man sighed. "Can I convince you not to?"

"You're sure trying."

"Honestly, it just gives me the creeps. Not just because it's a blood gun. I've seen those before. This . . . this is something else. It turns my stomach, just standing five feet from it. The air curdles around it, like milk left out in the sun. It feels . . . I don't know. It feels radioactive somehow, like being near it takes away a piece of you."

He's just trying to scare me.

I held up a palm but didn't feel any evil radiation coming off it. Just the musty odor of gun preservative and ancient solvent.

"I kept it in the bag the Dyson widow mailed it in," he said. "I haven't physically touched it, with my bare skin, since it arrived. And I never will."

"Okay."

"I'm also not selling you any cartridges for it."

"Understood."

"And I swear to God, you'd better not shoot up a shopping mall with it."

I shrugged. "If so, I'd be better off throwing it like a javelin, right?"

Not Joe didn't laugh.

The new customer was hovering with his hands in his pockets by the wall of luxurious black rifles (the Lexus of the gun world, apparently), so Not Joe huffed and scooted a handful of yellow paperwork at me before moving on. The pens here had little *Don't Tread on Me* flags. I listened to the two men talk while I initialed boxes on the carbon-paper NICS background-check forms. When I knew the old man wasn't looking, I leaned forward and pressed the sticky plastic flat against the Mosin Nagant to read the serial numbers engraved on the barrel. I matched this to the writing on my palm, scribbled earlier that morning in black Sharpie: B5066.

This was the one. No doubts left.

I found you.

But this antiquated weapon didn't seem haunted or cursed. Nothing felt off-kilter or wrong to me. The air wasn't curdling around it (can air even curdle?). It was just a battered hunk of ancient wood and milled metal, surprisingly heavy but surprising in no other way. For all the gory photographs and digital campfire stories, it was still just a gun. An object. Hard to believe it made W. Louis's book.

"Yo." The other customer eyed the bag. "Is that a Mosin?"

I nodded. "Good eye."

"Good gun." He grinned wolfishly. "That's Ruskie tech — ugly and beautiful at the same time. Helped 'em boot the Krauts back to Berlin. Did you know that during the Space Race, they shot the first dog into orbit?"

I shook my head. His breath was aggressively foul, even at ten feet, which must've been some kind of record. An acrid ammonia stench, like cat litter clumped with urine (so maybe air *can* curdle).

"Dog's name was Laika." He shouldered a black rifle with a holographic sight and aimed it at the wall. "She was this cute husky-terrier. The Soviets, they crammed Laika into a three-foot pressurized capsule, Sputnik II, and fired her off into space. After they made human history, you know how they brought little Laika back down to earth?"

I shook my head again.

He dry-fired with a click. "They didn't."

The old man snatched the paperwork from under my hand, startling me. Then Joe's Guns ran my background check through a nineties-era landline, and in ten minutes, the Mosin Nagant was mine for a total of two-hundred-and-four dollars. It was the first firearm I'd ever purchased. I had zero interest in shooting paper targets with it, or cans, or whitetail. Or myself, if that's what you're thinking.

I carried it out in a taped cardboard box.

"Shoot safe," Not Joe said as I left. It was probably a standard parting phrase, but to me it sounded like a barbed joke.

The Ben Dyson suicide stuff was all true, but it was only the beginning. The real gruesome business happened on the other side of the ocean, before the Mosin even reached our American civilian market. Not Joe didn't know about it. If he had, he wouldn't have sold me the rifle at all.

He'd also missed a small tertiary detail — before Mr. Dyson mail-ordered this Mosin Nagant as a cheapie to be cannibalized, it spent several years sitting mothballed in a warehouse in West Virginia. A forklift driver who worked the graveyard shift there apparently walked off his shift one night and drove home. His wife awoke to find him standing in their driveway at 3 a.m., in a strange trance, chugging what she thought was a two-liter bottle of diet cola. Until she got closer and read the container — concentrated lye solution. The stuff they sanitize industrial ovens with. He was a walking DOA by the time the paramedics arrived, his lips turning bubbly red, his organs dissolving. But, you never know — that could just be unrelated, right?

9

I didn't believe in ghosts. Or curses. Or poltergeists. Or demons, or possessions, or any of the pleasant fantasies we like to scare ourselves with. That's not horror — that's wish fulfillment. Because even the cruelest, most heinous supernatural terrors imply a higher order. You can't fear the devil without also acknowledging God.

I'd been searching for God for a while now.

Not Joe must've recognized my name from the NICS check, because as I stepped outside into the parking lot, he called through the swinging door. "Wait, I *knew it*. Dan! You're one of the guys from the ghost-hunting show on channel eleven, right?"

I let the door close. I hadn't been on *Haunted* in over two months. This was my extended leave of absence, after what happened on New Year's Eve.

"Asshole," I heard him grumble.

I carried it out into the parking lot under a watery sky. I put the rifle in my trunk. As I climbed into my black Toyota Celica, I fumbled for my phone and set a countdown timer, beginning now. Twenty-four hours: BEEP.

24:00:00

23:59:59

23:59:58 . . .

I'd almost forgotten — but according to the original Russian legend, no owner of this cursed rifle had ever survived longer than a single day. So there's that.

Thus far, this quirk had held true in America, too. Exactly twenty-four hours after Ben Dyson signed a little UPS tablet for his mail order, his wife heard a concussive bang from his workshop. She'd found him with the Mosin Nagant cradled in his lap and a 7.62 mm hole in the ceiling. Through some minor miracle of physics, he'd remained seated on his stool. The photos were all digitally scrubbed of gore, but you could see browned blood speckling the workbench, dripping down solvent bottles and Ziploc bags bulging with brass casings. A camouflage hat on the floor. His laptop was there, too, but it was pixelated by a censor. Meaning a chunk of Mr. Dyson's scalp had likely landed on it. The cops and medics on the scene were all wearing shorts and tees darkened with sweat; it had been over a hundred-and-five degrees, mid-August under a blistering Georgia sun.

Minutes before putting the barrel under his chin, Dyson had logged into his WordPress blog and typed: SO COLD IN HERE.

As I drove home with that very same rifle in my trunk, the first flecks of snow hit my windshield. With my phone quietly counting down in my pocket, I promised myself that if in the next twenty-four hours I couldn't find anything legitimately supernatural with this old, Russian *blood gun*, I'd stop searching forever.

And move on.

23 Hours, 11 Minutes

"Dan, this is the dumbest thing you've ever done," Holden said.

I stopped mid-sentence. I hadn't even told him about the lye.

Holden H. Hume was a crucial element to our *Haunted* investigative team: the true believer. The heart and soul. The one your mom probably likes. Holden can't cross the street without having a paranormal encounter. You name it, he probably believes in it. He's the only guy I know who could go out hiking to search for Bigfoot, and spot the Jersey Devil on the drive out there. He's also my best friend, which is why I was telling him — and only him — about this.

And this was a bizarre reversal. When the DVC tapes were rolling, I was usually the one ridiculing *his* ideas.

"This isn't for *Haunted*," I clarified. "This is just for me."

We'd met for coffee at Jitters, a little place in downtown Farwell known for its superb Mexican hot chocolate and godawful live poetry readings. After what happened on New Year's Eve, this had become a weekly ritual of ours. Through Windex-streaked windows we watched eighteen-wheelers haul dismantled chunks of blue papier-mâché ox; debris from last weekend's Winter Bunyan Days. The snow kept falling but didn't stick, swirling on updrafts like dry cotton.

Holden stirred his pale drink. It was more creamer than coffee. "So . . . what equipment do you need to check out?"

I sipped mine — jet black. "Nothing."

"Not even a camera?"

"Like I said. This is just for me."

Holden made a sour face.

Yes, I was jaded, but I'd never actually seen a ghost before. And eighteen months of televised ghost hunting had given me a healthy disrespect for all the flashy tech vendors that sponsored our website. It's basically electronic cloud-watching. On *Haunted* we'd hit our possessed motels and lighthouses fully loaded with full-spectrum cameras for infrared night vision, electromagnetic field detectors for spiritual 'hot spots,' and microphones for electronic voice phenomena. Overnight we'd record hours of raw footage and our bafflingly enthusiastic production assistants would then comb through terabytes of digital slush, searching with bloodshot eyes for the odd creak or incongruous shadow. And sure, we'd find them, usually at least one per episode to keep the viewers (and, more importantly, the Nielsen ratings diaries) happy. But anomalies are cheap, and still explainable. I wasn't after anomalies.

Now that I'd tracked down the Moby Dick of haunted objects, the cursed Soviet rifle that W. Louis's book had declared to be 'the single most infamous military relic since the Spear of Destiny,' I sure as hell wasn't going to settle for an electronic fart on an EMF meter.

"So . . ." Holden looked guilty and stared up at the warm paper lights hanging from Jitters' ceiling of exposed ductwork. They looked like CGI pollen from an allergy medicine commercial. "LJ is wondering if you want in on the Old Briar Mine investigation. We'll meet at the park-and-ride, tomorrow at noon—"

"Old Briar," I said. "That's the one with the ghost of the coal miner with the black tar gurgling from his eye sockets. Right?"

"No." He read off his phone. "It's the . . . ghost of a screaming baby, carried around the tunnels by a floating, legless man."

"Meh. I'll pass."

He scrolled. "Over a dozen sightings. Sounds legit—"

"They always do."

"Are we really having this argument now?"

I shrugged. "Want to?"

"Disappointment Bay Lighthouse," Holden said with a flourish, dropping an invisible microphone. He needn't say more, because what our thermal camera had recorded on the summit of that rusty little lighthouse in Seaflats, Washington was the highlight of his career. Three orange-yellow splotches in a sea of cold blues.

"Just warm glass," I said, sipping my coffee.

"Warmed by what?"

"Probably the big-ass rotating light."

"Dan, I *heard* footsteps on those stairs."

"I didn't."

"You weren't there."

"I was," I said. "I was *everywhere* you were. I've spent the last eighteen months of my life with you and Kale and LJ, poking through every haunted house, haunted hotel, haunted lumber mill, haunted Hostess factory, haunted library, and haunted water treatment plant in the Pacific Northwest, and I have exactly zero paranormal experiences to show for it. So maybe . . . maybe it's just you, Holden."

Dusty snow flurried outside, blowing sideways down the street.

I shouldn't have said that. It was different when the cameras were on us and we were bickering over creaking floorboards and dust specks on the lens (excuse me, *orbs*). People watch ghost shows for that. It was part of an act; a contagious good humor powered by sulfurous energy drinks, fun company, and the adrenaline of exploring a deserted locale at night. I love the hunt. But here, right now, we were just old college friends having coffee and the words stung.

He softened. "I wish I could make you see the things I've seen."

I remembered the time he'd claimed to see the Mothman while taking out his trash, and I nodded sincerely. "Me, too."

When you lose a loved one, everyone else in your life swoops in to support you with hugs and cookies, and paradoxically, that's the single loneliest feeling I've ever experienced. Family and coworkers grin like teary-eyed Cheshire Cats and tell you *it's okay, everything's okay, you'll be okay* — but that only made me feel guilty for mourning her death. Like I needed to forget her, catch up with everyone else, and climb aboard the Everything's Okay Train before it left the station. You can't fast-forward through grief; it's a multi-stage process and step one is being *not okay*. Step one is suffering.

Holden understood this. He knew I smelled her old shirts and listened to her old voicemails. Yes, he pressured me in other ways (since I'd been stuck on step one for almost three months now), but he never, *ever* tried to tell me that everything was okay, because he knew it wasn't.

Leave it to the guy who believed in Bigfoot, I guess.

He turned now to watch Paul Bunyan's grinning, severed head drive by, caged by two-by-fours. Holden's a big guy; he looked a little bit like a blonde giant himself, clutching a teacup of Jitters coffee. "As for your new gun," he said. "Well, haunted objects are generally bad."

I gulped my coffee. "So I've heard."

"Evil and matter are entwined, pretty much by definition," he said. "To accept God means to let go of the material, the tactile. The worldly things. So if you've got a spirit clinging to a physical object like a gun, dug into it like a hermit crab . . . well, it's almost a guarantee that it's gonna be an asshole."

"Cool."

"Yeah, Dan. This . . . *thing* you just purchased could be a lot more dangerous than some haunted lighthouse."

"Also, it's a gun."

"Hopefully, I wasn't putting too fine a point on it when I told you this is the dumbest thing you've ever done."

"It's certainly cracked the top ten."

His eyes narrowed. "How long since you bought it?"

"One hour."

"That gives you—"

"Twenty-three."

Survive the next twenty-three hours to beat Ben Dyson's record. Easy, right?

"Jesus." He shuddered, like an electric current had just slithered up his spine. He popped the cap off his keychain inhaler and took a pressurized hit. "And after all of that, you still don't believe it's haunted?"

I couldn't lie. I shrugged.

"Why'd you buy it, then?"

Again, I shrugged. "I . . . I think that if there's really an afterlife, if we really go somewhere after we die, then that ugly old Mosin Nagant is my best chance at finding proof. Real proof."

"That'd look funny on your tombstone."

"Seriously. It's got the nastiest, most disturbing background story of anything I've ever seen. More than any site we've ever tapped for *Haunted*. If the guy at Joe's Guns knew about the weapon's history back in Russia, he'd be exorcist-shopping. With all the nightmare fuel I've read about this rifle, if I don't personally witness something paranormal in the next . . ." I checked my cracked iPhone. ". . . Twenty-two hours and fifty-eight minutes, then souls and ghosts *don't exist*. Period."

Someone clicked a microphone stand. I remembered it was Friday; some truly rancid poetry would soon fill the air like tear gas. More Bunyan Days bits and pieces trucked past the windows, heavy tires rattling the glass, but Holden just stared into me, clutching his milkshake coffee with two hands. Call Holden a kook all you want — but don't you dare call him stupid. He knew what I was really saying: *I have to know.*

I have to know if I'll see her again.

"I'm coming," he finally said.

"Coming where?"

"To your house."

"Why?"

"I can't leave you alone with it."

I shrugged. "I'm fine."

"Dan, you just bought a *suicide gun*."

"Yes, but for a non-suicide purpose."

"That depends," he said icily.

At that same moment, a barista was scrawling something on the blackboard menu and the chalk broke. Her thumbnail scraped the blackboard. The hellish squeal made everyone in the coffee shop flinch.

A tumor of strange, irrational fear took hold in my stomach. My mind darted to, of all things, the censored chunk of Mr. Dyson's scalp that had plopped onto his laptop keyboard, where he'd typed his last blog post to over six thousand followers. Had he been prone to suicidal thoughts? My phone still obediently counted time in my pocket. The gun was mine now; you can't put the pin back in the grenade. For a wobbly half-second, I wondered if I was ready to be proven wrong on this.

I have a fail-safe, I reminded myself. *And besides—*

"Tonight," Holden said abruptly. "My car's already loaded for Old Briar tomorrow. So we'll have the full-

17

spectrum camera, the EMF meter, and audio. We'll ghost-hunt that little Russian bastard, just you and me, and assuming you found the right rifle, maybe we'll find your paranormal proof. Obviously no bullets in the house or anything?"

"Obviously," I lied.

And besides, ghosts aren't real.

"It'll be just like the good old days, Dan-O, before we sold out and went Hollywood."

I smiled. The pitted streets and toothpick trees of Farwell, Idaho were a long way from Tinseltown.

"And speaking of . . ." he checked his phone again. "Gotta beat the dead horse one last time. Motion is life. We need you back on *Haunted* before the April sweeps. LJ is sick of making it a two-man show. He says you can take all the time you need, I know, but yesterday I saw him interviewing fill-ins for your—"

"*Motion is life*," I echoed. "Cute. Did you make that up?"

"No," he said sourly. "Hippocrates did."

Something went unsaid, passing between us like electricity. The rush of displaced air following a near miss.

He'd almost mentioned Adelaide.

Sent: 3/19 2:59PM
Sender: dskagit23@webmail
Subject: Viewer Feedback (redirect)

Dear Dan,

So sorry for your loss. Ive been a loyal viewer of haunted ever since that first pilot and I hope to see u on it again soon. Luckily with all the ghosts your team has found, u of all people know that an afterlife really exists, and that your fiancée is waiting for you on the other side.

You'll see her again.

-ds

21 Hours, 48 Minutes

Grieving isn't what I expected. You don't see your loved one's face wherever you go, haunting you on billboards and strangers. That's a cliché. The reality is simpler, less melodramatic, and far worse. You just start to forget.

So, in a way, it felt like I was already running out of time.

I unlocked my front door and carried the brown-boxed Mosin Nagant inside. The security system cooed: "Front door is ajar."

I shut it with my foot.

I was distracted. For weeks I'd been trying (and failing) to dream about her, and to trigger a lucid dream, you're supposed to focus on a specific thought as you fall asleep. Memories are best. The secret to fish-hooking a memory into your subconscious? Repetition, repetition, repetition.

So a few times a day I'd daydream about the night I first met Adelaide Radnor, back at the 2011 Halloween FrightFest on a boardwalk in Anacortes, Washington. Sense memories are a good start — the sharp odor of low tide, of barnacles and knotted kelp. Among the patrolling monster costumes and funnel cake stands, they had this low-budget version of a haunted house called the Total Darkness Maze, and it was exactly what it sounded like. You and your party fumble through a pitch-black plywood maze, groping your fingertips against walls lined with dangling eyeballs and rubber snakes. It's as terrifying as a broom closet and costs six dollars. It's only scary if you're claustrophobic — which Adelaide was.

No joke. She Incredible-Hulked her way out of that place. In her panic she'd broken down a weak section of plywood and somehow opened a locked maintenance door leading to an off-limits part of the dock. Don't ask how that's possible. I like to imagine her crashing through the cheap walls like the Kool-Aid Man.

Meanwhile, from the dark guts of the maze, I'd spotted the glow of outside harbor lights and assumed it was the exit, so I followed this blonde girl's path of destruction to the dock outside. We ended up in this storage area where all the costumed ghouls and zombies of FrightFest ducked out to smoke, and I remember blinking in the haze of foggy lights and seeing her for the first time; the girl I'd spend the next four years of my life with. She was doubled over the dock railing, hyperventilating into the salty Pacific air. In the harbor lights, her hair looked ash-white. I'm not ashamed that I noticed her legs first. She'd run her first half-marathon that summer, she later told me.

Then something tore in my hands. A ripping snarl—

Adelaide whirled to face me, startled—

The Mosin Nagant box. The mailing tape on the cardboard bottom gave out and the bagged Soviet rifle dropped to the floor—

"Shit—"

Back in my kitchen, circa 2015, I fumbled for it. Too late. The stock banged off the floor and left an eye-shaped bruise. I caught it on the bounce — grabbing the weapon

21

by its birch handguard, knuckles clenched — and I carried it to the dining-room table, cursing through my teeth.

She turned around.

No.

She didn't. It had been a daydream.

But she turned. Somehow, I saw her turn. It was impossible, but in some weird temporal bubble, a place neither remembered nor imagined, at once real and unreal, I was powerfully certain that my dead fiancée had heard the rifle tear through its box, and spun around and looked at me on that dock—

I was halfway to the table when I noticed the blood.

A spreading warmth in my palm. No pain, no discomfort, just *heat* where my skin was touching the rifle. Like hot soup, sticking between my fingers and dribbling down my wrist. My first thought was that the rifle's handguard had cracked open like a hollow clamshell and was leaking some kind of putrid, warm fluid. Even when I blinked and saw the fresh oxygenated blood on my skin, I had a hard time telling myself it was mine.

Mine. My blood.

She turned around. That was new.

Red drops tapped the floor, perfect little circles.

My mind shuttered, dizzy thoughts coming in blinks. I unwrapped my fingers from the weapon and identified the culprit. The Mosin's sinister bayonet, a whites-of-their-eyes CQB infantry weapon, had pierced the plastic. And the pad of my thumb. Still no pain. I couldn't see how deep, exactly, the ancient Soviet spike had gone — and then through the semi-transparent part of my thumbnail, I saw a black dot. Okay. Question answered.

The world wobbled. I tasted stomach acid in the back of my throat.

That synthetic voice: "Front door is ajar."

Our home alarm system does that sometimes — if you don't fully close the front door, the lock doesn't engage and it can be pushed open by the slightest change in air pressure. Obviously, I didn't give two shits about the front door right then.

I gritted my teeth and slid the seventy-year-old Soviet bayonet out of my thumb. Maybe it was the blur of shock, but I swore it took longer than it should have. Inches and inches of black metal kept coming out of me, like an optical illusion, like ribbons unfurling from a magician's sleeve, before the tip finally slurped out. The *pop* echoed up the veins in my arm. Still no real pain or discomfort, just the unsettling knowledge that it should hurt and didn't. My blood stained the Mosin Nagant's plastic bag in a gratuitous B-movie splash of shiny beads. I couldn't drop the rifle — that would leave another dent in the wood — so I leaned it against the fridge.

"Stay," I told it.

"Front door is ajar—"

"Shut up."

I saw her turn—

I reached the bathroom sink, my mind a churn of half-thoughts, and the first rolling wave of pain hit. Viciously sharp, like a scalpel jammed under my thumbnail. My knees jellied and I grabbed the sink. I hoped the antique bayonet hadn't left a shard in there, like stabbing yourself with a graphite pencil. I ran the faucet full blast, filling the sink bowl with pink water.

Tetanus? I doubted it. The blade wasn't rusty; too much Soviet preservative slopped on it. But I wondered what sorts of decades-old industrial solvents and chemicals had sloughed off inside my thumb. Circulating in my bloodstream right now.

A bang reverberated from the kitchen, startling me. The rifle must've fallen over anyway. Another dent.

"Front door is ajar."

From the living room I heard a reptilian hiss. Adelaide's pet lizard sometimes reacted to commotion.

In the fogging bathroom mirror I fought a stupid, crooked smile. It was kind of funny. I hadn't even taken the Mosin Nagant out of its mailing bag yet and it had already ruined my kitchen flooring and cost me half a thumbnail. Of course, I knew it was an accident and nothing supernatural. And, obviously, I'd only imagined Adelaide turning to face me on that dock; you can't affect a memory of 2011 with a loud noise from 2015. I was depressed, not crazy. But the adrenaline was intoxicating, and maybe — just maybe — this could turn into an interesting twenty-four hours.

What were Holden's words, back at Jitters?

Let's ghost-hunt this little Russian bastard.

Amen to that.

And as for my very first encounter with Adelaide Radnor, back on that FrightFest dock? The little area had no other exit, so I'd taken her hand and led her back into the claustrophobic plywood maze. She'd been reluctant but there was no other way. We had to backtrack. Backward is forward, I'd told her.

Backward is forward.

Outside, I heard the lope of a motor and gravel crunching underneath tires. Holden was here now.

* * *

"What happened to your hand?"

I'd mummified my thumb in a hasty bandage of gauze and scotch tape before coming out to meet him in my driveway. I didn't answer his question. I watched him pull something from his back seat, and it wasn't a camera bag. "What's that?"

He hoisted a weighty cardboard box over his shoulder. "A surprise."

He'd accidentally parked his Ford Explorer (affectionately nicknamed Dora, as in *Dora the Explorer*) on the planter where Adelaide had planned on growing pumpkins this spring. It was full of dry weeds. The eastern sky was cloudless, bruising purple through scraggly trees.

My breath curled in the porch light. It was cold enough out here to kill you, but it would take a while.

I led Holden up the steps and inside.

The security system chirped again: "Front door is ajar."

"Where's the rifle?" he asked.

I closed the door and made sure it shut all the way. "The kitchen."

But Holden hovered there in the foyer, sheepish, like a child in an antique store. I knew the feeling. This was the first time he'd been over since New Year's.

Yeah, I still had all of Adelaide's stuff in our house.

I didn't know what to keep or toss, so I just kept everything. I'm told you're not supposed to rush this part of the process, so in that respect I'm doing just fabulous. At night, the house felt like a museum. Every room had that posed look of a home décor section at Sears. It felt like every surface I touched, I left fingerprints on.

Holden gingerly pulled off his tennis shoes, right next to Adelaide's.

I wanted to explain to him that this was normal — I'd read online that it's perfectly natural to leave a dead spouse's belongings in plain view until you're ready to box them up — but honestly, coming up on three months, it didn't feel normal. It felt like denial. Or cowardice. I was embarrassed, and I think he was, too.

But grief is a process. It's surprising, and a little disturbing, how fast you scab over and grow numb to the major reminders. Her work-issued laptop became part of the coffee table, the battery long dead. Her stupid pet lizard became my stupid pet lizard. Framed photos of our trips to Astoria, Maui, and the Mount St. Helens blast zone ached, but only when you stopped to look at them. After a few weeks, it's all white noise. You gain some momentum and you think you're doing okay. Not good, because *good* is still months away, but *okay* is a reasonable goal.

Then last week I opened the fridge and saw her coffee creamer, caramel macchiato, sitting forgotten in the very back. It had gone chunky and sour. For some stupid reason, it was the expired half-quart of her favorite coffee creamer that nearly broke me. The subtle things blindside you like that. All of January, February, and March had been like this, some torturous inner circle of Hell, where you're forced to tediously rediscover the worst event of your life, over and over, from every oblique angle.

Like the junk mail. She's dead, and she gets more mail than I do. A monthly subscription for Exotic Pets, a warranty statement for her latest tablet, a student loan statement. She needs to renew her vehicle tabs in April. Good to know, right? The tedious clockwork of life just sort of grinds on.

Like Baby, Adelaide's pet savannah monitor, named after Jennifer Grey's character from *Dirty Dancing*. Perhaps I shouldn't call it a lizard, because *lizard* implies something small and amiable, like that gecko that sells insurance. Baby was almost five feet long. Let that sink in a moment — Adelaide's savannah monitor was bigger than some dogs. She'd been our 'practice-child,' and now she was my problem; a shambling, bow-legged dinosaur with a serpentine black tongue and a whip-like tail. Every two days I'd feed her a dead mouse (humanely pre-killed) with barbecue tongs and watch her shake it like a pit bull thrashing a chew toy. Then she throws her head back and swallows in these gurgling, goose-like motions. Thank God it was mammals that inherited the earth. That meteorite came just in time.

Still, during these weekly rituals I'd formed a bit of a grudging bond with Baby. We resented each other, but we both missed Addie. We suffered together, squatting in a house that had become a minefield of freeze-dried memories.

But the weird part?

I had never cried for Adelaide. Not once. Not even the night it happened. I suck at grieving, I guess, and perhaps it was just another form of procrastination. But like I said, I'm not good with emotions. I compartmentalize everything. Addie used to say that if you cracked my brain open you'd just find carefully organized Tupperware.

Acres and acres of Tupperware.

As Holden and I lingered in the foyer like intruders, he glanced into the living room at the plywood corner enclosure we'd had built for Baby (yes, we put Baby in the corner), and chewed his lip. "So . . . how long can savannah monitors live?"

"Twenty years."

* * *

I lifted the plastic-wrapped Mosin Nagant with both hands. Nine pounds, dense as granite, still freezer-cold from sitting in my trunk. It was right where I'd left it, bundled up like a greasy corpse at the foot of the fridge. It had left a cracked dent on the checkered parquet where it fell. Twice.

Holden froze. "Is that blood?"

I showed him where the bayonet had pierced a slit in the bag. My blood had already crusted and darkened to a muddy brown, which was strange, because I'd impaled my thumb on it just minutes ago. I didn't think blood could dry that fast.

He folded his arms. "Seriously?"

"I dropped it."

"And . . . *stabbed* yourself on it?"

"Trying to catch it, yes."

"Choke on any small parts, too?"

I elbowed past him and carried the heavy thing to the dining table, flicking on the chandelier light and setting it sideways on the wood right by Adelaide's glass fruit bowl. Like an autopsy slab.

He followed. "What are you doing?"

I didn't answer and unwrapped the loose end. The bag came crinkling off, clinging and damp, and the rifle's barrel and circular front sight slipped out. Glistening with moisture. A sharp odor rushed out with it, like an exhaled breath.

Holden stepped back and gagged.

I coughed, my throat tightening. It was awful in a rich, concentrated way, like black centipede musk; the staleness of pungent air concentrated into the plastic vessel for years and finally escaping.

"No wonder he kept it in the bag."

Holden breathed through his Bigfoot t-shirt. "Are old guns supposed to stink?"

I had no idea. It was like opening a hellish diaper. I unrolled more clammy plastic, peeling it back over itself the way you'd unroll a sweaty gym sock, but it was catching on something. The knobbed bolt, probably. Chemicals glued my fingers together in clots. Half the gun was visible now, from the bayoneted muzzle all the way down to the triangular back-leaf sight, and the rancid odor kept bleeding off the thing in eye-watering waves. I could taste it.

"Man, that bag . . ." Holden watched from a few feet away. "Did the gun take a shit in there or something?"

My eyes blurred with irritated tears, but I didn't dare rub them. As I tore away the last rumple of plastic, a pool of drained slime squelched between my fingers. A drop squirted on the table — mustard-yellow.

The bag slapped to the floor at my feet. Like moist snakeskin.

Now I held the Second World War-era rifle in one outstretched hand, the stock at my hip, the barrel aimed up at the chandelier. That's the thing about guns — they're always aimed at something. It rattled slightly as I hefted it under the light.

"Wow," Holden said.

I nodded.

Cat-Litter-Breath-Guy at Joe's Guns had been right; the Mosin Nagant design is both ugly and beautiful. It's a hand-cranked killing machine, the Soviet sniper's weapon of choice. You may have seen the Jude Law movie. Of course it's a genius platform — you don't engineer one of the most prolific battle rifles of the last century if you're an idiot — but there was also something . . . I don't know . . . something *stupid* about this old, single-shot beast. It shoots people, and in close quarters, it can also stab people. That's it. Nothing fancy to it. The Red Army men and women who carried it into Stalingrad may have accomplished great things with it — true acts of bravery — but without them here, and stripped of context, this Mosin Nagant was just a dumb stick.

I turned it over and the slimy bolt hung open with a slippery KA-CHUNK, revealing an empty chamber. Unloaded. Still, I poked a finger inside, because if there was ever a time to make sure, this was it.

Still unloaded.

I thumbed yellow-brown sludge off the manufacturer's stamp on the barrel. It was pea-sized but crisply detailed; a five-pointed star pierced by an arrow. Collectors call it the Tula. Under it, the rifle's serial number: B53066. In the Russian Cyrillic alphabet, the *B* actually has a *V* sound.

I waved a hand in the soupy air, wishing we'd opened the bag in the garage instead of the dining room. The fumes were needling into my sinuses. There wasn't enough Febreze in the world for this. "Maybe the smell made Dyson kill himself."

"Dan, what does the odor remind you of?"

"Ass."

"Break it down." He circled the table. "Into individual scents."

I inhaled again and let the fetid air crawl up my nostrils. "It seems biological," I said, like the world's unluckiest wine taster. "Like digestion, breaking something down, creating waste. Like gum disease . . . or mildew . . . or yeast."

Yeast, definitely. I knew yeast. Adelaide and I used to homebrew five-gallon batches of beer in our kitchen pantry, and to trigger the fermentation process, you dump in a little vial of dormant yeast. That stuff *reeks*. Like a grim omen, the weekend Addie died, we'd had our Belgian wheat batch overflow and flood the pantry, and the rank odor had fogged the kitchen windows. Fungal and goatish.

He looked at me. "You can't smell it?"

"Smell what?"

"Rotten flesh."

I rolled my eyes so hard I almost saw my own brain.

Don't get Holden started down that road. At our season-premiere investigation of an abandoned Hostess factory last year, we'd opened the sliding bay doors and immediately gagged at the odor of decaying meat. Kale and I had breathed through our sleeves and soldiered on, but Holden panicked. According to most psychic mediums, he explained breathlessly to camera B as we ventured out into the cavernous production floor, the odor of rotting flesh signals the presence of the most hateful and dangerous force known to ghost hunting. A demon.

Then: a wet crunch. Camera B pans down, and we see Holden has just stepped through the maggoty ribcage of a dead raccoon.

"Smell it?" he asked again.

"No." I slid the rifle bolt up and down its tracks like a toy train. Oily sludge beaded between contact points, burbling and dripping. Up close, the clockwork of the weapon formed a sinister maze of crannies, crevices, and dark spots. A morbid thought slithered into my mind: *Maybe there are still some year-old chunks of Ben Dyson's splattered brain in here?*

Maybe that's the decay Holden smells?

30

That led to another one. This Mosin Nagant was almost eight decades old, and if properly maintained, could survive many more. Centuries, even. Guns aren't biodegradable like us soft, fleshy humans.

"Well." Holden clapped his hands with false cheer. "At least it's not loaded."

"Yep."

"And we don't have any ammunition."

This made for a convenient segue. I reached into my back pocket and with a guilty flourish, placed a single bullet on the table.

Click.

18 Hours, 55 Minutes

Holden backed against the wall. "Worst. Idea. *Ever*."

"Hear me out."

The M91/30 Mosin Nagant fires a 7.62x54R cartridge, sold at most sporting goods outlets for plinking and medium game. It's a stout thing about the size of a swisher cigar. More missile than bullet. A brass-cased railroad spike with an explosive chemical primer at its base, and accelerated to three thousand feet per second, I couldn't fathom what it would do to a human skull.

This particular round was special, though. Its pointed tip was slopped with a dollop of bright red candle wax. I palmed it and held it out to Holden, who flinched away as if it were an eyeball. "This is my backup plan," I said.

"*Really?* Because it looks like a bullet."

"It is."

"Dan, this is nuts."

"Sit down. Let me explain."

He stayed standing. His hands were raised a little, like he half-expected me to thumb the round into the Mosin's breech right then. Worse than being merely frightened, he looked deeply sad. Like this whole spectacle was heartbreaking to witness. Maybe it was. It gave me a twisty stomach pang to imagine how utterly, self-destructively crazy I must've looked to my closest friend.

I also realized I'd never told him the rifle's full story. He only knew about Ben Dyson's suicide last year on that southern-fried afternoon.

"What's the backup plan?" he deadpanned. "Suicide?"

"Do you really think this gun would be famous for just killing one guy in Georgia?"

"It's *famous*?"

"Okay," I said. "Let's work backwards. Before Dyson mail-ordered it, before this rifle even touched North American soil, it was kept mothballed in a government armory in Saint Petersburg. For decades. The building was nicknamed the Kalash, after the philanthropist who invented the AK-47—"

"Can you at least put down the bullet?"

I set it upright on the table. "At the Kalash, they broke down decommissioned military small arms for storage or disposal, and they kept all the parts separated by type and immersed in big tubs of grease. So you've got an industrial bathtub of Mosin bolts, and a bathtub full of Mosin magazine springs, and so on. All sitting out there on acres of warehouse floor. Like cryosleep, for obsolete guns."

Holden nodded absently. He was staring at the red-tipped bullet on the table, and several inches beyond it, that rifle. Like he expected it to grow hands and load itself.

"The Kalash armory was notoriously haunted," I said. "Pretty much the Russian equivalent of the Winchester house. You can Google it. It could've been a pop-culture curiosity over there, if it were a public place like a library or a hotel. But it wasn't. It was a military complex. The only people who had access were employees, and they *hated* the place."

"Any suicides?"

"Maybe. Researching Cold War-era Russia is like sticking your head into a black hole. Even if everything wasn't all redacted to hell, the motherland was too busy shooting dogs into space to keep up the bookkeeping."

"Is that a joke, or did they literally do that?"

From the counter I grabbed a sloppy heap of papers and let it crash down onto the dining table. Filing cabinets aren't really my thing. From the bibliography of W. Louis's book I'd worked upstream — tracing sources of sources — and much of it was clumsily auto-translated from Russian with gaping holes and missing prepositions. I pushed the stack toward him and papers fanned out on the wood like a hand of playing cards. It would've been a great cutaway, a perfect segment lead-in after a commercial break, but the cameras weren't rolling.

Because this wasn't *Haunted*, and this Mosin Nagant sure as hell wasn't a lighthouse or hotel. Sure, nothing genuinely paranormal had happened yet, but there was definitely a sort of . . . *malice* to the way the bayonet pierced my thumb. I sensed ill will, somehow. Like the cursed weapon wished to attack me any way it could, and right now it had to settle for drawing blood and denting my kitchen floor (twice). It had only been a few hours since I'd picked it up from Joe's Guns. What would happen as Dyson's twenty-four-hour record inched closer? What could happen?

Sure, maybe I'd die. Maybe it had already reached its lucid tendrils into my brain and started to squeeze (which would explain the headache). But as concerned as I was about this allegedly cursed Mosin Nagant on my dining table, I was even more afraid of finding nothing paranormal at all. The ultimate lose/lose situation.

Holden flipped through pages. I'd highlighted the best bits in orange.

I couldn't hide my enthusiasm here; it bubbled up under my words. "If only a *third* of this is true, the Kalash was the most haunted building in human history. You name it, somebody claimed to see it. Gruesome accidents. Crushed fingers. Exploding lights. Illness, strokes, heart attacks. It was said that if you brought a wristwatch in, it would start to tick backwards. Compasses didn't work in there; the needle pointed south instead of north. Neither did most recording devices, or radios, or keycards. And cold spots galore — the temperature in the building fluctuated so severely, pipes would freeze while the boiler ran full blast five feet away. A loud voice, too, that spoke to workers at night."

"Saying what?"

"Weird things. The translations get iffy."

The stories were wildly different and even contradictory, so I wasn't going to delve into it. Some claimed to hear references to food (*yeda*) or candy (*konfety*). Others heard premonitions. One guy learned that his pregnant wife would miscarry. The most detailed account was an interview arranged by ParaNews, where two former Kalash guards recounted hearing the same voice echoing up the elevator shaft. First they thought it had originated downstairs, so they chased it, but the source seemed to move freely around the building. They'd described it as *progorklyy* — which loosely translates to 'spoiled,' or 'rancid.' I imagined a slippery voice, as soggy as a gutter full of dead leaves, like a meth addict chanting through wiggly teeth and ulcerated gums, shivering with breathless glee: *Yes, please, thank you . . . Yes, please, thank you . . .*

Yes, please, thank you . . .

Yes, please, thank you . . .

Holden straightened a page. "Visual manifestations?"

"Early eighties," I said. "One watchman was doing his patrol on the Kalash floor in the middle of the night. Cavernous open space around all the tubs of oily gun parts. And he hears these whispering voices in English. He whirls around, aims his flashlight, and sees two apparitions. A man and a woman. Drenched with blood and ice. Frightened, weary, tired, speaking in English. These two

35

ghosts, this man and woman, they urgently pass him by, and they keep snapping green glow sticks—"

He looked at me. "Glow sticks?"

"Dropping them on the floor. Leaving a trail of them, spaced every twenty feet or so. Like green cave worms in the darkness. And this baffled watchman follows them, because I guess I would, too. Eventually, this path of green lights just leads right into a wall, like these blood-soaked ghosts just . . . walked right through it."

"And you believe that?"

"No," I said. "I don't believe any single *one* of these accounts. But an entire haystack of them starts to gain credibility."

"Of course it looks legit," he said, flipping crinkled pages. "I'm not doubting that something really vicious haunted that armory. I'm just wondering why this rifle is better than any other place we've investigated. Why not come with us to Old Briar tomorrow? That mine sounds plenty haunted, too, and—"

He froze. He'd stopped at a page. A black-and-white photo.

I knew which one.

His eyes thinned. "I wish I could un-see that."

I continued: "The Kalash was also a magnet for transients. Bums, drunks, criminals, the general fringe of society. They were drawn to the building like mosquitos to a zapper. This was a military complex, with guards and barbed-wire fences, and Vlad Six-Pack still wandered right in. There was one story about a homeless guy from Moscow in the seventies. Just cheerfully telling his friends out of the blue one day, *Well, the Gasman has summoned me*, and walking off on his own to—"

"The Gasman?"

"He hitchhiked over three time zones to Saint Petersburg. And when he got inside the Kalash, he climbed up to the metal beams on the ceiling and did the same thing everyone else did."

Holden set the photo on the table, looking nauseous.

It was a corpse, dangling upside-down from the high ceiling, hung crookedly by one leg. A human Christmas ornament, zebra-striped with drips of black blood. The details were blurry and the lighting was murky, but you could just make out the thorns of barbed wire knotted around his ankle (stolen from the outside perimeter fence). With his limp head and fingertips hanging over the storage tubs below, he looked like a whitetail being drained of blood in someone's garage.

"Died of blood loss?"

"No. Gravity."

"*Gravity*?"

"Hanging upside-down. Blood pressure in the brain."

He swallowed. "I didn't know that could kill you."

I thought of that *The More You Know* shooting star.

And even now, I felt my eyes tugging to that black-and-white photo. It was wrong; an illogical and painful way to commit suicide. And then there was the way the corpse seemed to be . . . well, reaching. Hanging by a leg pivots your body weight, so it made sense that one arm would hang a little lower, but it still looked like this poor guy was consciously straining, *reaching* downward for something. Like he'd hung himself from the ankle — instead of the neck — for that very purpose. I guess he'd be reaching forever.

Well, the Gasman has summoned me.

And who the hell was the Gasman? He sounded like an anesthetist, or a gas meter reader, or a superhero with a dismal superpower. W. Louis's book didn't know, either. Did it even matter? It was all fiction. I knew it was fiction, just the workings of many separate, overactive imaginations hardened into legend by groupthink, but still I couldn't help but imagine being alone in the Kalash after midnight. Now *that* would be a ghost hunt. Patrolling acres of interior space, slicing darkness with a cheap-ass flashlight, and suddenly hearing that rotten voice echo from the elevator shaft, giddy with anticipation, like a starved dog watching a food bowl finally arrive: *Yes, please, thank you . . .*

Yes, please, thank you . . .

Yes, right up there, please, with the barbed wire. Thank you . .
.

Holden couldn't take his eyes off the photo, either. "How many . . . how many people hung themselves like that?"

"You're happier not knowing."

"And . . ." He glanced across the dining table, at the Mosin Nagant. "And this gun was stored there, during the Kalash hauntings, and you suspect it absorbed some of the—"

"No," I said. "This rifle was believed to be the *culprit*."

He looked at me.

I lowered my voice, my words cleanly spaced: "Everyone who has ever been issued this rifle has shot themselves with it."

As if on cue, the chandelier flickered.

"Every. Last. One." On the kitchen counter, I spread out black-and-white photos — mug shots of flinty, unsmiling farm boys in fox hats with nothing in their futures to smile about. "As an infantry rifle manufactured during World War II, it passed between at least four different enlisted men. Two artilleries, one motor, and one undefined, which probably meant something classified, like a gulag or something. Guess how every last one of them died."

Holden held an index finger to his temple.

"Twenty-four hours," I said. "That's the record."

"How long have *you* had it?"

"This Mosin Nagant was a legend," I said. "A sort of Red Army boogeyman that passed from corpse to corpse. Rumor has it the Nazis even captured it on the battlefield — and *gave it back*. Everyone checked the serial numbers of their rifles to make sure it hadn't gotten to them next. They called it the Head-Scratching Rifle."

"Why would you scratch your head with it?"

"It's a joke."

"Oh."

"So fast-forward to 1995," I said. "One of the Kalash's engineer guys — Nikolai Something-Or-Other — puts two and two together. He suspects that this legendary *Head-Scratching Rifle* from five decades ago was actually one of the outdated guns being stored in the armory, and that's the cause of the suicides, the nasty voices, et cetera. People believe him. He claims, to a TV station, that his brother works in archives somewhere and that he even knows the serial number of the Head-Scratching Rifle. 'B3065,' he tells the camera. And he and his buddies pull some strings and go through the armory and rebuild that Mosin Nagant. And then they take it to a foundry and melt it down."

"So . . . did the Kalash's paranormal activity stop?"

"No way to tell," I said. "The depot shut down pretty soon afterward, and the Mosins were imported into the US surplus market."

Holden leaned over the rifle, squinting in the light, and studied the stenciled numbers on the receiver, just under the five-pointed Tula star. He read aloud: "B3066."

I nodded.

He looked up at me. "One digit off."

"Exactly. I think they screwed up." I felt a grin tighten my face. "I think Nikolai What's-His-Name had the right idea, but then he reassembled and destroyed the wrong gun. And the real Head-Scratching Rifle got imported to America with the others. Just ask Ben Dyson."

Or that unfortunate forklift driver in West Virginia.

I caught another whiff of the Mosin Nagant's stench — that yeasty odor of digestion — and nearly gagged. It seemed to come and go, like a sentient cloud, scouting the rest of the house and returning. It had a way of creeping up your nostrils and ambushing you. My headache was intensifying; I plucked an ibuprofen bottle from the junk drawer and swallowed two.

"Well." Holden glanced at the red-tipped bullet on the table. "You're right, Dan. That makes me feel much better about the live ammunition resting a few inches from the demonic gun."

I picked the round up with my good hand and rolled it over my palm. It should've felt subtly heavier than the other 7.62x54R rounds I'd handled last week, but I just couldn't tell. The difference was fractions of an ounce. "Like I said, this is my backup plan."

"How so?"

"You don't have to be a part of this—"

"Yeah, well, I am now. What's with the bullet, Dan?"

"Addie showed me this once." I held the brass cartridge up to the dining-room chandelier, which flickered again. "The casing is full of explosive gunpowder, which is ignited by the little circular primer here, at the base. The pointed metal tip is the actual projectile. The true *bullet*; the part that flies out and kills Bambi's mom. Everything else is just the delivery system—"

I paused. I thought I'd detected motion in the corner of my eye. In the decorative mirror Adelaide hung by the pantry door—

"Dan?"

It had been nothing, I decided. Just a shadow, or reflected glint.

"You can pull the bullet out." I looked back at Holden and brushed my thumb over the marred copper jacketing where my pliers had left ugly divots. "And the gunpowder just pours right out, like black sand. I cannibalized a few, and consolidated their powder into this one. This special cartridge, Holden, contains almost *twice* as much explosive force as the Mosin Nagant is designed to handle."

I'd been careful to avoid the phrase *bullet bomb*. But I think he got it. He sat down, shoulders sagging, rubbing his eyes. "Jesus, Dan."

The blot of red candle wax was just to mark the cartridge, since black Sharpie kept rubbing off the curved metal. Still, I thought as I rolled it between my fingers, it did give the round an oddly fatalistic quality. The wax was a brilliant tomato-red, as red as freshly splashed blood, still hot and pulsing with oxygenated life.

"I'm not going to load it into the Mosin Nagant," I felt the need to clarify. "I never will. But in the million-to-one event that this rifle really is cursed, possessed, self-aware, *whatever* — if it makes me shoot myself, it'll also blow itself into shrapnel and split the barrel like a banana peel. I can die satisfied that the Head-Scratching Rifle won't take any more lives. And again, Holden, I'm okay with risking my own ass, but I don't like having you here. This is my stupid ghost hunt. Not yours."

I set the red-tipped bullet back on the table for emphasis. Click.

Holden eyed it like it was a grenade.

I wished he'd go home. I felt guilty for allowing him into this. And in the descending silence, I wondered again exactly how crazy I must've sounded. It's tough to appear rational when your backup plan involves an explosion. Being an on-air ghost hunter requires a special, reckless curiosity — we all had it — but this was something darker. More desperate, more self-destructive. Emotions were tangled up in it.

And worse, I'd already made a cardinal error. I'd allowed myself to believe in the Head-Scratching Rifle's intoxicating little legend. I would've called BS an hour ago if we'd been scouting this rifle for an episode of *Haunted*, because nothing in real life was ever this clear-cut. From the soldier-suicides in the Siberian district, to the bizarre manifestations at the Kalash, to Mr. Dyson's blood-splattered workshop — it all felt as tidy and plotted as a movie script. Hell, there was even a sadistic little cherry on top that I'd forgotten to mention: Nikolai What's-His-Name, the aforementioned worker who believed he'd ended the curse and melted the rifle into a glowing puddle, killed himself in 1996. The year afterward. Apparently he'd gotten shit-the-bed-drunk one night, staggered outside, and passed out with his head on some railroad tracks. Not a pretty photo (in color, of course). By that time, the murderous rifle was six pallets deep into a West Virginian warehouse, but like the Corleone family, it didn't forgive or forget. Convenient, right? Like a movie script, it all just felt too good (bad?) to be true.

And I needed it to be true.

Yes, I know it was crazy. And stupid, and selfish, and beyond reckless. But in a way, this was also my first honest ghost hunt in years.

Holden huffed. "Wouldn't it have been easier to just buy blanks?"

"Blanks can still kill you."

"Jesus Christ—"

"It takes free will to load a bullet," I said. "I'm not loading it. Are you?"

He shook his head rapidly.

"Terrific. We'll be fine."

He had a sad look in his eyes. I recognized it. I'd seen it in my parents, my coworkers, and my boss. Like they're watching me adrift in space. Everyone wanted to rescue me, but no one knew how to build the rocket.

Finally, he spoke. "I don't think Ben Dyson or those Russian soldiers shot themselves out of their own free will," he hissed. "I think that's pretty much *the point*."

I forced a grin.

After all, that was what I hoped to find out.

* * *

Holden and I started the proper investigation just after eight o'clock. After nineteen webcasts and two seasons of televised ghost hunting, it was all muscle memory. We unzipped the same duffel bags, clacked in the same batteries, and double-checked the same digital cassette tapes and thumb drives. For electronic voice phenomena (EVP) capture, we placed an analog microphone on the table. For apparitions, we telescoped a tripod and ran a full-spectrum DVC camera. Last, we powered up the EMF meter to detect any electromagnetic or thermal fluctuations.

Like I told Holden, I wasn't interested in mere anomalies tonight. But, I supposed, there was no harm in being ready to capture them for our fans.

Haunted had a surprisingly active online forum, and you could learn a lot from the anonymous viewer comments. Apparently I was a dead ringer for Jim from the sitcom *The Office* (the American version). Our John Carpenter-esque synth soundtrack was almost universally mocked. And they were especially vicious about Holden's weight:

> *Maybe Holden should ghost-hunt a gym next.*
> *Do they have to pick haunted places without much stairs?*
> *Hey holden hume, maybe theres a ghost in that CHEESBURGER!*

My best friend had always laughed these off, saying that the world is full of critics and short on artists, but since last season he'd switched to a low-carb diet and lost almost sixty pounds. Not that it helped:

> *Hey anyone notice that the fat one looks slightly less fat now?*

As we set up our equipment in my dining room, he only spoke twice. The first was his customary *Haunted* prayer, but with a minor addition on my account: "Dear Lord in Heaven, in Your infinite wisdom and grace, please bless our investigation, protect us from unclean and hateful spirits, and forgive Dan here . . . for being a complete idiot."

I'd nodded absently, staring at the cursed Mosin Nagant and my wax-tipped, exploding bullet on the table. If God existed, He'd probably agree.

I hoped He existed.

The second thing Holden said was barely a whisper, exhaled through his teeth as he thumbed tiny buttons to white-balance the camera, but the words hung in the air like smoke: "That's a nice idea and a cute little backup plan, Dan. But it won't un-splatter your brains from the ceiling."

I ignored him and popped two more ibuprofen.

For a second, it had sounded like he was going to say something different.

That's a cute little backup plan, Dan. But it won't bring Adelaide back.

Sent: 3/19 7:09PM
Sender: kale@haunted
Subject: FYI

Hi Dan,

Hope you're okay. Sorry to bother you but apparently you have a new #1 fan.

Jake says a guy wearing a gas mask came into the production office this afternoon looking for you. Like one of those full-face, bulgy HazMat masks, for poison gas or radiation. He didn't give a name. He just asked to see DAN RUPLEY on the courtesy phone, over and over.

The receptionist didn't let him inside, and Jake couldn't see the man's face (due to said gas mask) and the outdoor footage is too grainy to be any good. But I had them make a police report.

A really weird police report.

Stay safe. Holden said we might see you at Old Briar tomorrow?

Kale Wong
Talent/Tech Coordinator
Haunted (Sundays at 11pm and Wednesdays at 2am, only on KSPM)

14 Hours, 15 Minutes

Nothing happened for the next four hours.

Well, technically, lots of things happened. I went to the bathroom. Holden scribbled up shot lists for tomorrow's Old Briar investigation. The Keurig burbled and made Italian Roast. We played War with a deck of fifty-one and speculated about LJ's podcast plans for the third season. The baseboard heater popped. Baby scurried inside her enclosure. A barred owl screamed outside.

But nothing paranormal happened.

The audio recorder? Just our voices.

The full-spectrum camera? Just us.

The EMF meter? Don't even ask.

As for Holden's surprise in the moth-eaten cardboard box? It was a last-ditch attempt to contact the entity — a Ouija board. Our production manager LJ never allowed them on *Haunted* — "too occulty," he'd said — but I've never believed in them, anyway. They're powered by unconscious movement. Like dowsing rods. People love to pretend the Ouija board is a dangerous portal to a writhing, Lovecraftian darkness beyond our known world, while conveniently forgetting it's a party game manufactured by Mattel. Like Mousetrap. Is Mousetrap also a gateway to unknowable horror? If it is, I've been playing it wrong.

But I'd seen Holden's Ouija board once before, and it had some history. It was a dense wooden slab, walnut-colored, like my uncle's antique poker table. Veneered with a gray film of ancient dust, as sticky as tree sap in spots. It smelled like old people. The black letters were scorched into the grain; a YES and a NO on the top, a HELLO and GOODBYE on the bottom, and in the exact center of the board, between two lines of alphabet: TURN. The planchette was the size of a hockey puck, a pale arrowhead with a cloudy glass lens. Mostly just the same standard-issue Ouija board you might recognize from your own misspent youth. But, I admit — the TURN was unique.

"It belonged to my grandmother," Holden said. "She was a medium. A claircognizant."

"A *what*?"

"A claircognizant."

"What's that?"

He lowered his eyes. "A phone psychic."

I nodded. At least there was no Mattel logo on the board.

And the Mosin Nagant just sat there, like the dumb, inanimate object it was. The legendary Soviet rifle that had punched a 7.62x54R round through the skull of every last man who'd possessed it, here and abroad. The cursed relic that summoned innocents from thousands of miles to hang inverted from the ceiling of the Kalash like pagan offerings, and compelled some poor West Virginian man to chug industrial lye. The most infamous object since the Spear of Destiny had been sitting on my dining-room table for four uneventful hours now. Was there an on/off switch?

My headache had intensified, but any more ibuprofen might burn a hole in my stomach lining. And my right thumb still ached under the scotch-taped bandage — but that had been just an unlucky fumble. Nothing paranormal about dropping a gun.

"We each put our fingers on the planchette," Holden said. "Like this."

You're supposed to stare at the Ouija while you operate it, but I just glowered over the table at that stupid rifle, wishing it would suddenly move, or slimy ectoplasm tentacles would sprout from it. Something. Anything. Even more than that, I was wishing I hadn't poisoned myself with false hope.

Come on, Head-Scratching Rifle.

Do something scary.

I'm waiting.

Holden explained that his grandmother's board was an Icelandic type called a *mirror board*, because it allegedly existed on multiple planes of reality at once (good luck proving that to the Better Business Bureau). Really, that's just a fancy way of saying it functioned like an eighteenth-century walkie-talkie. You spell out your message on the board, and then you move the token to the TURN in the center. That means you're ready for the spirit, on another realm of existence, to move the planchette and answer. Like ending a radio transmission with *over*.

"She was a *really* good phone psychic," Holden assured me.

I nodded again. "Okay."

Gently pushing the planchette in unison, we agreed upon and sent our first message to the world behind this one, initiating contact with the entity that inhabited the Head-Scratching Rifle.

HELLO?

AREYOUTHERE?

PLEASESIGNALYOURPRESENCE.

We had no idea what would happen in the next hour . . .

* * *

Again, absolutely nothing.

"God-freaking-damnit."

We were both exhausted now. Two home-brewed porters sat half-gone on the tabletop between us. Shadows under our eyes. It was well past midnight, technically Saturday now, and I knew he'd have to leave soon so he could hit the park-and-ride for Bozeman early in the morning.

I bent the playing cards and sprayed them, chattering, into the air. Holden jolted in his chair; he'd almost fallen asleep.

Cards click-clacked onto the table. One landed in the Mosin's bolt, sticking upright, oddly perfect. For some reason it reminded me of the time Holden and I were teenagers — long before meeting Adelaide on that dock — and practicing that Starsky and Hutch hood-slide move on his old Honda Accord. I'd ripped a button from my cargo pants and left it wedged in the seam of the vehicle's hood, perfectly upright. We'd laughed hysterically. What're the odds?

My world had lost a lot of its magic since then. I rubbed my eyes.

Holden squinted at me. "Why's it so hard to believe in ghosts?"

I didn't answer.

"I know . . . the thermal signature at the lighthouse might've just been a glitch, or warm glass." He plucked the card from the Mosin's bolt — a Four of Hearts. "But the reasoning behind ghosts? It's solid, Dan. Millions of people have seen them, across cultures, across centuries. Even if you haven't, personally. Why can't you just . . . allow yourself to believe?"

"I don't want to believe," I said. "I want to *know*."

Silence.

"Okay," Holden said. "Fine. Screw it. Let's be hypothetical and say ghosts aren't real, and Addie's really gone. And what we call *souls* is really just energy. And

49

when we die, that energy just . . . scatters, like a shotgun blast of atoms, into a lonely universe of dead stars, and Adelaide is really gone and you'll never see her again. Ever."

I couldn't look at him. I stared at the cursed rifle on my dinner table and pushed the Ouija planchette, hurling idle stones into the void:

HELLO?

HELLO?

BUELLER?

"If that's the case, Dan, if that's true — it doesn't change the fact that *you're still here*." He leaned forward into the light and his voice softened, nearly pleading. "Your life is happening, right now. You're here. She isn't, but you are."

A playing card fluttered to the floor.

Something about his words shot a chill down my spine. I glanced at my own reflection in Adelaide's gothic little wall mirror and remembered — I was growing older and she wasn't. Eventually I would be thirty and she would be forever twenty-five. She wasn't a person anymore; she didn't age like us. Someday I'd be an old man and even if an afterlife existed, even if I could somehow find her address in Heaven and be reunited with her eternal soul after death — would she even recognize me?

Holden's voice broke. "Dan, I've been praying for you every day. I've been asking God so many times, in so many ways, to help you through this. And I've had to watch you go to shit before my eyes, and cut ties with your job and friends, and I don't know how to help, and God's not telling me *anything*." He sighed. "That's hard for me, Dan."

I nodded.

For a long moment we sat in silence, sipping our porters. They'd been home-brewed in November; the last complete batch Adelaide and I had made together. We were drinking beers brewed by a dead woman.

I finished mine and decided that my best friend was right. Self-pity is easy, but motion is hard. And motion is life.

I needed to move on.

So I'd start boxing her things tomorrow. I knew her parents were planning to fly in from the UK sometime next month to take what they wanted, and then I'd give away whatever remained. I wasn't looking forward to seeing them again. Her father had always resented me for not finishing college like Adelaide, not making eighty grand a year like Adelaide, and for calling him out on those two things one awkward Christmas in 2011. Some people are gifted at reading maps, some are natural chefs — my talent is ruining Christmases. I'm a man with very particular skills.

Photos, too. I would archive every image from her phone. Ditto for her work laptop. Everything on her Facebook page as well, which had already staged a digital funeral in January and would now only see a slow trickle of remembrance on birthdays and holidays. You could almost see the electronic cobwebs forming. And as for Baby? I hoped Adelaide's parents would ask for custody of that five-foot salmonella carrier, but they probably wouldn't. I wondered: is it illegal to drive up to White Bend, open the passenger door, and let a five-foot African savannah monitor loose in the wild? If so, how illegal?

Still, it was progress. Forward motion. Maybe this stupid failed ghost hunt was it — my turning point — and after nine weeks of doggedly attacking rock bottom with a ten-ton excavating machine, I had no choice but to move forward and resume being alive.

I helped Holden pack up our equipment and load the backseats of Dora the Explorer. The Ouija board took the passenger seat. But he halted abruptly in my front doorway. One more thing, whispered through gritted teeth: "Dan."

"Yeah?"

"I'm taking the rifle, too."

I understood; he didn't want to leave me alone with a firearm and an exploding bullet. But I didn't want him alone with it, either. It didn't matter. He gave me no time to argue. He doubled back into the dining room to grab the Mosin Nagant . . . and instead ducked into the kitchen pantry to pick up something else.

A broom.

I thought he was joking at first.

But he carried the red broom outside to his car. Carefully, with both hands, conscious to keep the handle aimed skyward, like it actually was a firearm. I followed in surreal silence, hairs prickling on my arms. The night outside was frigid, gray with shadowless starlight. Gravel crunched underfoot. Ten seconds, twenty, thirty. We reached Dora the Explorer. He was really drawing out the joke.

It was now almost one-thirty a.m. March 20.

I watched him delicately place my broom in his trunk, shut it, and then we exchanged our goodbyes — I can't remember our exact words. I couldn't focus on anything else. I kept waiting for him to reveal that it had been a tasteless joke. It felt like a joke. It had to be a joke. But he closed his door. Twisted the key. Gunned the engine. And then Holden Hume drove home with my kitchen broom in Dora's trunk, his headlights splashing down the driveway, his taillights fading into the darkness like a pair of spectral red eyes.

Leaving me alone.

With the real Head-Scratching Rifle.

11 Hours, 59 Minutes

It was still on the dining table.

I lingered at the edge of the kitchen, my fingertips gripping the countertop. Half-fascinated, half-horrified. Without thinking to, I'd stood with my body shielded behind the lower cabinets, like the rifle was emitting radiation. Not Joe had voiced a similar sentiment, earlier that day: *Being near it takes away a piece of you.*

I cleared my throat, shattering the silence.

"Okay," I said aloud. "You've got my attention."

I gave the rifle a few moments to respond before considering how crazy that was. But I knew — it had chosen to stay with me. Like a sentient creature, the Head-Scratching Rifle had understood Holden's intentions and exerted a subtle force to stay in the house. The same way it had forced Nikolai What's-His-Name to misremember its serial number. It seemed to *want* me, which was at once exhilarating and terrifying. I should've left the house then and there. But, who knows — would it have allowed me to?

"What are you?" I asked.

No answer.

The air curdles around it. Like milk left out in the sun—

"Hey. What happens now?"

I tried to think logically, untainted by the supernatural. But Occam's razor didn't really work here. There was zero chance of Holden just coincidentally confusing a broom for a Soviet battle rifle.

I shivered and felt goosebumps rise under a layer of icy sweat. I heard a low creak somewhere in the kitchen — a floorboard, maybe, flexing in the changing temperature — and it was instantly gone.

Silence.

"You stayed with me," I spoke to the empty kitchen. "Here I am."

Nothing.

Why do I keep expecting it to speak?

Habit, I guess — on *Haunted* we'd spend hours calling out to cobwebbed ballrooms and rusted-out hospital wards, politely asking spirits to manifest themselves for our thermal cameras and EVP microphones, but standing alone in my kitchen while addressing an inanimate object felt different. Crazy, even.

Then again, so was spending four hours playing a kids' go-cart racing videogame by myself. That'd been last Sunday, when I drank too much and exhumed Addie's childhood Nintendo 64. Stored on the dusty cartridge were her high scores on every racetrack. The game saved the fastest lap time as a semi-transparent 'ghost' that you could play against — so I'd seized the opportunity and raced my dead fiancée up and down twenty-four candy-colored racetracks. Until a heart-wrenching moment after midnight, when I'd noticed that her racer's silhouette seemed to mimic my driving more than hers, and I'd realized that if you 'beat' a top time, you overwrote the ghost. I was the new ghost.

On every single track, I'd erased her.

And—

I heard that creaking sound again. Much louder. It wasn't a floorboard. It was biological. Like bones bending under mummified skin. A chorus of slow, groaning croaks; a multi-limbed, spiderlike body of joints and kneecaps carefully untangling itself. It was in the room with me.

I've had these moments before on-camera — these fight-or-flight pauses when you suspect you really are sharing the room with an unknown entity. It's an addictive rush. Our *Haunted* mantra was the three S's — *stop, stay calm*, and *see* (Holden used to joke that there's a fourth: *shit your pants*) — so I held my breath, swallowed my heartbeat, and like a lighthouse, scanned a wary three hundred and sixty degrees. Inch by cautious inch. The tabletop with the Mosin Nagant, the red-tipped bullet, and the homebrews I'd drunk with Holden. The glass patio door. The slab counter, covered with printed research and a potted ball cactus. Behind me, the empty kitchen. The sink, the dishwasher. My own reflection on Adelaide's horn-rimmed mirror. Then the pantry door, the fridge, the whiteboard—

Wait.

I froze like an ice sculpture. The lights flickered.

Wait-wait-wait—

My eyes tracked back to the mirror. To my reflection. It was holding the Head-Scratching Rifle.

That's interesting.

I blinked and glanced into the dining room. The rifle was still on the tabletop.

I looked back.

My reflection still held it, now carefully pivoting the thing in a slow, baton-like twirl. Muzzle aimed upward. Paralyzed, I watched myself lean forward and extend my chin so I could nestle the black barrel under my jaw. Just like Ben Dyson, I realized as my stomach turned. Just like that poor gunsmith in his workshop in Macon, Georgia, seconds before peppering his laptop with red-salsa chunks.

The chandelier flickered twice.

My doppelganger was already reaching for the rifle's trigger. And I — the real Dan Rupley — was standing empty-handed in my kitchen, staring in agape silence, my thoughts unrolling in panicked tugs: *I must've fallen asleep.*

In the stuttering light, I watched my own thumb slink into the rifle's safety guard. My knuckle bent ninety degrees. The gauze-wrapped wound burst open, leaking a hot dollop of blood down my wrist—

This is a dream. I'm dreaming.

And my thumb kept bending, and hooked around the trigger and tightened, squeezing it—

This isn't—

The rifle fired.

THWAP.

A strange, slurping sound. Like a silenced pistol in a Bond movie. I flinched, and a bead of sweat tapped the floor, but my duplicate in the mirror remained unharmed and monotone, gripping the rifle with two hands. What had happened? No explosion. No blood splatter. No real gunshot, even. Just that bizarre misfire, like a firecracker detonating underwater, no louder than a child's cap pistol—

Then the chandelier went out, dropping the room into darkness.

And a prickly voice spoke behind me:

"Front door is ajar."

Part II

A TRAIN OF THOUGHTS

. . . Less than a day afterward, Arkady was seen crouching at the bottom of a steep berm. Witnesses described trance-like movements as he removed the Mosin Nagant's bolt and checked the barrel for obstructions. He studied every inch of the weapon, inside and out, even applying careful blots of oil here and there, before inserting a round, pressing the weapon under his chin, and pulling the trigger.

Three of the four confirmed victims killed themselves in view of others, and all witnesses described this same, eerily ritualistic "safety check" before death. Like a supernatural force was guiding each man's fingers, first ensuring that the gun wouldn't damage itself while firing. It's particularly telling that all victims died crouching over snow, carpet, or insulation . . . a yielding surface for the rifle to land upon.

Excerpt from "Cursed Objects of the New Century" (W. Louis), Haunted Inn Press, 2002.

11 Hours, 53 Minutes

The security system repeated: "Front door is ajar."

I couldn't see the door from where I was. I could hear the outside air, though — the deepened ambience of the forest — and felt the chill of the night creeping through the empty house. The doorknob tapped the wall once.

I looked back at the mirror. It now showed only darkness; my doppelganger had left the frame.

The kitchen was pitch black.

It had happened so quickly. It wasn't just the chandelier; all of the lights were off now — every last one of them — and I didn't remember switching them off. Despite that, and despite witnessing my own attempted suicide in the mirror, my mind darted to the mundane and took shaky refuge there. Maybe . . . maybe I'd imagined everything? And the front door had been opened by the wind?

It wasn't windy. Through the window above the kitchen sink I saw paper birch trees standing in darkness beyond the overgrown lawn, pale ghosts with blistered trunks. The branches were still, rigidly fixed, like models on a train set. I crept two paces toward the fridge, to the mouth of the kitchen, and from there I'd be able to see the front doorway. I flattened one palm on the cold wall, feeling my heartbeat in my skin, and peered around the corner.

The front door hung wide open. Doorway empty. Darkness outside.

And I heard footsteps.

Heavy, ponderous footsteps already inside, scuffing on hardwood and softening on carpet. From the other side of the house. As though whoever had pushed open the front door had taken an immediate right, passed in front of the stairs, and walked into the living room. I'd missed them by a second. My blood turned cold.

Someone is inside my house.

I exhaled through my teeth. Cold air came down the hallway and licked my face. The footsteps continued through the living room at a comfortable pace. This intruder was in no hurry, and felt no need for stealth. Even on carpet, the footfalls sounded creaking and leathery. Stiff boots, maybe.

This wasn't an apparition. This was a real person, wearing real boots, inside my house. And it wasn't Holden. My first thought was to call 911 — but we had no landline and my iPhone was on the coffee table, in the living room, with my undocumented houseguest. My second thought was Adelaide's gun safe. Upstairs, under our mattress. The keypad combination was 1024, the date we first met outside that Total Darkness Maze. I considered bolting for the stairs, swinging a hard left around the banister, and racing for that safe — Addie kept a Beretta something-or-other for her range club — but it was unloaded, with a manual safety and a de-cocking lever and a bunch of other crap I wouldn't remember how to operate. Moving upstairs would also make a lot of noise, so I decided it would be my last resort. If all other exits were compromised—

I realized the footsteps had stopped.

"Front door is ajar."

I clutched the corner with both hands, head low, listening. The intruder was still in my living room, but he'd stopped walking. He must've found something of interest.

Silence.

I waited with swollen lungs. I held each breath until my chest burned, and let each one in and out through my teeth. Like an airlock. A careful build and release, to minimize noise, so the man in my living room wouldn't hear me.

Nothing happened.

I peered and checked the front door again. Still open. Another current of night air breathed in, bracingly cold, and my arms goose-bumped again. It's tough to judge minutes and seconds on an adrenaline high, but after at least a minute of silence from the living room, I started to wonder . . . had I really heard those footsteps? Had I really seen myself in the mirror?

I spoke: "Hello?"

My voice rattled through the dark house. No answer.

"I called the cops," I said weakly.

Nothing.

From the living room, I heard a scraping hiss and recognized Baby, shuffling around in her enclosure on disjointed little claws. I'd forgotten about her. In the haze of panic, could I have been mistaking her sounds for footprints? That thirty-pound creature made all sorts of bizarre noises. Lately she'd been fond of nuzzling her head under her big water bowl, raising it forty-five degrees, and letting it crash down flat. To a steady rhythm . . . maybe that could sound like a footprint?

"Front door is ajar," the security system helpfully reminded me.

I counted to fifty. Nothing else moved in the living room.

I kept counting and reached a hundred.

There's no one in my house.

A hundred and fifty. My heart rate was back to normal.

To hell with it; let there be light. I was tired of waiting and second-guessing. I backtracked to the dining room and palmed all of the lights switches in a row. CLICK — the kitchen fluorescents triggered first, bathing the room in scalding light. Then — CLICK, CLICK — the dining room and living room went nuclear. I had to squint and lower my eyes, so at first all I saw was the dented wood floor, which looked much worse in the unforgiving brightness—

Holden's Ouija board was on the dining table.

I jolted.

Not just the board. *Everything* was back. The EMF meter. The audio recorder, its little gearbox spokes quietly turning. I bumped something with my hip — the tripod. The *Haunted* production's full-spectrum camera, worth over a thousand dollars, wobbled precariously but I caught it. The red light blinked; its HD tape was still recording.

Everything's back.

Everything's back, just as it was.

I'd carried all of these things to Holden's car before he'd left, twenty minutes ago. But everything had been restored, *defaulted*, to the start of Friday night's ghost hunt. Like a reset video game.

I was so taken by this brazen violation of physics that it took a good second for me to remember my initial reason for flicking on the lights — to ensure there wasn't a man in the living room — and turn my head to check.

Yeah, there was also definitely a man in the living room.

* * *

He was seven feet tall, draped in a charcoal-gray greatcoat that hung off his shoulders and fanned behind his legs like a wool superhero cape. Pale buttons. Black boots. I couldn't see his face. He was hunched over, his gloved hands on his knees, peering intently into Baby's plywood enclosure.

My stomach coiled. I stood rigidly still, a breath trapped in my throat like a hot bubble, terrified to make a sound. The intruder hadn't noticed me yet, but he would if he glanced to his left. Even turned away from me, I could tell something about his face was wrong. The shape of his head seemed off, in a lumpy, jack-o-lantern way.

He touched Baby's sliding glass door.

Not a tap, like a kid at a zoo exhibit. He was *testing* it, exploring every inch, listening to it creak under the pressure of his fingertips. Like the transparent surface was an unknown force field to him, and he was searching for the edges. In another moment he found them — the sliding metal frame — and tugged the door out. It shattered, spraying the living room with shards.

The report echoed twice.

A chunk of glass skittered past my foot, into the dining room.

He crouched now, coat flaps touching the carpet, and reached inside with both hands to scoop Adelaide's savannah monitor up and out. Baby struggled; her tail flopped against the wall and one crocodile foot kicked in the air. There's no graceful way to pick up a lizard that big. Not even Addie could do it.

The man — or ghost, whatever — fumbled with Baby for a second, still facing away from me. He hefted her from one hand to the other, then back, and then raised the thirty-pound savannah monitor to his mountainous chest. I saw one cloaked elbow rise, like he was about to try and pet her, which was inadvisable. You don't pet most monitor lizards, any more than you'd pet a landmine. Addie had a special way with her, of course, but for everyone else, Baby doesn't really have moods — just a sliding gradient of how likely she is to bite your hand.

But, by all means, try.

The man's elbow raised higher—

Go ahead. This'll be fun to watch—

But he made a gripping, twisting motion, like he was opening a pickle jar, and I realized with a nauseous jolt what was really happening. And it happened fast. Adelaide's lizard made a strangled, gurgling hiss, like air escaping a wet balloon, and I saw her hind legs flailing harder now, desperately, her toes scratching and slicing. Her tail whipped right and left, knocking a lamp to the floor, filling the room with strange shadows.

The first sound was a wet *pop*.

Then . . . a *tearing*. Like fabric, stretched and ripping in a long, slow schism. The man's elbow rose higher, and higher, and then he snapped through some final knot of meat and sinew. The animal came apart. The hissing stopped. I could see Baby's back legs still kicking and her tail still thrashing, but slower now, in contracting jerks.

The intruder spun to face me, with two bloodied halves of Baby flopping in his gloved hands, and the lamp's light bulb exploded. The room went black.

Well, holy shit.

I stepped backward and with cat-like grace, tripped over a chair. The world inverted. I crashed down on my back, staring up at the chandelier, sucking in a mouthful of displaced air. The full-spectrum *Haunted* camera toppled over and broke beside my head. Plastic bits skittered on the floor.

Move.

Footsteps from the darkened living room . . .

Move. He's coming.

I rolled over, socks slipping on wood, and thrashed upright on my elbows and knees, my eardrums filling with blood. The kitchen lights fizzled out, too. I heard the man's heavy footsteps approaching from the living room. Boots on carpet. No time for shock or horror; he'd killed our pet and he was coming for me. I heard a squishy thump on the carpet as he dropped one half of Baby.

Up. On my feet. Escape—

Back door.

His next footstep clicked on parquet floor. He was inside the dining room with me, towering over me, turning the room small, a reaching shadow with blood-slick fingers—

Backdoorbackdoorbackdoor—

I scrambled away, shouldered hard into the back door, feeling the glass bend in its frame, and flicked the lock, twisting a doorknob slippery with gun oil and panic sweat—

"Rear door is ajar—"

Sausage-fingers clawed at my back. They didn't feel human. They felt boneless, jellylike, like a gloved hand made of slugs, squeezing my shirt—

I tore free, hurled myself outside. The back porch wasn't finished yet, so I dropped through a plywood skeleton and hit my knees on crunchy frozen weeds. The coldness of the night air lashed my skin, shocking and powerful. Like breaking through lake ice, being immersed in frigid water. It physically hurt.

The dining room light died behind me. My shadow vanished.

I didn't look back. I scrambled to my feet and bolted into the starlit woods, hearing the back door swing shut behind me. The paper birch trees came fast, white and peeling, whooshing past me. Dry sticks broke against my palms and face, slashing skin. I staggered and stumbled in the general direction of our nearest neighbors (the Mullins, at the end of the cul-de-sac) but I couldn't find their porch light in the darkness. Had theirs burned out, too?

Mostly I was just moving for the sake of movement, without a true plan or tactics, because *motion is life*. I forgot about Adelaide, about Baby, about the Head-Scratching Rifle, about everything, and Holden's little offhand Hippocrates quote became a chant in my mind, underlining every raw breath, every crackling step, every skeletal chill of subzero air.

Motion is life. Motion is life. Motion is—

Twenty feet back, I heard the back door break in two hard impacts.

* * *

I woke up.

Sitting in a chair.

I was back at Jitters. Back at Farwell's premier coffee shop with the best house blend in the panhandle and bay windows peppered with dusty snow. It was daytime and the little place vibrated with life. A cappuccino machine gurgled. A barista laughed. The smell of apple fritters, Windex, ground coffee beans. My chair leg must've squealed when I'd jerked awake; an old couple glanced up at me from another table.

"You okay?"

I whipped back to face Holden, seated across from me. Looking at me sideways in the warm glow of those stupid paper lanterns, sipping his familiar milkshake-coffee.

I froze.

"Dan. Are you okay?"

"I . . ." My lips stuck together.

"You dozed off."

I blinked, my eyelids dry as paper, and recognized my black coffee on the tabletop, half-gone and cold. "Just now?"

"Yep."

"What . . . what day is it?"

He misunderstood. "About three."

"What *day* is it?"

One table over, a conversation hushed. Had I raised my voice? I hadn't meant to. The windows were a bright gray headache, filling my brain with afternoon sunlight. Holden leaned forward on his creaking chair, as if bracing to deliver bad news.

He's going to say Friday, he's going to say Friday, he's going to say—

"Friday."

I stood up, my thoughts running together. I didn't feel it but my knee must've bumped the edge of the table; our coffees splashed. Holden guarded his paperwork. My eardrums rang and the little java house seemed to fall silent, like a theatre after the curtain rises. A horrible, pressurizing silence.

"Dan—"

"I have to go the bathroom."

He pointed.

Jitters' unisex bathroom had a perfectly good toilet but I took the liberty of vomiting in the sink. It was just more convenient. I was still in shock; still in shaky, post-car accident mode, assessing damage and counting fingers. I needed to stay alert and on my feet. Besides, the sink drain could handle it.

I slurped from the faucet and caught my face in the mirror. I looked like I felt, my eye sockets shadowing like bruises under the buzzing electric light. I could've passed for ten years older. But — according to Holden, and the blazing sunlight outside — I was really *twelve hours* younger.

Friday.

It's Friday afternoon, March 19.

Which meant Friday night's ghost hunt hadn't happened yet. I hadn't even brought the Mosin Nagant home yet. It was still in my trunk. Everything — Holden's antique Ouija board, myself attempting suicide in the mirror, the late-night visitor in the winter coat — had all been a dream. An intricately detailed, *twelve-hour* nightmare. Even the part where the Head-Scratching Rifle's spike bayonet had pierced under my thumbnail.

I checked my thumb.

Intact.

The Jitters bathroom seemed to wobble. The checkerboard floor was slick; recently mopped. An air-conditioner kicked on. Outside I heard muffled voices — a stranger asking Holden if I was okay. I took another swig of metallic sink water and knew my best friend would come in and check on me in thirty seconds, tops. He's dependable. He's the guy who texts you after a night of dollar beers to ensure you got home safe.

I cupped a cold handful of water and splashed it in my face. All a dream, right? I'd never had one like that before. I rarely dreamt at all, and when I did it was usually about locations, not events. My dreams were never *plot-driven*, you could say. Just nonsense dreamscapes — vast Jerusalem catacombs sculpted of sand, mile-wide warehouses with illogical conveyer belts, titanic ocean storm walls guarding nothing.

But this? This had been real. As vivid as an HD camera. Tactile in awful ways. I could still hear the twisting tear of Baby ripping in half, the detailed pop of those little reptile vertebrae, the rip of sinew and tendons. There was something disturbing about the way the man in the gray coat had just pulled and pulled, applying more and more pressure, like a curious child testing the physical limits of a savannah monitor's skeleton until he broke them. He wasn't there to kill. He was there to *play*.

But Addie's stupid lizard was fine. Safe at home. In her enclosure. Right?

Right.

I twisted off the faucet.

Just a nightmare.

It's jarring, trying to write off half a day of detailed memories. Your body resists it, like jet lag. I couldn't believe it was Friday afternoon again; it felt like early Saturday morning. What if it had been a flash-forward of some sort? A premonition? Or something knottier and more complex, like time travel?

Time travel. I recalled the urban legend Holden once told me of the young honeymooning couple driving through the New Mexico scablands, right through some sort of temporal blister. Their watches stopped working. They fell five hours out of synch with the rest of the world. So when they stopped for food at some trucker diner, they were horrified when the waitress who seated them was just empty skin. A hollow bag of dried-out skin and nothing else — no bones or tissue inside. The entire diner had been like that, a crowd of grinning human taxidermies, gaping eye sockets and mouths, seated in their booths. Moral of the story? Don't fall out of synch with time, I guess. I don't know what happened to the couple afterward.

Hell, I didn't know what was happening to me *right now*.

Shadows moved under the door. Holden tapped twice. "Dan, you okay?"

"I'm fine."

"What're you doing?"

"Heroin."

Muffled voices outside, and I heard Holden again: "No, no, he's joking; he's not actually doing heroin in there—"

I checked my phone out of mindless habit — and promptly wished I hadn't. Because according to my iPhone, it wasn't Friday at all. It was Saturday, March 20. The time was 3:36 a.m. I even had an hour-old text message from Holden, sent after he took my broom home at the conclusion of our Friday night ghost hunt.

The screen trembled in my hands.

The twenty-four hour countdown was still ticking.

NEW TEXT MESSAGE
SENDER: "Holden" (509) 555-8727
SENT: 2:01 a.m. Mar 20 2015

Glad you're OK. Still got the rifle in my trunk will destroy it tomorrow just to be safe. Get some sleep buddy see u tomorrow for briar mine.

10 Hours, 31 Minutes

I returned to my seat, taking careful steps.

Everyone in Jitters seemed to be watching me. Even the baristas fell silent, eyeing me between stacked cups on the counter. I was hyper-aware of my own heartbeat, the mechanical push and pull of my breathing, the scuff of my footsteps on hardwood. Not frightened or panicked, because those were unproductive emotions. Just . . . alert. Aware. Like a deer that may — or may *not* — have just heard the distant snick of a rifle's disengaging safety.

I sat back down with Holden, squealing my chair, and sipped my coffee with shaky hands. As cold as tap water.

"Second thoughts?" he asked me.

"About what?"

"Your new gun."

Right. I remembered that although I'd jumped back twelve hours in time, the Head-Scratching Rifle was still in my possession. In the trunk of my Celica parked outside. I'd just detailed my intentions to Holden, and he'd invited himself along. I'd been too gentle — or maybe too lonely — to sway him. He'd show up at my house with *Haunted* equipment and his Ouija board. History was set to repeat itself.

Outside, Paul Bunyan's grinning head trucked past on an eighteen-wheeler. A chug of diesel fumes and a flash of piano-white teeth in the sunlight. Just like before.

"Creepy," Holden murmured this time, watching it go.

Maybe I'd wake up again, I supposed. This would turn out to be another blistering salvia-trip of a dream. That was the only way to describe it. My cell phone said it was Saturday morning, the rest of the world said it was Friday afternoon, and I was in the throes of another mind-bending nightmare.

But the big man who killed Baby did make some sort of sense. I recognized the greatcoat; it was trademark winter-wear for the armed forces of the Soviet Union. I'd thumbed over hundreds of black and white photos of men cloaked in these things, warming their wrapped hands over barrel fires, fiddling with their Mosins and SKS's, grinning for impromptu group shots. You can buy Russian greatcoats at army surplus stores; stiff, itchy robes that chafe your skin and reek of mildew and spray-on mite killer. They weren't pretty, but they'd keep you alive when the wind chill hit the negatives.

So that was it. I'd dreamt a uniformed Red Army ghost walked into my house and tore Adelaide's savannah monitor in half. One of the Head-Scratching Rifle's prior victims, maybe? Trapped in a hateful, mind-melting eternity, seeking gory revenge on all living creatures, great and small? Sure, sounded good.

Step one complete. Ghost seen.

Step two: how do I avoid becoming one, myself?

"Holden, I have a hypothetical question." I ran out of air and remembered to breathe, sucking in a coldness that stung my throat. "In theory, if we . . . if we proceed with this investigation tonight and we do find a demonic entity attached to the Mosin Nagant, how would we fight it?"

He put down his pen. "You don't *fight* demons, Dan."

Rookie mistake. I adjusted my goals. "How would we . . . survive it, then?"

"We'd destroy the rifle, obviously, because that's the demon's vessel. The physical object that anchors it in our world. We'd bury the pieces, or better yet, drive up to White Bend and throw them in the river—"

"Why is that better?"

"Some mediums believe . . ." He looked embarrassed. "Well, that unclean spirits can't cross bodies of water."

I shook my head. "It already did. It's from Russia."

"Surviving it, though . . ." He sipped his coffee and stared out at the teriyaki place across the street. "There's a lot of popular misconception about demons, Dan. People think that they're just asshole ghosts. They're not. They're not even human. Never have been. They don't just regard us the way we regard insects, because . . . well, we don't dump salt on slugs for fun. Cruelty is their language. They feed off human pain, weakness, sin . . ."

"Well, excellent." That pretty much summed up my life after Addie died.

"The biggest mistake you can make is trying to understand one," he said. "Don't even try to wrap your mind around them. Your mind will stretch, rip and bleed. They exist outside of time, on lower dimensions, in dark, cold places incompatible with human life. Places far from God. If a demon, well, *has* you, it's like crossing the event horizon of a black hole. Doesn't matter if you move up, forward, back, or even go *backward in time*, because when you're in it, all routes take you in the same direction. Down."

"To Hell?"

"Like I said, your brain will bleed—"

"Do you believe in Hell?"

"I believe in God." He finished his coffee. "And I covered all this demon stuff at the Hostess factory. Remember?"

I didn't. But it had been one of our highest-rated episodes, raccoon corpse and all. I stood up, wobbling on slushy knees. "I . . . I left my wallet in my car."

I was lying, of course. I told myself that my migraine was pounding and I just needed fresh air, but that was also a lie. My headache had vanished. I really just wanted to pop my trunk and get another look at that Mosin Nagant. I needed to see it with my own eyes, to verify that the rancid, plastic-wrapped thing was here in my trunk on Friday afternoon and not on my dining-room table on Saturday morning. It was my link, a sinister thread connecting dream and reality.

"You're sure you're okay?"

I pushed through Jitters' front door and out into the parking lot. The coldness pierced my hoodie and my skin erupted in goose bumps. Gritty snowflakes stung my eyes. The afternoon sun burned lantern-like, lost behind a thick cataract of clouds.

I checked my phone again. 3:45 a.m.

Not good.

Apparently I'd broken time and space so severely that the sun was shining at three in the morning. I tried to laugh but couldn't.

My black Toyota was alone in the parking lot, just a shadow behind sheets of falling static. A film of dry snow had already overtaken the slope of my windshield.

I opened the trunk but the metal surface scalded my bare fingers. I tore my hand away, gasping gray mist. This wasn't a normal coldness for early spring in the inland northwest. This was something else. I found myself wishing for that Soviet ghost's ass-ugly wool coat.

I propped the trunk open with my elbows.

There it was.

The infamous Head-Scratching Rifle was still in its cardboard mailing box. I opened the top flap and peered inside at the gooey, wrapped rifle. I could see the pointed barrel and front sight, and underneath, the tucked bayonet. The ancient bolt-action weapon was dormant, still slumbering in its cocoon of jellied chemicals.

"This is all real," I said aloud.

I'm not dreaming.

"It's Friday afternoon. And I'm in the Jitters parking lot."

Because this is real—

But I noticed something.

Inside the bag, a powdery substance was caked on the Mosin Nagant, raising the plastic in gray clumps. All over it, from barrel to stock. This was new. This strange powder — whatever it was — hadn't been on the rifle when I'd opened the bag in my house with Holden. In my dream.

So I peeled off the skin-like plastic (again) for a closer look. Handling a firearm in a public place is Darwin Award-worthy, yes, but I was alone in the parking lot. The snowy whiteout had reduced visibility to silhouettes. Keeping the weapon in the trunk, I palmed off a clump of sludgy powder, like wet sand, and recoiled at the pungent odor — ammonia. Like cat urine.

It was cat litter.

The Mosin Nagant was coated in cat litter.

Like it had been buried for two weeks in a neglected litterbox. Clumps of sand hardened to the rifle's seams in damp globs. Something rattled inside the barrel and dropped out, bouncing off my foot — a blackened cat turd, bumpy with grains of litter. Adelaide called them Kitty Rocas.

I suppressed a violent gag. The ammonia odor was so dense, I was almost nostalgic for the yeasty foulness from before. I dropped the Head-Scratching Rifle back in my trunk, but my fingers were already slick with acrid cat piss. Seriously, to hell with that thing. I wished it had a face so I could punch it. And I knew it was attacking me, in whatever ways it could. Big or small. Any way it could get to me — by being repulsive, by being eerie, by stabbing my thumb, by warping time — it was going to work on me, busily attacking my sanity. Bleeding out my willpower with a thousand little papercuts.

That Kitty Roca in the barrel? Just one more mental papercut, I guess.

I slammed the trunk.

Another blade of freezing wind slashed at me. Plates of snow crunched under my footsteps as I returned to Jitters, one hand raised against the sudden blizzard. Scabs of cat litter stuck between my fingers, crunchy and moist.

Cruelty is its language.

When I got back inside Jitters, I'd wash my hands about fifty times, order another coffee, and tell Holden everything. I'd describe the twelve-hour dream, or premonition, or whatever it was. And this time, on this bizarrely reset version of Friday, I wouldn't investigate the rifle or risk Holden's life by stupidly permitting him to drag himself into it. I'd destroy the thing, and hurl the pieces into the White River, just like he'd suggested, and that'd be that. Right?

What if I just wake up in Jitters again? With the rifle in my trunk?

Hell, I'd already lost twelve hours.

. . . Or somewhere worse?

I shivered and pushed open Jitters' front door with both hands, leaving a butterfly pattern of smears on the glass. Maybe this wasn't really a Groundhog Day-esque temporal nightmare, and I was just losing my mind. Detaching from reality, like an untethered astronaut falling into the void. That's what happened to everyone else, right? Ben Dyson and the others? Maybe right now, it was really Saturday morning and I was pressing the Head-Scratching Rifle to my chin and reaching for the trigger—

I froze in the doorway.

I'd entered Jitters. But I wasn't inside Jitters.

I saw a different room entirely. No Holden. No baristas. No paper lights. Just a squared storefront with prison-gray walls. Center aisles lined with red solvent bottles, leather holsters, and little square patches. A long glass counter packed with tagged semi-automatics and revolvers. Behind it, a back wall bristling with shotguns and rifles. And the sudden, disarming comfort of room temperature. This place ran its thermostat much hotter than Jitters.

I was back in Joe's Guns.

My stomach turned to water and tugged my throat in contracting pulls. I felt ants crawling on my skin. The prickle of millions of insect feet. And a powerful wrongness somewhere deep inside me; a wrenching dislocation between time and space. I didn't even notice the old man standing by the cash register, eyeballing me —

it was Not Joe, the tired old guy who'd sold me the Mosin Nagant on behalf of Ben Dyson's surviving family — until he exhaled and muttered something under his breath.

It sounded like: "Well, *shit*."

10 Hours, 2 Minutes

I'd entered a coffee shop and ended up in a gun store six miles away. So, yes, this was definitely getting worse.

"I have it," Not Joe said.

I jolted.

"I have it, I have it," he echoed, ducking into the back room to get something. I knew what it was. I knew exactly what he was talking about, because we'd had this conversation before. All of it. Even his annoyed grunt as I entered the store — "Well, shit" — because that was exactly what he'd said the first time. He knew I was here to pick up the Mosin Nagant that killed Mr. Dyson last year in Georgia. The creepy blood gun. Déjà vu didn't even begin to describe it.

The jail-barred front door whooshed shut behind me, with JOE'S GUNS stenciled backwards on the glass. Under it, accompanied by a silhouette of a ghillied sniper shouldering his rifle: REACH OUT AND TOUCH SOMEONE. Outside, the blizzard was gone. No pelting waves of snow, no arctic winds. Just the same watery sky I remembered from Friday morning, dumping sporadic handfuls of slush. And my black Toyota Celica, now with no snow on the windshield, parked beside a blue Ford pickup.

This is time travel, I thought numbly.

Like wristwatches running backwards in the Kalash. I'm falling back in time—

Something clanked harshly on glass and I whirled, my throat tightening. Not Joe was back at the counter, setting the rifle on the surface. The Head-Scratching Rifle was once again bundled in its slimy, skin-like cocoon, because Not Joe couldn't bring himself to touch it with his bare skin. Because, as he would shortly explain to me, it had just felt *wrong, radioactive somehow.*

At least there was no cat piss on it this time.

He looked up at me again. "You know what this is?"

Last time, I'd played dumb and said: *An M44?* This time I just hesitated dumbly on the spot, words lumping on my tongue. My brain was a squirming coil of loose thoughts.

Free-falling backwards in time . . .

Time travel is always so clean in movies — our heroes punch a precise time and date into their magic device and away they go. Like selecting floors on an elevator. It was never like this; sporadic, uncontrolled, like plunging down a dark shaft to an unknown dark floor. I tasted slippery terror. I'd already barfed in the bathroom sink at Jitters two hours in the future, but who knows how this worked? Maybe my stomach was full again.

"I asked you a question." Not Joe pointed at the rifle with two fingers, hooked in an arthritic claw. "Do you know what this is?"

Oh, God, I sure don't.

I'd thought I did. But I'd been wrong.

The rifle lay between us like a bagged corpse. Smeared with those gummy clots of yellow-brown sludge I knew all too well. I could smell it again, that familiar stew of yeast and insect musk, and under it — yes, maybe Holden had been right — the sharp stench of decay? Putrid flesh, souring and bulging with trapped bacterial gases. Had it been hiding from me before? How did I miss it the first time? More importantly, when *was* the first time? Like a snake eating its tail, time was a dizzying loop.

"It's a blood gun," Not Joe answered his own question.

"Yeah. I know. It's killed someone." This was a deviation from Friday's first timeline; I'd jumped the dialogue forward a few beats and stolen his line.

He didn't seem to mind. "Do I know you?"

I didn't have time to recite the script. "What time is it?"

"Twelve thirty."

I checked my cell phone: 4:01 a.m.

Yep. Time and space is still broken.

"I . . . I don't want to buy the gun," I blurted out. "I changed my mind."

The air thickened between us.

Not Joe eyed me crookedly, like I was an alien wrapped in human skin. He was right to be suspicious; I was an imposter in this world of Friday, March 19. I looked the part, I sounded the part, I literally *was* the part, but I felt stranded on the moon. Wearing my body as a spacesuit. In the corner of the store, a fluorescent light buzzed like a hornet, then flickered and died.

"Just now?" he asked. "You changed your mind?"

I shrugged aimlessly and leaned on the counter, as chilly as lake ice. "Like you said. It just feels . . . wrong, somehow."

He looked puzzled. "I didn't say that."

"Believe me, you did."

If this really was time travel, I supposed wishfully, perhaps I could just rewrite the past here by not purchasing that damn thing and simply leaving the store empty-handed. Maybe the Head-Scratching Rifle would retcon itself out of my life. Like entering the Cretaceous period and stomping on the right butterfly — *squish* — and then I could stand back and let Ray Bradbury's temporal physics do the rest—

He shrugged. "Sure."

"Sure?"

"But you still owe the transfer fee. To reimburse us for—"

"Deal." I scooted my debit card across the glass. He punched buttons and tore a receipt. Thirty-nine dollars. I signed with a half-assed Nike swoosh and threw the pen down, glancing over at the rifle. "Done?"

"Done."

"Transaction canceled?"

He nodded, making a sour face. "Something smells like cat pee."

I wiped my hands on my jeans. I remembered that leering customer — the guy with cat piss on his breath who'd told me the story of Laika, the Soviet Union's unlucky first cosmonaut — and wondered with a nervous tremor if that had been his breath after all. Time seemed to be porous; maybe odors seeped through. Was that even the first time I'd been here?

I stepped back, away from the Mosin Nagant on the counter. Technically, it wasn't mine — not anymore — but that didn't make me feel any better. Demonic evil probably doesn't abide by Federal Firearms License paperwork. Somehow I knew with a grim certainty; I could flee Joe's Guns right now and never look back, but the Head-Scratching Rifle would remain with me, its tendrils hooked inside me, its alien cells quietly multiplying in my brain like cancer.

I glanced up at a wall bristling with cutting-edge tech — P90's, SCAR's, F2000's decked out with red lasers and holographic sights — and found it darkly amusing that the most dangerous thing in this room full of assault rifles was a wooden, single-shot clunker. Then again, I remembered, *assault rifle* is a misnomer. Adelaide had corrected me once, in this very same gun store: *Those are just scary-looking semi-*

automatics, Dan. Real military "assault weapons" have fire selectors for automatic fire, and they've been illegal in the US since the 1930s. So when you hear people wring their hands about how we need to ban those evil "assault rifles," it tells you that they have no idea what they're talking about.

Yes, she'd been a bit of a know-it-all. But her words stuck in my mind; an American gun nut with an oh-so-proper English accent. Sometimes I wondered if she ever felt like a cultural orphan, forsaken by both sides of the pond.

I shivered.

The temperature in Joe's Guns was now plunging. I could feel the air change around us; a gathering chill that seemed to originate on the floor and rise in drafts. Cold pillows. Not as bad as the subzero heat-death of the Jitters parking lot, or the woods outside my house, but it was getting there. Fast. Like something else, something not of this world, was greedily siphoning the warmth.

I wondered: *why is it always so cold?*

"You look familiar," Not Joe said, his breath fogging the air between us. "You on TV?"

I wasn't listening. Something else had occurred to me, something monumentally terrifying. Just one sentence. But the most terrifying sentence I'd ever read, because now I understood its meaning. The last thing Ben Dyson ever typed on that sweltering July afternoon in Macon, Georgia, via a WordPress post on his laptop, seconds before blowing his face off with the cursed Mosin Nagant I'd so willingly introduced into my life.

SO COLD IN HERE.

Not Joe paused and looked over my shoulder.

As I turned around, my mind whispered: *The ghost in the Soviet greatcoat. He's here.*

* * *

He was standing at the door.

Perfectly still, statuesque, as if he'd been out there for hours, peering eagerly into Joe's Guns like a Black Friday shopper. Today's milky daylight exposed every inch of him in crisp detail. I'd been right; that greatcoat was definitely Russian military-issue, worn in patches to reveal tufts of decayed yellow. So was the leather-brown utility belt encircling his belly, bulging with flapped pouches, pockets, and a dirty oilcan. All things I'd only seen before in black and white.

He wore a gas mask. It encircled his head in flattened walls like a half-crushed beer can, and two round eye apertures gave it a vaguely insectoid look. The nose of the mask was protracted, snout-like, and from it dangled a flaccid air tube. About a foot and a half of corrugated black rubber, attached to nothing. It looked like the design of the apparatus — some antique trench-warfare thing designed to guard against mustard gas or blister agents — called for the breathing tube to coil around the cheek, into a goiter-like filter box on the neck. This creature was wearing the mask incorrectly, but it hardly seemed to matter. I don't think it breathed.

And it was standing outside the door. Staring at us, through the jail-barred glass, right over the REACH OUT AND TOUCH SOMEONE sniper sticker.

I shivered.

Not Joe regarded the man in the gas mask with dull suspicion, like he'd seen much worse, and glanced at me. "You know this guy?"

My throat dried up.

"*Hey*. You know him?"

"Kinda," I managed.

"You don't *kinda* know someone. Yes or no?"

I hesitated — actually, this could be the literal definition of *kinda*.

"I think he's here for you," Not Joe said.

I remembered the poor homeless guy who'd hitchhiked three time zones just to hang himself upside-down from the Kalash ceiling with barbed wire. And his nonsensical final words to his buddies: *Well, the Gasman has summoned me.*

This was the Gasman.

He still held the severed upper half of Adelaide's savannah monitor in one fist, like a toddler clutching a favorite toy. I recognized Baby's front legs, her toe claws hanging limp. Several inches of bloody spine dangled from her torso, making her resemble a two-foot tadpole. With his other hand, the Gasman reached for the door.

"Oh, *shit*—"

I lurched backward, off-balance, bumping a rack of blue gun manuals—

THUNK. The front door clicked.

Not Joe rolled his eyes.

I looked back and the door was still shut. The apparition was still outside. It took me a moment to realize — the Gasman had pushed it with his gloved hand. It hadn't budged. So he adjusted his hulking stance, reached, and pushed again.

THUNK.

"Pull the door," Not Joe said. "Don't push it."

The Gasman pushed again, harder.

THUNK.

"*Pull* the damn door. It's on the sign—"

THUNK. THUNK.

The old man sighed. "Jesus Christ—"

"Don't let him in," I whispered.

"Son, he seems to be not letting himself in."

"If he gets inside, shoot him."

THUNK. THUNK. THUNK.

The Gasman kept forcing the door — the same identical motion, each time a little harder. A little rougher. The frame creaked. His head didn't move; his mask stayed focused on us, studying us. Maybe just studying me. This thing had followed me, *stalked* me — from Saturday morning to Friday afternoon, from the twentieth of March to the nineteenth, like an extra-dimensional predator.

Who was, at the moment, baffled by a door.

THUNK-THUNK.

There was a frightening stupidity to those flat eyes. Maybe it was the way the eyeholes seemed to stare out in slightly opposite directions. Maybe it was the goofy snout-like profile of the mask, like a sports mascot. Or maybe it was the simple fact that it had spent the last ninety seconds pushing a door clearly marked PULL. But morbidly, I wondered if a human face even existed underneath that shaped rubber. My arms prickled and my next breath fogged the air.

The coldness, I realized. *The Gasman brings it.*

Like rancid meat brings flies.

Not Joe bunched up his flannel shirt to reveal a holstered pistol on his hip. "Hey!"

The Gasman paused.

"Yeah, you." The old man's voice boomed. "Take a big step back."

The Gasman did. Then he kicked the door.

CRUNCH. The glass spider-webbed with icy cracks and the dangling open/closed sign clattered to the linoleum.

I backed up to the counter. "*Now* can you shoot him?"

"Not unless you're gonna help me drag a giant-ass corpse inside." It took me a second to grasp what Not Joe meant by that. His pistol was out now, held at his side, a boxy little automatic with a checkered grip. Through the corner of his mouth he hissed: "Go out the back and call 911."

"What?"

"The fire exit. Take it—"

THUNK-CRASH.

The Gasman punched the door with his gloved fists. An exploding circle of cracks. The door sagged and a hinge blew out.

Not Joe aimed, his finger on trigger. "Go!"

It was about to get loud. I vaulted the gun counter, kicking over a cup of *Don't Tread on Me* pens, and bolted for the back office, my eardrums pressurizing, my veins surging with blood. Another ice-tray light fizzled overhead.

His raw voice chased me: "Go, go, *go*!"

CRUNCH-THUNK—

I hurtled through the back room, a dingy little office with a Windows 95 box monitor and last year's wall calendar swarmed with yellow Post-its. I pivoted, tripping over a surge protector, my shoes squealing on bare cement foundation (*where is it, where is it?*) and found the emergency exit door behind two flattened cardboard boxes. ALARM WILL SOUND, said a red stencil. I wrenched it open, a ponderous thing that squealed on gritty hinges. Alarm didn't sound.

Also, it didn't lead outside.

It led into another building, miles away.

* * *

At my feet, the floor morphed from cement foundation to itchy blue carpet. The back exit of the gun shop looked out into the *Haunted* production office.

Where I worked.

Our show's base of operations is the Ferguson complex, a dried-out corpse of a building. A cavernous hollow of vacant office suites; a mega-corporate office without a mega-corporation — chopped up and divvied among local businesses so we could squat under its giant bones. Plastic plants, fake skylights, and a drained water fountain in the lobby that stank of bug spray. I was looking down the long hallway into our cubicle farm.

To reiterate — from the back exit of Joe's Guns, I could see my work desk. This was problematic.

Free-falling through time . . .

I hesitated there, between times and places, my fingers tightly gripping the doorframe and brick exterior wall. In the gun store behind me, I heard the cymbal crash of disintegrating glass. The Gasman was coming in.

Down the hallway ahead of me, a ponytailed head prairie-dogged up from the gray cube walls. A production assistant (usually a community college intern because they'll work for free). This one's name was either Sarah, Amy, or Casey. She stared agape at me, and at the gun store I'd apparently brought in with me. She dropped something — I heard papers fluttering onto carpet. Then the chattering thud of a stapler.

I waved. "Hi."

I knew what this was. *When* this was. This was last Tuesday, a few days before I'd purchased the Head-Scratching Rifle from Joe's Guns. I'd skulked into the production office to grab a paycheck from my inbox. I'd planned to take the freight doors and discreetly SEAL-Team-Six my way in and out, but of course I'd been immediately spotted by Sarah/Amy/Casey, whose corner cube guarded the hallway. At least that time, I hadn't brought a gun store into the office with me. This was much more awkward.

She clasped her hands to her mouth. "Oh my God—"

CRUNCH-THUD. The front door to Joe's Guns crashed down flat somewhere behind me, the sound wobbling strangely between dimensions. An echo trapped forever between Friday and Tuesday. I expected to hear the pop of Not Joe's gunshots — but heard only the Gasman's incoming footsteps, boots crunching kernels of glass . . .

I stepped forward, into the *Haunted* production office, and slammed the emergency exit door to Joe's Guns. Doors seemed to give the Gasman momentary trouble, but somehow I knew — he'd always get through. He'd always follow.

"Oh my God," the intern gasped again.

"Uh . . ." I pressed the door, making sure it clicked shut. "Yeah, don't go in there."

But Sarah/Amy/Casey just stared, shaking her head in slow disbelief. Now that I was fully inside the production office I could see it, too — the brick exterior wall of (Friday's) Joe's Guns was crammed into the hallway of (Tuesday's) Ferguson building, like two dollhouses violently mashed into the same space. The office walls were bowed, exploding windows and exposing rebar bones. The floor sagged under my feet. Ceiling tiles dropped and a sprinkler pipe leaked overhead, drizzling gray water. I was pretty sure I'd either proven or disproven Einstein's Theory of General Relativity. Not sure which.

I pointed weakly. "Sorry about . . . all that."

Her eyes welled with shocked tears. Fingertips raking against her cheeks: "You . . . oh, holy shit, is that a *building*?"

I brushed drywall powder from my hair. "Yes. Yes, it is."

"Is that Discount Guns?"

"Joe's Guns."

"How did you . . . do that?"

I almost laughed. I didn't *do* it. I had no control over this. If I did, I would've parked Joe's Guns somewhere else. And I had to keep moving. The Gasman was coming. So I raced on through the *Haunted* production office, grabbing a handful of M&M's from the Sasquatch bowl on Holden's desk.

"Don't stay here," I shouted over my shoulder. "Something *really bad* is going to come through that door after me."

Her eyes followed me over cubicle walls. "Where . . . where are you going?"

I passed my empty desk, passed the crooked doorway to LJ's office marked UNIT PRODUCTION MANAGER, and elbowed through the fire escape door.

For the first time in a long time (I couldn't specify exactly how long, since time had become so bizarrely malleable), I had a plan. An objective. A relentless, pulsing thought that crowded out all others. All paths lead backwards in time, right? Never mind the gas-masked creature behind me — I felt a strange excitement building in my guts. A shivery, reckless glee.

"Dan, where are you going?" Sarah/Amy/Casey shouted after me, but I'd left the fire door swinging and I was already going, going, gone. Vanishing over the next event horizon, deeper into the rabbit hole. Hell, I've always had a self-destructive streak.

Adelaide.

Yep, she was my goal. My race against time. Before the dream dissipated, before the salvia trip burned off, before the Gasman caught me.

Oh my God, I can actually see Addie again.

If I hurry.

8 Hours, 4 Minutes

The *Haunted* production office led to my kitchen, where I'd found Addie's soured coffee creamer in the fridge.

My kitchen led to my parents' rancher in Astoria.

My parents' living room led to the cramped interior of a Greyhound bus, bumping shoulders with greasy strangers and runaways.

I hurtled from locale to locale, memory to memory, as if I were running down a passenger train. Bolting down the center aisle, crashing through each connecting door, on to the next car down. A literal train of thoughts. Somehow I knew this bizarre suspension of physics could evaporate at any moment, that my time was running out.

The Greyhound's side exit led to the post office lobby, where I'd waited in line to fill out a yellow form to update Adelaide's mailing address to *dead*.

The post office led to my dining room (I think we're back to late February now) where I'd gritted my teeth and pried bullets from their casings with needle-nose pliers, pouring gunpowder in a black hourglass heap on the table. The rifle itself was still in bureaucratic limbo, awaiting its transfer from Ben Dyson's widow to Joe's Guns, but in the meantime I'd mail-ordered a cheap box of Czechoslovakian 7.62x54R ammo to engineer my backup plan. Because *backup plan* sounded more rational than *bullet bomb*.

This led to more nights of research, of lying belly-down on the living-room carpet, submerged in the wan blue glow of my laptop. Frozen pizzas, Wild Turkey, and sinus headaches. Hunting the Russian legend of the Head-Scratching Rifle (which was now, ironically, hunting me), hacking through a tedious snarl of Creepypasta myths and serial number databases while missed calls and well-meaning voicemails accumulated on my phone.

Now reliving all of it in reverse, I couldn't believe I'd worked so hard to track down this obscure evil and willfully introduce it into my already fractured life. Like turning a hurricane loose against a sandcastle. I pretty much deserved this. Adelaide would've laughed.

She will. She *will* laugh. When I tell her.

Maybe I was losing it. But I kept running, kept barreling down my own train of thoughts, rewinding the depressing movie of Dan J. Rupley's life, and the Gasman was always a car or two behind me. I saw his circular glass eyes approaching from the darkness of my backyard, glinting in the porch light like cat irises, and before the rest of his body came into view he'd looked like a floating head. I saw him again in my parents' kitchen. He nearly cornered me in the Farwell Thrift Mart, coming down the frozen food aisle. He followed. He never stopped. He was always there, the slow tsunami at my back, pursuing me deeper and deeper into my past. To stand still was to die. Motion is life, right?

Adelaide died an hour before midnight on New Year's Eve. If I could push through the rest of January and break into 2014, I could see her again. Before the accident. That was all I wanted. To find her, to see her again, to smell the mango shampoo in her hair, to hear her laugh, to feel her fingertips on my shoulder, to live a moment with her one last time. Any moment. It's chillingly convenient when you think about it — my goal with the Head-Scratching Rifle had been to find evidence of the afterlife, so I'd know that I might someday be reunited with Addie's eternal soul. Now, I was on my way to see her right now. I practically had her address. Almost too easy, right? Just a few cars to go . . .

Maybe Addie was onto something when she'd said my brain was over-compartmentalized; filled with Tupperware. We're into early January now. Like being funneled through an Ikea, through room after room of dioramas, all unnaturally conjoined.

The Farwell Thrift Mart led to Holden's driveway.

Holden's driveway led to the cemetery.

The cemetery led to that church on Pine, where we'd held Addie's funeral service. Her stateside one, at least (her parents had put on a much fancier burial in the Edgbaston suburb of Birmingham, far beyond the reach of us American yokels). So this was Farwell Methodist, a small-town church with peeling paint, a yellow lawn, and amusingly snarky signboard messages. Addie and I used to pass it on our workday carpool, and every Monday we'd crane our necks to see the week's new message: THAT CARRIE UNDERWOOD SONG IS A METAPHOR, DON'T EXPECT JESUS TO LITERALLY TAKE THE WHEEL.

I came in through the side entrance, from the restrooms, dodging the bottleneck of mourners. I didn't want to be seen — this time or the last. I passed a folding table stocked with untouched lemon bars and four carafes of room-temperature coffee. The auditorium hummed with murmured voices and creaking chairs, all hushing in unison. Before Adelaide's parents spoke, they put on an iMovie slideshow and scored it to Green Day's *Time of Your Life*, because she wasn't alive to point out how much of a cliché that was. I knew the funeral's exact date because I'd helped circulate the e-invites — January sixth.

I was almost back to her. I only had to free-fall six more days into the past.

Keep on falling . . .

It occurred to me then, as the first guitar strums crackled through the cheapo speakers — when I returned to 2014, would I find the real Adelaide? When I finally reached her, before the accident, at LJ's lake house on New Year's Eve — would it really be her? Her soul, I mean. I suppose that was the million-dollar question: would she be a ghost, a memory, or something else?

I was afraid of the answer.

And the Gasman. That bulbous face and ragged greatcoat would always be a step behind me, like an inescapable figure from a nightmare. But I'd worry about all of that later, because I couldn't stop now. I was too close to her.

Keep going . . .

Green Day was mourning *tattoos, memories, and dead skin on trial* when I passed through the assembly. Rows of gray folding chairs loaded with friends, coworkers, distant family. Someone sobbed in the back, and someone else munched chips (who eats *chips* at a funeral?). Photos of Adelaide clicked through the blue-tinted projector at fifteen-second intervals, and I was conspicuously absent from each one. Yes, whenever possible, her parents had cropped me out.

I crept behind the back row, trying to remain unseen — but heard a collective gasp from the crowd. Shock. I turned around, expecting to see the Gasman's insectoid face looming in the hallway behind me.

The hall was empty.

And I realized that on the pull-down screen, the projector had clicked to *that* photo. I remembered it because I'd taken it. A dumb-luck accident, shot from the hip at the Mount St. Helens National Monument. Addie and I were hiking inside the volcanic blast zone, on that ridge where some poor volcanologist was made famous in

1980 for his last words, breathlessly cried into his radio: *Vancouver, Vancouver, this is it!* The mountain loomed in our background; a sad, cavernous shell cloaked in rainclouds. Even after decades of recovery, the land was still a beaten slurry of logs and damp mud. There's regrowth and foliage, but it's clumpy, scrubby, like the stuff you'd find in the Mojave. Millions of fallen trees, bleached as white as exposed bones.

And here's Adelaide Radnor, stepping over a particularly thick trunk, profiled against the gray ruin and dome of churned clouds, in her sundress and hiking boots, her sunglasses on her forehead and her blonde hair whipped up by a sudden breeze. She was about to turn to face the camera — face me, as I snapped the spontaneous picture — but the image had frozen her in this moment, this fragile half-second of almost. We could almost see her face. She could almost see us. *Almost*, forever.

It shattered me. It hurt worse than a million preppy yearbook photos, because she was real in it. She's not smiling, she's not posing, she's not wearing mascara, she's not even aware she's being immortalized for her own funeral slideshow. She's just Addie, just the woman I wanted to marry, with the sun in her eyes and a red zit on her cheek, leaning to step over a dead tree.

I'll find you, I promised her.

I'll see you again.

Someone blew his nose, an abrupt goose honk.

Now Green Day closed the final chorus about hoping you've had the time of your life, and sure enough, that haunting Mount St. Helens pic was the one her parents had chosen to end the slideshow on. Fading in, stenciled in white Tahoma font: ADELAIDE LYNNE RADNOR. ALIVE IN OUR MEMORY.

As I kept going and crashed through the church's double doors, on to the next train car down, I realized that was literally the plan. I couldn't have put it better myself. Alive in memory? Let's hope so.

Keep going . . .

But I looked back — one final sidelong glance at Addie's funeral, to see if the Gasman's snouted face had joined the grieving crowd behind me — and I noticed another message had appeared on the projector screen, below the original. Same Tahoma font. But this one was new, unpunctuated, shouting in breathless caps-lock:

DAN TURN AROUND DON'T GO ANY FURTHER—

Nope. I let the heavy church doors swing shut behind me.

I'm coming, Addie.
I'll see you again.

* * *

From the funeral on, times and places smear together. I didn't stop for anything. I couldn't. The emotions were too fresh, too new. I just kept sprinting from place to place, kept hurtling forward (which was really backward); no time to examine my surroundings, no time to think or even change direction. The past is sticky. Like a basilisk running on water, you have to keep going or you sink.

Just flashes; embedded sense memories. The jungle-green linoleum and cheaply lacquered wood panels of the ICU. The rhythmic chime of a heart monitor. The sigh of a ventilator. Whispers, stiff hugs, greasy fast-food breakfasts. Motel lobbies in Boise, an ugly city of exposed brick and potholes. Myself, alone in my Celica, punching my steering wheel until a knuckle pops and bleeds. The heart-plunging way the trauma doctor had hesitated when Adelaide's mother asked about brain damage, and then said: *We're not really concerned about that right now.* The starchy odors of pressed bed sheets, bleach, and urine. The way her dad had to leave the room, stand in the cornered hallway by the restrooms, and cry where no one could see.

She was somewhere ahead. The Gasman was somewhere behind.

You know how if you watch a movie in reverse, the meaning changes? This would be like watching Addie slowly come back to life. In a sick way, it was exhilarating, and I ran faster, sprinting, barreling dangerously through time and space.

Don't stop. Don't look.

Somehow, I was everywhere at once. I was in the waiting room but I wasn't. I was in the aid car but I wasn't. I could feel the bruised car door, the whiplash of impact, the gummy cubes of safety glass the paramedics had picked out of her blonde hair, tangled and matted in clots of hardening blood. It hadn't even looked like Addie on that bed, her colorless skin pierced with needles, IV tubes and hanging bags, and her head had been *so collapsed*. Like a stomped beach ball. I remember not believing her face could possibly be attached to it. I remember being certain they had the wrong person. I remember wishing they had.

I was everywhere, and nowhere, and *almost there—*

NEW TEXT MESSAGE
SENDER: "Holden" (509) 555-8727
SENT: 7:18 a.m. Mar 20 2015

Dan wake up turn on the news. Clerk at joes guns shot himself with pistol last night. They're showing a photo was he the one who sold u that mosinnagant????

5 Hours, 9 Minutes

Burning skin.

I smelled burning skin. It's a dense, unmistakable odor. It turns the air solid, burns your eyes, and congeals on your tongue. Most disturbingly, it smells just a little bit like food. Like a hamburger thrown into a fireplace.

Burnt skin. Burnt hair. Burnt chemicals.

A guttural scream right beside me, loud enough to rupture eardrums. It exploded inside the confined space, a pressure-cooker roar ringing off tile walls, cut off by a wheezing gasp. Something ice-cold splashed my face.

I was in a bathroom. A man was doubled over the sink faucet beside me, hurling cupped handfuls of water into his beet-red face. Dirty smoke curled in the air. Black whiskers, scorched dead, fluttered to the sink like bugs. This was all okay. This was Kale Wong, and five seconds ago Kale's face had been on fire. Because on this New Year's Eve, he'd attempted 'fire breathing' out on the *Haunted* production manager's back porch. Apparently there's a special chemical that the professionals use, and it's not a water bottle of tiki torch fuel. No one had captured it on video, but they say that for a few transcendent seconds, Kale Wong looked just like the Ghost Rider.

He screamed a four-letter word into the sink, with sixteen extra vowels.

A crowd bottlenecked by the bathroom door. "Kale. You okay?"

He grabbed a fluffy white towel and mashed it to his face. It came back smeared muddy black. "I regret nothing."

"He's okay." I brushed soot from his shoulder.

He spat in the sink and looked up at me, the lower half of his face a mask of furious red. "How bad is it?"

"Not awful," I said. "Like a sunburn."

"Will it scar?"

As a time traveler, I knew it wouldn't. It would peel in crispy sheets — he'd look like an Asian Freddy Krueger at Addie's funeral — but the long-term damage was minimal. The real issue would be *Haunted*'s production schedule. Between my absence and his blistered face, LJ's financiers at the station would be biting their nails all January.

Kale rubbed his temple and an eyebrow came off.

"He's alright!" someone shouted in the hall, and good news passed through LJ's lake house one voice at a time. This would have become the story of the evening — if not for Adelaide's car accident. That happened an hour later, give or take.

Kale slapped a blackened towel to the floor and grabbed another. "I want to know where LJ bought these little towels, man. They're heavenly soft. Like baby butts—"

"I'm going to see her," I said.

"What?"

"I'm . . . I'm going to see Addie."

He nodded, dropping more burnt whiskers.

Oh my God. I felt a pull in my stomach. I hadn't thought about it — I'd just blurted it out, because memories seemed to have a strange, subtle momentum to them, like stepping into a waist-deep river current — but yes, I would see Adelaide now. She was here, at the party. She was downstairs.

Right now.

I pushed through the gathering crowd at the bathroom doorway, like elbowing through the ground floor of a concert. The acrid smell of scorched chemicals hung in the hall, a foggy haze of trapped smoke—

"Tell LJ he's out of tiki torch fuel!" Kale shouted behind me.

Down the hall. Gaining speed. I rounded a corner and side-scooted past Holden, drunk and happy. This Holden knew nothing of the Head-Scratching Rifle, Addie's death, or any of the bitter realities 2015 would bring. This Holden was still in 2014, and 2014 was the best year we'd ever had. It was the year we'd made it, the year *Haunted* indexed on the Nielsen ratings book (three times!), the year the Boise-based TV affiliate ordered a third season, the year the paychecks became regular. What a year 2014 had been.

I bumped his beer as I passed, splashing the wall. He was talking to some girl I didn't recognize. "Dan! Yes, Dan can verify. Remember the Deer Cap Dude? Three thermal signatures, on top of the lighthouse—"

"Warm glass," I said.

At the top of the stairs I passed Sarah/Amy/Casey, coming up with a fruity blue drink. She shouted in my ear — a question about Kale's face, I think — but I pretended not to hear her and kept going. My feet turned sideways, clomping down carpeted stairs, my hand squealing on the banister. Still chalky with sawdust, like the entire house was built yesterday.

Kale's voice boomed from upstairs: "KALE WONG REQUIRES ANOTHER DRINK!"

I descended fast, and LJ's first floor living room came into view, stretching up from the bottom like a stage revealed by a rising curtain. I saw sneakers, heels, jeans, legs in skirts — down, down the stairs — and then hands in pockets, hands nursing beers, sleeves rolled up to the elbow. Then faces, a sea of mixed faces, some turning to look at me as I stomped down the L-shaped staircase.

"Kale's okay, right?"

I scanned from face to face. I had to find her.

An iPod on the mantel played something by Snow Patrol; drowned out by a surge of hard laughter from LJ's dining room. They were playing Apples to Apples in there, and someone had just turned over the Hitler card. The Hitler card always wins.

A hand slapped my back.

It was Holden, wobbling downstairs: "Dan!"

I gripped the banister and craned my neck; from here I could see the red and green playing cards on the dining table. No Adelaide. If she wasn't in the dining room or the living room, that left the backyard. Plus the patio where Kale had attempted his disastrous fire breathing stunt. Or maybe she—

Holden's warm breath in my ear: "*Dan!*"

"Yeah?"

He took another swaying step downstairs, gripping my collarbone for balance. "I just . . . I just want you to know you're my best friend."

"You're my best friend, too."

"And . . . whatever happens. Whatever you need. I'm here for you. I will *fight a demon* for you, if you ask me to—"

I grabbed his wrist and squeezed, a sort of drunk Roman handshake. His words were oddly prophetic. Oddly loaded. He hadn't said this last time — in the original timeline of our New Year's party, I'd remained upstairs with Kale while he dabbed his face and some smartass handed him a shot glass burbling with Fireball whiskey — but Holden's words were real. The emotions behind them were real. Memories or not, this all felt *real,* somehow, and that gave me hope.

"Now, if you'll excuse me." Holden lurched past. "I must go outside and seize a once-in-a-lifetime opportunity to pee in my boss's birdbath."

It wasn't LJ's birdbath. It belonged to a neighbor. Property lines are messy around Lake Paiute; houses, yards, and bark gardens blend together. But on that time-locked staircase I watched past-Holden leave, feeling a strange melancholy wash over me. A strange sense of heartbreak. This world had no idea what was coming. No year would ever be better than 2014. And it was almost over.

Upstairs, through a cloud of laughter. "THE JUDGMENT OF KALE WONG IS NOT SUFFICIENTLY IMPAIRED! BRING ME A DRINK!"

That was when I saw her.

She'd materialized in the living room, backlit by LJ's fireplace full of candles. Suddenly, impossibly, she was just there. Like a *ghost*, if we're being ironic. Maybe she'd stepped out from behind someone taller. Maybe she'd been in the guest bedroom, or kneeling behind the sectional couch to fidget with her heel. But if she'd been visible, I would've seen her.

I couldn't have missed her.

4 Hours, 59 Minutes

Adelaide Lynne Radnor has a timid smile that flickers over her face like lightning. It's there, and then it's gone. Her eyes are big, open, alert; windows to a fierce intelligence. That'd been my first read on her, on that closed-off dock outside the Total Darkness Maze in Anacortes — this girl's eyes were always open. She was always looking, scanning, calculating. Running contingencies. She always knew where she was. I used to marvel at how someone could appear so vulnerable — and so frighteningly smart.

She'd curled her hair in wisps. One bang slid over her brow and required constant, self-conscious adjustment. She wore a yellow sundress that she'd fidgeted with the entire drive here. The birthmark on her shoulder was visible; a brown, inverted C the size of a quarter. This was a big deal. She hated that birthmark. This was only the second or third time she'd ever worn clothing that revealed it.

The entire party moved, a shifting blur of arms and legs, spilling drinks, all grins and guffaws, but I stood still on that staircase, and she stood still by the fireplace loaded with candles, and we both saw each other at the same time.

She smiled — that cautious lightning flash.

I smiled, too — dumb and puppyish.

She was here. She was real. All of this was real, as sharp as nails. And nothing, not even the Gasman, could take this moment away from me.

"Did Kale set his face on fire?" she asked over the crowd.

Kind of a mood-killer, I know.

I don't remember closing the distance. I just sort of freight-trained into her, squeezing her into a bear hug, and she entwined her fingers on the back of my neck as she always did. I was over a foot taller than her. She'd stand on her toes when we kissed. She smelled like perfume, shampoo, cigarette smoke from the patio outside. I felt her push into me, all soft skin and the fragile bones beneath, and realized she would be dead in forty minutes. Give or take.

"I love you," I whispered into her hair.

"That's nice," she said. "But what happened to Kale?"

Her voice was both familiar and chillingly alien. Six years in the states and she'd still kept her angular British accent, as sharp and poised as she was. I'd thought I'd never hear it again, outside of the voicemails I kept on my phone. My eyes blurred with tears — she was warm, alive, generating heat and wit. I wasn't imagining her. I'd tried, of course. I'd tried for weeks to relive our first meeting outside the Total Darkness Maze, where I'd taken her hand and guided her back through it (*Backward is forward*, I'd told her. How eerily right I'd been). But my imagination wasn't fertile enough for the vivid details I marveled at now — the way she kneaded her fingers on the back of my neck, kitten-like. The way her blonde hair spilled over her shoulders, tickling my wrists. The way she pushed upright, angled her head back, and surprised me with a spontaneous kiss. White zinfandel on her lips.

She drew back and saw tears in my eyes. "Are you okay?"

I nodded.

"Dan—"

"I'm okay."

"Is *he* okay?" She wrestled past but I held her. "What happened to Kale?"

"He's okay," I said, my voice coming in shallow breaths. "I'm okay, and you're okay. Everything is okay right now."

A brief window of expectant silence — the iPod was loading the next song. For a moment, the world turned unstable, and she looked at me, blinking, and I had to marvel at the IMAX depth of her eyes. Freckles of green on brown, melding in firework splashes of hazel. There's no way I could be imagining this, or remembering this. It was too real.

Then the next song triggered — Green Day's *Time of Your Life*. The song her parents had picked for her funeral slideshow. It knocked the wind out of me. It was a coincidence, but a coincidence you'd only notice from the future. Here we were, on the jagged edge of 2014, lovers out of time.

"Dan. What's going on?"

"A SHOT OF *FIREBALL*?" Kale bellowed from the second floor. "WHAT IS THIS, FUCKING KINDERGARTEN? KALE WONG REQUIRES BOURBON!"

"Addie," I whispered. "What day is it?"

"You're scaring me."

"Answer me. Please."

"It's . . . December thirty-first."

"What year?"

"2014." She checked the ebony clock on LJ's mantel. "For one more hour."

"How'd we meet?"

"Halloween Fright Fest. October twenty-fourth. The Total Darkness Maze." She smiled crookedly. "Backward is forward."

105

Backward is forward.
Yes, yes, it really is.

"I have to explain something to you." My mouth dried up. "It's going to sound crazy, like an acid trip. I'm not sure . . . I'm not even sure if I believe it yet—"

An explosion thumped outside and I flinched. No one else did.

She looked at me.

It was . . . thank God, it was just pre-celebratory fireworks over the lake. LJ's neighbors had a whole crate of illegal Indian reservation stuff on their dock. I remembered seeing it. So far, so good. The hollow report rattled through pine trees, and a fireball of orange and white bloomed outside the bay windows, embers sinking to the glittering water in slow motion.

She pulled in close. "What, Dan?"

Someone flicked off the living-room lights to better appreciate the show, and for a frightening second I couldn't see her. It was irrational but it terrified me. She'd been gone almost three months, and I'd bent time and space to find her, and I couldn't lose her again. I couldn't lose sight of her, or she'd cease being real. She'd crumble to bones and dust. I squeezed her hand, all knuckles, a trembling promise. If this were all a dream to be woken up from, by God, I'd take her with me. Somehow. I felt her exhaled breath in the darkness, and her voice, rising with alarm: "What's wrong?"

"You were dead," I whispered. "I dreamt you were dead."

"I'm right here."

Another firework exploded over Lake Pauite, scanning the room with an X-ray of purple light. Shadows skittered across the carpet, raced along paneled walls and bookshelves lined with model battleships. I saw her face again, sharp as daylight, shadowed in incendiary violet, those scary-smart eyes locked on mine. She was so real.

"You ate breakfast?" she asked me.

"What?"

"You ate breakfast this morning. Right?"

Her question hit me between the eyes. I strained. From almost three months in the future, that was a tough detail to remember. "I . . . I think so—"

"This is life and death, Dan. How *sure* are you?"

"Fifty-fifty."

"Bad dreams only come true if you talk about them before eating breakfast," she said matter-of-factly in the sinking darkness. "So, nicely done. There's a fifty-fifty chance you doomed me."

That's right. Addie never walked under ladders, opened umbrellas indoors, or shared a table with parties of twelve. Whenever she spilled salt, she threw a handful over her left shoulder. She was a mathlete software engineer who co-owned a pending patent, but she was also as superstitious as the Dark Ages. God, I love her.

I kissed the top of her head as two more illegal fireworks launched off the neighbor's dock. Twin bursts of neon lit up the house. Then a white one, almost as bright as the sun, filled the living room with synthetic daylight. I saw stains on the carpet. In another instant, it was all gone, and I remembered LJ once telling me that as gorgeous as this house was, he'd gotten a hell of a deal for it, because the hill was limestone. In fifty years, give or take, it'll slough into the lake. I could remember his toothy grin, inside his red Corvette pocked with cigarette burns, as he said: *But until then? Frickin' gorgeous.*

"How'd I die?" Adelaide asked me.

I didn't want to talk about it.

The warmth drained from the room. I could almost feel it exhaling between us. The overhead light in the kitchen buzzed and dimmed orange, and everyone at the table squinted into their Apples to Apples cards. Something was already here, absorbing the energy from LJ's lake house. I thought of parasites, suckerfish, leeches; slimy things that grip you, puncture your skin with needle-

107

teeth, and suck. Addie moved closer to me, drawing in a breath.

"You feel that?" I asked.

"Yeah," she said. "Maybe someone left the back door open?"

I held back a bitter laugh. *If only.*

Murmuring behind us. Doug, one of the show's camera operators, complaining to his wife about a piercing migraine. A beer clanked against a glass coffee table; a nerve-jangling sound that rattled through the house. Another firework ignited the sky, flooding the room with a new color. Blood red.

She was looking at me. "Why? What else could it be?"

I didn't have an answer for that. I spoke softly, my words carefully spaced, like a surgeon delivering bad news: "We have to leave the party. We have to leave now."

"Right now?"

"Yep." I pulled her by the elbow to the foyer.

"Can you drive?"

Strange question, but I nodded.

"Good," she said with a bashful shrug. "I can't."

I looked at her.

Outside, a string of firecrackers rattled like machine gun fire.

She cocked her head. "What, Dan?"

"How many drinks have you had?"

"You explain first. Why we're leaving all of sudden—"

A ceiling light exploded in LJ's kitchen, and the walls flattened the report into something like a champagne cork popping. The jingle of glass shards hitting the floor. Someone yelped and dropped a handful of cards.

In another fireburst of arterial red, I saw it in Addie's eyes. A slight glaze. Only a highway patrolman would have detected it. She didn't seem drunk — she never, *ever* seemed drunk, just sleepy — but it was there. She might have skated through a breathalyzer, but she wasn't good to drive. Except she did. Twenty minutes later, to retrieve her cell phone charger from our house, five miles away.

The idiot who'd hit her? He was sloshed. It was New Year's Eve — if you believe the PSAs, the entire highway system of Idaho was one booze-soaked bumper car arena. His pickup had barreled right through a four-way stop as she crossed it, less than a half-mile from our house, and rammed her driver-side door, concentrating the full kinetic force of the impact into the left side of Addie's face and body. A hit like that, and airbags don't even factor in the equation. The trauma doctor likened it to falling onto a cement sidewalk from a ten-story building. Even reduced to a turnip with a shaved head two floors above us, I'd always hated the guy, and quietly wished for a janitor's vacuum to accidentally unplug his breathing machine. I guess I'd imagined him as this roving, destructive force, a two-ton meteorite powered by vodka, Red Bull, and stupidity, as impossible to anticipate as blue-sky lightning. I'd imagined there was no earthly way Addie could've avoided the grill of that truck racing toward her window.

But she'd been drinking, too.

The report had mentioned alcohol in her system, but I'd never seen the BAC or cared to find out. I'd assumed there'd be a trace amount, since I'd seen her sip a wineglass with her Cubek friends, Corey and Jamie, when we'd arrived at eight. But that was it. Adelaide was too smart, too responsible, too in-control, to drive drunk. Or buzzed.

So? They say hindsight is twenty-twenty. It isn't.

She gripped my shoulder and I whiffed the fruity-aspirin smell of white zinfandel on her breath again. I guess that explained that. "Dan. You're acting weird."

I tugged her arm. "Come on."

"It was just a dream—"

A woman screamed in the dining room.

It echoed off the bay windows, harsh as a buzz saw, shrill and utterly out of place here. It sounded prerecorded, like a radio sound bite. It couldn't be real, but I knew it was. The crowd in the living room parted, arms and legs and elbows staggering backwards and dropping beers. Someone fell ass-first over an end table. A chorus of terrified gasps. The firework embers over the lake faded and for a moment the house fell into a perfect darkness. The kitchen and dining-room lights were both out, their electricity sapped. The candles in the fireplace, too.

The Gasman was inside the house with us.

I groped behind me, finding Addie's slender wrist with one hand and LJ's front door with the other. I pulled her but she planted her feet into the hardwood. "Oh my God," she said. "Oh my God. Oh *my God*—"

She'd seen him.

Her night vision had always been sharper than mine.

Then a brilliant green fireball lit the house and I saw him, too. The Gasman was standing where the living room meets the dining room, silhouetted as a black shadow against sparkling green water. I saw everything — that tattered wool greatcoat, the pudgy skinhead boots, the bulging gear belt, that nonsensical gas mask. The dangling hose that connected to nothing. Here he was, a transplanted nightmare, a beer-bellied bottom feeder with a snouted face.

Addie panicked behind me. "Who is he?"

"I don't know," I said. "But he's an asshole."

Green shadows deepened and stretched as embers wafted down to the water. In the swirl of moving light I didn't even notice the woman crouched beside the Gasman until he raised one thick arm, his gloved hand clenched, squeezing a fistful of her hair. She screamed again — another buzz-saw shriek — and wobbled upright on her tiptoes, punching and kicking to no effect. I couldn't tell who she was. The Gasman held her there for a moment, like an angler studying a hooked fish, and then fastened his other hand around the nape of her neck. For leverage, I realized.

"Let her go!" I shouted. "I'm here. You don't want her—"

Oh, but he did. The green backlight died just as the seven-foot Gasman started to pull out a gripping handful of her hair, and I heard her wailing in agony, the horrified group scream of onlookers, and worst of all, the rip of her scalp tearing off. It sounded like old carpet being pulled up.

Addie clasped her hands to her face.

"Hey! I'm *right here.*" But all I heard was that nauseating carpet sound. The Gasman was just tearing and tearing, ignoring me, like a fussy child occupied with a favorite toy.

I pulled Addie to the front door. I'd spent much too long here already, and given the Gasman enough time to ambush us. This was a stupid mistake, and it was time to leave New Year's Eve. But Addie struggled every inch of the way, fighting me, bumping over a coat rack with her shoulder—

"Stop him," she hissed in my ear. "Someone has to—"

"He won't."

"What?"

"He *won't stop.*"

Her eyes widened in an orange flash. "How? How do you—"

"PUT HER DOWN." I whirled just in time to see red-faced Kale Wong stomping down the stairs, hurling a shot glass over the bannister. It shattered off the Gasman's chest. The hulking thing dropped the woman, wobbled on those big boots, and leveled those circular eyes on *Haunted*'s third co-host. The creature behind the gas mask wasn't injured, frightened, or even really all that surprised. Just deeply curious, like an astronaut navigating a foreign planet, still clutching a fistful of bloody hair. The last shards of glass chattered on the floor as darkness reclaimed the room.

I realized what was going to happen. "Kale, *no*! Don't touch him!"

He didn't hear.

Adelaide stepped out behind me, too — she'd already ducked into LJ's coat closet and wheeled back out with an aluminum baseball bat. Even buzzed, she could think and act fast — but action was useless here. I know it sounds like an excuse, but whatever ancient evil lived behind that bug-eyed Soviet mask wasn't going to be beaten to death with sports equipment.

I grabbed the bat — bracingly cold — and stopped her. Her heels squeaked. Then I spun back to face the dining room, my voice raw: "*Kale!*"

The crowd shoved into the foyer, blocking my view. Half-retreating, half-spectating, boxing Adelaide and I against the front door with a wall of bodies. I couldn't see the Gasman. Or Kale. I heard grunts, shouts, furious scuffling. The dining-room table legs scraping tile, overturning, spilling cards and breaking glass. Then a bloodcurdling shriek. I couldn't tell if it was male or female.

Addie wrenched the baseball bat from my grip. "What *is* he?"

"I don't know."

"Is he even human?"

Three wet *pops* from the dining room. Like someone was cracking knuckles, but much louder and meatier. Then a second scream, strangled and hoarse, muffled by gloved, gripping hands—

"Oh, God—"

The party exploded toward us. A frenzied crowd pummeling us against the front door. The Gasman had made a few horrific examples — Kale probably among them — and now everyone wanted to get out at once. The foyer became a mosh pit. Someone elbowed me in the teeth and I tasted blood. Addie yelped and the aluminum bat clanged to the hardwood, lost in a forest of knees and legs. "Dan!" I heard her scream, at once very close and very far.

I felt for the doorknob, pinned against the door by squirming bodies. It was our escape — but it opened inward. Against the human tide. I thought of that nightclub fire in Brazil, where faulty lights ignited the stage and hundreds of partygoers burned alive in a charred heap because the *goddamn emergency doors opened inward*. A perfectly functional pair of doors. If everyone had just taken one orderly step back, the doors could've opened and the entire nightclub could've been evacuated in seconds. It's the stupid things that kill you. Like drunk-driving for a cell phone charger.

"The door," Addie cried out—

I wrenched it open a few gasping inches, but someone else pile-drove into my spine and smashed me into it, slamming it back shut. Too many people, crushed too tight. My lungs squished inside my ribs. The doorframe creaked under our combined weight — under this human landslide — and the stained glass broke out of the porthole above the door, raining colored shards. A big one bounced off my shoulder. Someone screamed to my right — I think they caught a piece in the eye.

Another surge of purple light, and over the crowd, I glimpsed the Gasman's first victim, staggering toward us with her shell-shocked hands clasped to the crown of her skull. Most of her hair was gone. She wore a helmet of scalp meat, shadowed deep violet in the wash of fireworks light, her cheeks running with blood and tears.

It was the intern. Sarah/Amy/Casey.

Heavy footsteps. Boots. Too calm to be anyone else. The Gasman came up behind her like a towering shadow as the firelight dimmed again—

Someone screamed: "Darby, behind you!"

Darby, I managed to think. *I wasn't even close*—

Panicked voices: "He's coming—"

"Open the *door*—"

This time I planted one foot against the wall, forced it open six inches, and wedged my other foot inside the frame. When the next body crashed into the pile, the door slipped free but stopped on my shoe. Someone else's arms folded around my face, grabbing the door and pulling, and I realized it was Adelaide. She screamed something in my ear; I couldn't tell what. Panicked breaths clouded the air, blinding us with gray mist. The cold air stung my throat.

"Pull!"

Another pitched scream behind us — it sounded like Darby — but cut raggedly short by a bass thud, a skull slammed into hardwood. A new voice screamed, and a bone cracked like a gunshot. Another fresh voice, and another, and I felt a hot splash of droplets on the back of my neck. Blood.

"Oh, *holy shit*—"

"Pull the door—"

"He's right behind us—"

Something hard, like a pebble, pinged off my scalp. Another clacked off the door. One landed in my mouth and chattered between my teeth like gravel. I spat it out immediately but somehow I knew — from the bladed earwig shape of it, maybe — that it was someone's tooth. Something else bigger, *squishier*, landed in the crowd behind us, and I realized the floor was suddenly slick, wet, our shoes slip-sliding. More blood. Gallons of it.

"Dan," Addie snarled in the chaos, her forehead pressed to mine. "Pull—"

But pulling wasn't working. Hell, pulling got those partygoers in Brazil killed. So I repositioned myself, wedging my shoulder into the six inches of guillotine-space between the door and the doorframe, and this time I braced my elbows and *pushed*.

"Yes!"

"Door's open!"

Halfway, at least. Someone slipped out under my wedged arms, and another, and another, like kids on a playground playing bridge. The first few to escape.

Addie went next and I followed. I didn't have a choice; the crowd drove us through the tight space. Through the front door, to safety — and then immediately tumbling over an unexpected object lying on the porch. A heavy, rectangular thing. I rolled free of the current of escaping bodies, somersaulted hard on my back, and Addie's hand was in my face, pulling me to my feet.

"Get up. Get up—"

Behind us, more partygoers crashed through the propped door and stumbled over the obstacle — a green yard waste bin. A hundred-pound bin, wheeled up onto LJ's front porch and laid down flat against the door. Compost oozed from the lidded top, sludgy and thick as wet cement. I recognized that familiar, yeasty scent of digestion, of bacteria breaking down matter into hot gas, the scent of the Head-Scratching Rifle, implanted here in my New Year's Eve memory.

I blinked in the freezing air. *How did the recycling bin get here?*

Now it was Adelaide tugging me by the arm. "Come on!"

The Gasman. I knew it had been him. Hauling that heavy-ass recycling bin up five steps onto the porch was quite a physical feat for anyone normal. And it made sense. The Gasman had entered the house from the back, breaking through the patio doors overlooking the lake, but first he'd set up a neighbor's recycling bin to block off the front door and seal the exit route. To trap the crowd (or maybe just me) in the living room. Only problem: he was too stupid to understand that LJ's front door opened inward, not outward. So instead of dooming us, he only inconvenienced us on our way out, because even after our encounter at Joe's Guns, the Gasman still couldn't quite grasp the subtle nuances to how doors work.

"Dan," Adelaide screamed. "*Come on!*"

I glanced back at her, gathering my thoughts. I noticed a knot of blood in her wisped hair and my heart seized with panic — but it was just an ear. A severed, blood-soaked ear, belonging to someone who no longer needed it, that had landed in her hair and stuck there. I don't think she'd noticed it.

The last person — LJ's wife, it looked like — cartwheeled through the front door and over the recycling bin. Then the Gasman's broad shoulders filled the gap, a ragged shadow against another splash of fireworks light. In one clenched hand, I saw a dark piece of gore — a jawbone, maybe. His snouted face swiveled and found us. Maybe he was disappointed that his recycling bin ruse hadn't worked. Maybe he was enjoying the chase. Maybe he wasn't really thinking at all, and only a sentient mold colony lived behind those dumb glass eyes.

Now he shouldered through the doorframe and gave the recycling bin a monstrous kick, scooting it across the porch and splintering the Victorian railing. A hummingbird feeder dropped and shattered. Someone screamed.

Addie and I staggered down the front steps as the railing broke behind us. Hand in hand, we bolted down LJ's sloped front lawn, the grass blades turned brittle by the sudden, unnatural cold. It was like running on a field of crunchy glass. Flecks of snow peppered my face, as dry and abrasive as sand. Of course it was snowing now, because the Gasman *brings the cold with him*—

"He's not going to stop," I said.

She ran alongside me, huffing: "We need to call the police."

Others had the same idea. Throngs of traumatized survivors, blood-drenched and wide-eyed, congregated by the motor pool of cars in LJ's driveway, warily counting heads and swapping horror stories. I saw cell phones held skyward in the universal sign for *no signal.*

"We have to drive—"

"Driving won't work," I said.

We ran past the crowd, into the street. Our palms sliced the frigid air like track runners. Our scraping breaths echoed into the stillness and vanished. There were more houses to our left and right — bloated McMansions, doctors and lawyers perched all along Overlook Drive — but every last one was dark and silent, like a block of dollhouses. Not even the porch lights or driveway lamps burned. Just as the Gasman brought coldness, he brought darkness. I remembered the champagne-cork pop of LJ's kitchen lights going out, darkening the lake house for his arrival.

"What do you mean driving *won't work*?"

"He's . . . he's not real," I said. "None of this is real. It's not really New Year's Eve. And you're not real. Because you're dead."

"What?"

"You're dead, Addie."

We stopped to catch our breaths a few blocks from LJ's house. Racking gasps, mouthfuls of icy air. My eyelids stuck together. Neither of us had coats.

Her fingers dug into my arm. "Dan, you're making no sense."

"None of this makes sense. It's actually March of 2015, and you're actually *dead*." I spat it at her like it was an insult, and my words rattled down the deserted street. I hadn't meant to raise my voice. "You'll . . . Addie, you'll get killed by a drunk driver twenty minutes from now, because you leave LJ's party to grab your cell phone charger. So you can drink more and we can spend the night. That's it. There's no higher meaning, no JFK conspiracy. It's just a stupid mistake, and it kills you. And it happened already, almost *three months ago*."

She blinked. She was realizing that she had, in fact, forgotten her charger.

"You don't need it now," I said. "Trust me."

117

Not even brilliant Adelaide could keep up with this. "Why . . . why would I leave the party for a stupid charger? After all *that* happened?"

I could've explained that the Gasman was new, an unwanted tourist following my time travels, but I just didn't have the energy. Too much talk, too much wasted time already. The Gasman was still pursuing us. I hugged her again in this miserable little snowstorm on a deserted Garage-Majal block, our teeth chattering in unison. Everything was awful, this was a terrible obscenity of time and physics, and I'd just had someone's bloody tooth in my mouth, but I had her. I had beautiful Adelaide Radnor back, and I would fight to keep her. I wouldn't lose her again.

A sad corner of my mind was still certain that this was a dream. She was still dead, and rescuing her from her appointed death on New Year's Eve wouldn't really change a thing. Because it was really March, or maybe even later now, and she was still rotting in a wooden box, buried in dirt. Like a toxic little seed planted in my mind, I started to wonder: *What is actually real anymore?*

"We have to keep going," I told her with my hands on her shoulders. "You're not going to believe what comes next."

Another firework ignited the sky through a canvas of scratchy pines. In the throb of red light, I saw Adelaide still had someone else's severed ear in her hair. I brushed it off — as cold and slippery as a jellyfish.

"What was that?" she asked.

"Nothing."

NEW TEXT MESSAGE
SENDER: "Holden" (509) 555-8727
SENT: 8:36 a.m. Mar 20 2015

WTF did I grab a BROOM?

4 Hours, 21 Minutes

LJ's yuppie block on Overlook Drive led to our kitchen, and it nearly ruined Adelaide's mind. An exterior space funneled into an interior one like a carnival funhouse. The sky swooped down to become a ceiling, the mansions flanked in to form walls, and white-hot sunlight exploded in our faces, a nuclear flash. The narrowing transition was jarring, violent, all sharp edges and friction. Had the walls and floor not aligned just right around us, it seemed, we could've just as well been inside a giant sausage grinder.

So now Addie and I were home, in the hallway overlooking the kitchen, fumbling and blinking. Sunlight blasted through the back windows at a low morning angle and bounced off the countertops, splashing amber tesseracts on the walls. Parquet creaked underfoot. The Keurig machine chuffed. The refrigerator whiteboard read, in Addie's own elegant cursive: PAPRIKA, PAPRIKA, PAPRIKA, GODDAMN PAPRIKA (guess what I'd forgotten last time I'd been to Fred Meyer). The digital oven timer displayed 8:56 a.m. It was the morning of December 31, twelve hours before the party we'd just left.

I exhaled through chattering teeth. You never get used to it.

Addie still had snowflakes and beads of frozen blood in her hair. "Daylight," she whispered. "Where did daylight come from?"

I turned to her. "So . . . I can explain."

For a second she looked like she'd be fine. She quietly surveyed these new surroundings, recognizing her coat on the wall and her (duplicated) boots by the door, glancing outside into the hot wash of sunlight, nodding her head lightly in acceptance . . . then she slapped both hands to her mouth and screamed.

"Addie! It's fine—"

She juked me in the hallway, feinting right before springing left. She went for the kitchen and I followed. I grabbed her elbow but she twisted free.

"Addie—"

"Don't *touch* me."

I couldn't blame her for being terrified. Time was running backward. My mind shuttered — I needed to make some narrative sense of this and I didn't even know where to start. Where did the macabre sequence begin? At Jitters, with Holden? The New Year's Eve party Addie died at? Or that irreversible moment when I'd first purchased the haunted Mosin Nagant from—

Okay, Addie had a steak knife. She'd reached over her shoulder and drawn it sword-like from our magnetic cutlery stand. She held it out now, at me, her bare shoulders rising and falling.

"Explain everything," she snarled.

"I'm figuring out how."

"Where are we?"

"The kitchen."

"*Not what I meant*, Dan."

"This is the morning of . . . December thirty-first," I said, stepping forward. "We just woke up. Remember? You heard the airlock splitting, from the bedroom. We ran down here barefoot, and the beer was overflowing and flooding the pantry—"

On cue, a heavy glug echoed from across the kitchen.

Addie flinched and pointed the knife at the pantry door, and then back at me. Yesterday's homebrew batch (the last one we'd ever brewed together) had fermented aggressively and cracked the plastic airlock open. Frothy, contaminated pre-beer had dribbled down the slopes of the five-gallon carboy, soaked through the packed towels, and flooded our pantry. A total, smelly mess.

She stared at the milky brown puddle gathering under the pantry door. "But . . . we cleaned that up."

"We did."

"So why is it back?"

"*We're* back," I said. "I think it's like time travel."

"You think?"

"Just put the knife down."

The blade shivered between us, catching a flash of sunlight. She softened, just a bit. "You . . . wait a minute. You said I was dead?"

"Yes." I clasped my hands together. "But let's not start the story there. So there's this antique Russian rifle that—"

"Nope. Let's start with me being dead."

"Okay. You're dead."

She forced a laugh. "No. I'm not."

"You are."

"Clearly I'm not."

"We just walked from LJ's lake house on Sunday night to our kitchen on Sunday morning. Please, Addie, step out on a limb with me."

It was starting to hit her. She glanced outside, a harsh band of light on her face. A gauze-like mist coated our backyard, burning off through shafts of sunlight. Her lip quivered and she held a hand to her mouth, as if stifling a bitter laugh: "Nope."

I saw her grip on the knife slacken, and I went for it, but she firmed up her stabbing posture. I retreated, just half a step.

"Nope, nope, nope," she said with tears glimmering in her eyes. "This is a dream, Dan. Just a horrible, vivid, pants-on-head-crazy nightmare."

Glug. The beer puddle rippled, like a ticking clock.

"We need to keep moving." I reached again for the knife.

She pulled back. "Killed by a drunk driver?"

"Yes."

"On New Year's Eve?"

"Yes."

She sighed. "Bit of a cliché, huh?"

Something slithered snake-like between my ankles, tugging my jeans. Claws clicking on the floor. I recoiled, staggering — and saw a crawling blur of sequined gray and yellow scales. Baby the savannah monitor. On weekend mornings, like this one, Addie would sometimes just open the enclosure door and let our 'practice-child' roam the first floor of our house like a free-range crocodile.

She scooped up her lizard with one hand, keeping the knife pointed at me. She sagged a bit under Baby's thirty pounds, and her voice broke a little: "What . . . what was my funeral like?"

I shrugged. "There were lemon bars."

"I *hate* lemon bars."

"Well, you weren't there."

She flashed a wounded grin and squeezed Baby like a stuffed animal. The lizard plopped its big head on her shoulder and nuzzled, and in a grotesque way, Addie looked like a mother holding a cold-blooded child. The heavy tail swished left to right between her knees, a scaly pendulum marking our dwindling time.

"I guess I just . . . hoped you'd say it was something more dramatic." She stroked the leathery ridges along

Baby's backbone. "Like, I don't know . . . Died rescuing orphans from a school bus fire."

"Mauled by a Velociraptor," I suggested, watching the knife.

She rolled her eyes. "It'd have to be a Utahraptor, Dan. Velociraptors were actually much smaller than movies portray them—"

We'd had this conversation before, in many forms. Once, while camping out by White Bend, we'd spent half the night awake in our tent, drinking cheap beer and imagining exotic and amusing ways to buy the farm. Her favorite? Skydiving out of an airplane, bouncing off a fifty-foot trampoline, hurtling a half-mile back into the stratosphere, and being hit by a meteor. So, in light of that, I can understand how a DUI fatality was a little disappointing for her.

I shrugged emptily. "It's the everyday things that get you."

"Did my parents cry?"

"Of course."

"Did Holden cry?"

"Everyone cried."

"Did you?"

I should've lied. But my mind was stretched too thin; I was too exhausted and rattled. And impatient. We were losing time here, held up and bickering at knifepoint while the real threat caught up and approached. So, yes, I hesitated.

She noticed. "What? *Really,* Dan?"

Enough of this; I lunged again for the steak knife. She shouldered away, but too slow this time. I snatched it from her and hurled it into the living room. It stuck in the arm of the sofa.

She looked back at me, eyes wide.

"We need to keep moving," I said. "The man in the gas mask. He's going to keep following us, everywhere we go—"

"Who is he?"

"I don't know."

"Why does he want you?"

Something about her question — the way she suggested the Gasman *wanted* me — reminded me of the hobo suicides back in the Soviet Union. That one particular guy who'd hitchhiked all the way to the Kalash to hang himself with stolen barbed wire like a pagan sacrifice. All because the Gasman had *summoned* him; reached thousands of miles to dig its icy fingernails into his brain. Was I being summoned?

I sensed a cold presence in the house.

Addie saw something in the mirror — behind me — and gasped.

I whirled. "What?"

The living room? It was empty. Just the couch, the television, and Baby's plywood enclosure. The daylight was fading through the bay windows, graying out, like the sun was passing behind thick storm clouds.

She pointed. "You didn't . . . you *didn't* see that?"

"See what?"

She was shaking. Spasms. She squeezed Baby against her chest, and I worried the big reptile would lash out and bite with those fishhook teeth. I touched her shoulder — her bare skin felt like candle wax. "*What*, Addie?"

She flinched at my touch. "In the mirror. I saw us."

"Us?"

"I saw *us*," she said. "You and me, just now. We ran through the living room, behind you."

I looked again. Still empty.

"We were . . . covered in blood." She stroked Baby with trembling fingertips. "Blood and snow and ice. We were carrying neon-green glow sticks. Just running right back through the house. We looked scared, worn out—"

The chandelier bulbs exploded like a string of firecrackers. Addie yelped under a shower of sizzling sparks. The stink of burnt filaments. The house was filling

125

with shadows, and the outside daylight was dimming, fogging out.

"We're fine," I said, tugging her along. "But we need to get moving—"

"Are you sure I'm dead?"

It hit me then, delayed as a thunderclap. My mind jolted to ParaNews, to that bizarre eyewitness testimony from the Kalash back in the eighties — the night watchman who'd seen a ghostly man and woman crossing through the haunted armory. Speaking English. Carrying green glow sticks.

Oh my God.

It squeezed my stomach, like an invisible hand. So that was it, I guess. I was already part of the Head-Scratching Rifle's history. Addie and I, we were already trapped in its hellish Mobius strip, years before I'd purchased the thing from Ben Dyson's widow through Joe's Guns. Years before I was *born*, even.

She read it in my eyes. "What?"

The oven clock died with a hollow click. The house creaked around us in the changing temperature, a symphony of deep echoes. Like a U-boat descending to a depth it wasn't designed for, groaning and leaning inward under the force of millions of tons of frigid seawater. Pressing in on all sides. I noticed the yeasty beer puddle was now frozen to the floor, a bumpy sheet of brown ice.

"Time to go." I led her down the hallway.

She hauled Baby over her shoulder, the big lizard's tail clumsily thudding against the wall. A framed photo of her parents fell and broke. Her teeth chattered: "Go where?"

To the front of the house, I guess. To wherever this decaying memory of December 31 would blur and link into the next one. They always seemed to get fuzzy around the edges, the details running together like watercolors. And already I heard those telltale footsteps coming up on the unfinished back porch, heavy and methodical.

"It's freezing," she said. "All of a sudden—"

"He brings the cold with him."

Like rancid meat brings flies . . .

We reached the front door, stacked with my shoes and her boots. The glass window was opaque, frosted with blades of ice, but I already knew it wouldn't lead to our front yard on New Year's Eve morning. It led to the next car down on my train of thoughts, further back in time. On to the next memory. With the Gasman behind us.

THUNK.

On the other side of the house, the back door rattled noisily in its frame. Thank God for the subtleties of doors, right?

Addie spun. "Oh, crap—"

"Yep. That's our cue to leave," I said, pulling her.

"How do we stop him?"

"Doors."

"What?"

"He has trouble with doors," I said. "For a while, at least."

"*Can* we stop him?"

I didn't know. How many victims had tried before me? How many corpses had the Head-Scratching Rifle created? And somehow we were already a part of the legacy. We'd made a cameo appearance, carrying green glow sticks in Saint Petersburg's Kalash armory, a good ten years before either of us had even been born.

"Dan." Her voice shivered. "Something's wrong with Baby—"

But a chill shot up my spine and lingered between my shoulder blades. It was true; we were already deeply tangled in the rifle's sticky web. As for that free will thing I'd lectured Holden about? Maybe there was no such thing.

The Gasman forced the back door. THUNK—

"Dan. Oh my God, Baby is—"

"Keep moving." I opened the front door. "We have to stay ahead of—"

"*Dan*!" Addie shrieked. Raw horror.

I turned and realized Baby had gone as limp as a ragdoll in her arms. A dead sack. Beaded eyes unblinking, staring flatly at the ceiling. And the lizard's back half — hind legs, tail, and all — was sliding downward under the tug of gravity. Her torso just . . . stretching, lengthening, Gumby-like.

"No, no, no," she cried—

But her beloved pet of five years came apart before our eyes. The skin split like an overripe banana, a spurt of cold reptile blood darkened Addie's dress, and the bottom half of Baby thudded wetly to the floor at her feet. Leaving her holding the upper half in sickened disbelief.

We don't pour salt on slugs for fun. They do.
Cruelty is their language—

"Addie!"

She backed away, opening her mouth to scream—

THUNK-CRASH—

The back door splintered. The Gasman was inside the house.

* * *

I lost her between times and places.

"Addie. Wait!"

She'd whipped away from me, through the door. I reached for her and missed; her hair slashed my face. I stumbled, the world turned over, and then she was gone. In a mottled flash of rearranging light, I was alone again.

My knees hit cement.

Gunshots. I heard a deafening rattle of gunfire, like a line of broadside canons, reverberating endlessly. My eardrums throbbed with pressure. I clapped my hands to my ears, stumbling upright.

The shooting range?

Yes. Alright. Next memory down: the BullsEye indoor shooting range in Boise. November, maybe? A firing line of booths and a twenty-five yard shooting bay against a beveled steel backstop. Targets on motorized pulleys. Air thick with grit, smoke, and the chime of brass casings pinging off carpeted dividing walls. It was a bustling Saturday, "Date Night" (if you bring a girl, the range fees are halved), and Addie had attempted the thankless task of teaching me how to fire a pistol. I recognized our booth. On the table, her Beretta something-or-other, two red boxes of ammunition, a few illustrated targets. Her latest masterpiece hung on clothespins: a tight cluster of .40 caliber holes, right in Jar Jar Binks' brain.

Everything was there. Except her.

"Addie!" I shouted again, drowned out by more banging gunfire.

I searched the complex; bay one and then bay two. A safety class was in session there; quizzical heads turned. I stole earmuffs from the wall hangers and clamped them around my head, catching my breath.

"*Addie!*"

There she was.

I found her in the back, behind the red trash bin, sitting on the smooth cement floor. She rocked there with her fingers clasped around her knees. The front of her New Year's Eve dress stained with Baby's drying blood. Shallow, gulping breaths. Tears glistening on her cheeks. Her mascara was smeared; she had raccoon eyes.

She didn't look at me. I touched her knee.

"I'm fine," she said.

"This is just a dream," I told her, slipping my earmuffs over her head. "None of this is really happening."

"Baby's safe?"

"Baby's fine."

I left out the flip side of that statement: *And you're dead.*

"It's just a monitor lizard anyway," she said. "It's . . . stupid to cry over a lizard. Like crying over a goldfish—"

"It wasn't just a lizard. It was Baby. Our practice-child." I glanced down at the oily blood on her dress. "Man, *thank God* it wasn't a real one."

She laughed.

I held her hand and squeezed. She rubbed her eye.

"Sorry." She hated crying in front of me.

"It's fine."

"I love you, Dan."

"I love you, too." I raised my voice under another staccato rattle of gunfire. "This is just a horrible dream, and we'll survive it together."

She swallowed and nodded, her cheeks colorless.

"And I promise, Addie, we'll wake up together. Okay?"

"Okay."

I didn't have time to wonder if I was lying. I felt an odd coldness growing at my back, like standing near a walk-in freezer. I turned and Addie gasped.

Down the rectangular shooting range, the Gasman was approaching; a dark shadow in a tailed coat. He passed unnoticed behind the firing line of target shooters. Circular glass eyes fixed on us. Unhooked breathing hose swinging.

Addie grabbed my shoulder, pulling herself up. "He really won't stop, huh?"

"Nope."

"Is he, like, the Grim Reaper?"

I remembered the Gasman standing dumbly outside Joe's Guns, pushing a door clearly marked PULL. "God, I sure hope not."

She was stuck on the idea. "I think he's Death. Chasing us."

I studied our cloaked pursuer and strained to find human features — exposed hair, ears, or skin — but the gas mask was airtight. The seven-foot walking figure was entirely sealed in plastic and wool, gloves and boots. As faceless and impersonal as a spacesuit, coming ever closer. Shambling at us at Romero zombie-speed — slow enough to lull you into dropping your guard, and steady enough to punish you for it.

"Creepy," Addie said.

"Let's go." I took her hand and we ran together.

But over my shoulder I noticed — as he strode after us, the BullsEye's overhead lights hissing and sparking out behind him — something didn't seem quite right about the Gasman's proportions. His legs were just a little too long; his arms just a little too short. Like a child's drawing of a human body, where the biceps are longer than the forearms. Coming down the hall at us, it was a little like being chased by a fat man on stilts.

Addie stopped under the electric EXIT sign. "What happens if he catches us?"

"Nothing good," I said, tugging her on.

We bolted out of BullsEye's, and into . . .

* * *

. . . A log cabin.

"Leavenworth?" Addie gasped.

I slammed the solid wood door behind us. "Yeah. Oktoberfest."

The cabin was tiny. We'd rented a one-roomer up in the Cascade Mountains last year with three of Addie's work pals. Even without the beer, I don't remember much of the weekend — just duffel bags, toothbrushes, and hair curlers crammed into every inch of shelf space. The morning after, Addie and I had stayed entwined under the sleeping bag, hiding our faces from the growing daylight in the windows, just our whispered breaths under the taut blue nylon, her eyelashes touching my cheek:

I have a theory, Dan.

Yeah?

They say that before the Big Bang, the entire universe was compressed into one single point. Right? All atoms, all matter, squished up together—

Here and now, Addie tugged my hand. "Which way?"

She didn't yet understand — the direction wasn't important. Any direction seemed to work. Any direction away from the Gasman. But I wished we weren't being chased and we could stay here, in this cramped little cabin, in the aftermath of 2014's Oktoberfest. I liked this memory. I liked what she'd said to me here under the sleeping bag, her hushed, sleepy hangover-poetry:

I think our atoms were together. Side by side, before the Big Bang happened—

The Gasman rattled the cabin doorknob.

So that's why, through all our problems, all our fights, we're always pulled back together. We share the same atoms, Dan. We'll always . . . feel that pull, I guess.

"I can't believe you never cried," Addie huffed. "After I died."

"We'll discuss it later."

I took her wrist and led her out of Oktoberfest, on and on, backward through our memories, shutting every door behind us. Overturning objects to block doorways, twisting locks wherever they existed. Anything to delay the Gasman, to buy us time. That's what this was all about. Time.

"I think he's Fate," Addie said as we ran. "I think he's—"

I kissed my dead fiancée before taking the plunge into the next unknown place. White zinfandel from New Year's Eve still on her lips, her teeth chattering—

"Maybe he is," I said. "Maybe he isn't. But I sure hope the next memory takes place in the door section of a Home Depot."

She laughed.

God, I'd missed that sound.

NEW TEXT MESSAGE
SENDER: "Holden" (509) 555-8727
SENT: 9:11 a.m. Mar 20 2015

DAN ANSWER UR PHONE. Something is wrong I have a bad feeling about this.

3 Hours, 29 Minutes

"I have a bad feeling about this," Holden told me as we unpacked the *Haunted* production van under a sky of puffy red clouds. Citrus energy drinks on his breath, his pale hair matted with sweat from the five-hour drive.

I helped him lift an Arri crate. "How so?"

"There's just a . . . weirdness to that lighthouse. Like another dimension is pressing in from behind it. You don't feel it?"

"Nope."

From this parking lot we could see the (allegedly) haunted Disappointment Bay Lighthouse, towering over the nautical museum and keeper's quarters. A stout pillar of painted brick, with a signal light caged behind dirty glass panes and wire handrails. It was banded red and white, like a hundred-foot barber's pole. Somehow, in some intangible way, I'll admit that it didn't quite match the burnt sky or the clumped coastal evergreens around it. If this were a movie, I'd have sworn the lighthouse was CGI'd in. Maybe that's what Holden had meant.

We set the crate on the curb with a leaden thud and the soft-box light jingled inside. Fun fact: of all the moving parts to a guerilla film shoot, the lighting is always the most expensive, the most time-consuming, and comes in the heaviest damn boxes.

"Dan," Adelaide whispered. "When is this?"

"The Disappointment Bay Lighthouse investigation," I told her. "You weren't here. This is by Seaflats, Washington."

"Yeah, but *when*?"

"August, I think."

"Wait." Holden wiped his brow. "How'd she get here?"

Addie smiled shyly. "Hi."

"She carpooled with Kale," I said.

She nodded. "That's . . . yes. I definitely did that."

Holden looked between us. "Kale's van was full."

"She sat in the back."

"The back was full, too—"

"Magic," Addie snapped. "I got here by magic."

He shrugged and grabbed another box. "Whatever."

Production was already racing at double time. Up a slope of fresh-cut grass, LJ, Kale, and our crew were in the museum lobby, clasping lavalier microphones and propping up tripods. It would be our command center, since the ground floor of the lighthouse was too wet and cramped. One assistant with an HD-DVC camera was already prowling the grounds for daytime cutaways, but I'd already seen the episode and knew none of it would make the final cut. His shot compositions sucked.

Addie looked out into the gray ocean. "Why's it called Disappointment Bay?"

"Because it's near Disappointment Beach."

"Why's it called Disappointment Beach?"

"Because it's in Washington."

Spoiler alert: our *Haunted* investigation wouldn't find any actual ghosts tonight. Not for lack of trying, though. Holden would claim to hear spectral footsteps every five minutes or so, and Kale would be perplexed by an electromagnetic glitch that seemed to move up the spiral stairs. Plus, the thermal signature on the balcony that would become Holden's Exhibit A for the next seven months — three panels of warm glass.

"I . . ." Addie chewed her lip. "Wait. I think I've heard of this lighthouse."

"It's famous." I shrugged. "By lighthouse standards, at least."

She snapped her fingers. "The Deer Cap Dude. Right?"

I nodded. Yes, the lighthouse (and the nearby eight-dollar nautical museum) was famous for a collective apparition known as the Deer Cap Dude.

Seriously.

According to several decades of local legend, the Deer Cap Dude was a middle-aged, pot-bellied figure in red flannel and a camouflaged hat who frequently appeared atop the balcony. He'd been spotted from the museum, the coastal hiking trail, and by the occasional trucker via Highway 101. Even once from the sea. It was always the same account — a black silhouette against the rotating light, with that signature ear-flapped hat giving his head a square profile, sitting or standing by the handrail. Like he was waiting for something (and he'd been waiting for well over forty years now). A boarded-up tourist trap we'd passed down by the Shell station still had t-shirts in the windows that read: *I Saw The Deer Cap Dude.*

"Or, you know, it could just be an actual dude in a hunting cap," I said. "Just throwing that out there."

Addie smirked. "You're no fun, Dan."

I unzipped one of the duffel bags in the van's back seat and tossed her a black flashlight. She caught it backhand. These were heavy Maglites with checkered steel bodies. You could club someone to death with one of these.

"What's this for?"

"The Gasman," I said. "When he's close, lights burn out."

She clicked hers on. Fiery blue-white.

I tossed her a black *Haunted* hoodie. "For the cold."

"Thanks."

I slipped one on, too. Mine was personalized; the back read RUPLEY in yellow stencil. I leaned back into the van and grabbed a smaller plastic box, popped the shoulder clasps, and pulled out an EMF meter. Like a little walkie-talkie, marked #3 with Sharpie on duct tape. Resisting a sick little shiver, I realized this was the same one Holden had brought to my house in March of 2015. To investigate the Head-Scratching Rifle. Seven months in the future.

"What's that?"

"Electromagnetic field meter." I showed it to her. "Also a directional thermometer. Anything more than a three-degree change, and it beeps."

"Right, so we'll know when the Gasman is close." She checked the back of the production van and wrinkled her nose. "No proton packs?"

"What's a proton pack?"

"Man, you really need to watch *Ghostbusters*." She swung back out through the van's sliding door. "I'm thinking self-defense. Weapons."

"Not unless you brought any—"

She pulled a handgun from her purse. It looked comically oversized in her tiny hands. But I recognized it — the Beretta something-or-other she kept in a keypad safe under the bed. She must've snatched it from my memory of BullsEye's. She smiled now, in a teasing way, like she'd just drilled another .40 caliber round between the vacuous eyes of Jar Jar Binks. Her Cubek friends called her *Annie*, like Annie Oakley.

"You're such a showoff."

"Just once," she said. "I need to try shooting the gas mask guy. To see what happens."

"Nothing. Nothing will happen."

"I'm just saying, I've never shot a ghost before." She stuffed the pistol back in her purse. "So, this is time travel?"

"I'm not sure."

She watched Holden and Kale scurry uphill from the parking lot to the museum, hauling the last load of duffel bags and heavy light boxes. The sky was red now, slowly bruising blue as the sun dipped behind the ocean. "But we're . . . what, six months back in time now?"

"I don't think we're rewriting the past or anything," I said. "We're just in my memory. My thoughts. My recollection of the Disappointment Bay Lighthouse—"

"And we're going backward?"

I shrugged. "Backward is forward."

She forced a sickly half-grin. Our little throwaway joke from the night we first met outside the Total Darkness Maze — now coming literally true. And for how long? I read it in her eyes; she was wondering what would happen when we ran out of memories for the Gasman to chase us through.

Instead, she asked an equally terrifying question: "What's really happening? Right now, in the real world?"

I felt for my iPhone, but my pockets were empty. I must've lost it back during our merry chase. Whether you're having a normal day or being pursued backwards through time by a nightmarish gas-masked demon, rest assured — that stomach-fluttery feeling you get when you lose your cell phone is still the same.

"Shit."

Had I left it on the counter at Joe's Guns? Not that it mattered. I was afraid of the answer to her question, too, and I only had a few jigsaw fragments of it. If my iPhone had been telling the truth, it was almost ten o'clock on Saturday morning now. Last I'd heard, 2015-Holden was struggling to contact me. And I couldn't answer, because I was currently out time-traveling with my dead fiancée.

But in the real world?

It was Saturday morning, March of 2015, and I was alone in my house.

With the Head-Scratching Rifle.

"Uh, Dan?" Addie tapped my shoulder. "You guys never actually found any concrete evidence of the Deer Cap Dude, right?"

"Right."

She pointed up at the lighthouse. "Well, uh . . . there he is."

* * *

The apparition on the balcony didn't move. It just stared a hundred feet down at us with both hands on the railing. Every ten seconds or so, the beacon swiveled behind him and turned him into a black silhouette. A human sunspot. A standing shadow wearing an unmistakable, ear-flapped hat.

"So far I've seen two ghosts," Addie said behind me. "And they both have atrocious taste in headwear."

It took me a second to grasp what she meant — I didn't really see the Gasman as a ghost in the traditional sense. He was not human, certainly, but he was too real to be a phantom. He left footprints. Snow stuck to his coat. He punched down doors. He tore bodies apart and threw ears and teeth at us. He was too brutal, too *material* to be a spirit. And he was somewhere in the future behind us, a door or two back, drawing closer every second.

Meanwhile, the famous Deer Cap Dude just stared ten stories down at us. Neither interested nor disinterested. Just sort of there, motionless, like a JCPenney's mannequin propped up atop the lighthouse, backlit by a rotating brightness. I guess he fit the description perfectly. He sure as hell wasn't the Walking Deer Cap Dude.

I waved at him. No response.

I threw a rock. No response.

Addie reached for her Beretta but I stopped her. "No. *Please* don't do that."

I looked around the grounds to see if anyone else — Kale, Holden, LJ, or any of the crew or production assistants — had noticed the specter, but the team was indoors, busy consolidating equipment for the first huddle. I also checked the EMF meter. The temperature held steady at a realistic fifty degrees Fahrenheit. The Gasman was still trailing far behind us, for now.

Addie squinted at the museum, then the lighthouse. "Man, you guys suck at finding ghosts. He's *right there*."

"He wasn't there last time."

"Yeah? We should go up to him," she said abruptly, eyeing the EMF meter in my hand. "While there's still time."

"Why?"

"Why not?" She shielded her eyes from the turning light, which felt brighter as the cloudy sky darkened. "Come on, Dan. I thought you were a ghost hunter."

"Yeah. On TV."

"Well, ta-da! There's a real ghost."

I sighed. I didn't want to go up there — not with the Gasman still chasing us.

"Come on," she said. "He looks friendly."

"He looks like he should be haunting a Big 5."

She stepped back and missed the curb, catching herself against the van's taillight. She brushed her hair from her face with a palm. "Wow. I think I'm still tipsy."

"Tipsy?"

From the New Year's Eve party, I realized. A half-year in the future. She still had the leftover remnants of the buzz that might've killed her.

I was still furious about that. I wanted to grab her by the shoulders and yell at her. I'd never seen her drive impaired before, but I guess she'd picked a bad night to try it. It couldn't have been much wine, but maybe that was all she would have needed — an extra tenth of a second or so — to react to the incoming pickup. Not enough to avoid the wreck altogether, but enough to flinch away and brace, maybe, so her head wouldn't have whiplashed into the truck's grill through a hail of shattered glass. Enough to *survive*.

But what did that matter here and now? I wondered if she'd ever sober up or if the alcohol would linger in her forever, held captive in her Mobius strip of a bloodstream. How much longer could all this last? How many train cars left, until I ran out of memories? And when I did, the Gasman would corner us, and we'd be forced to draw a line, make our stand, and fight. I didn't anticipate that going well.

That settled it. Maybe the Deer Cap Dude would speak to us. Maybe he'd kill us. At the time I called it a calculated risk, but it was really closer to desperation. We were *screwed* if we couldn't learn something here.

She looked at me. "We're doing this?"

I tested my Maglite. "Lock and load."

She reached into her purse and racked the slide of her pistol. It click-clacked like a deadbolt, jingling amid makeup, keys and receipts.

"Jesus, Addie, I didn't mean *literally*."

"Don't be so specific with your figures of speech, then."

3 Hours, 20 Minutes

We approached the lighthouse's arched oak door — it looked like leftover set design from *Lord of the Rings*. Holden, Kale, and LJ didn't notice us pass the museum, and even if they had, we looked the part with our *Haunted* hoodies and Maglites. A second camera operator prowled the grounds now for exterior shots, and she paused to film Adelaide and I entering, and then panned up the red and white brick for an ominous Dutch angle against a darkening sky. Nice.

The big door closed behind us.

The Disappointment Bay Lighthouse felt like a cave — chilly, damp, dripping. Every surface was beaded with raindrops. You could feel the mildew growing on your skin. Falling droplets echoed strangely against the walls, like sonar pings. Above us, the spiral staircase — a creaking iron latticework — seemed to climb up and up forever.

Adelaide looked at me. "Like you remember?"

"Exactly."

Every detail was the same. Rubber galoshes and a yellow coat by the door. A radio desk with rumpled nautical maps, binoculars, and headphones. A Dell laptop, wrapped in a freezer bag. Every bizarre sound and musty, dripstone odor was exactly as I recalled from our investigation. Everything except the Deer Cap Dude, who was hopefully still waiting for us up top.

"I don't know why," she said. "But it still bothers me that they served lemon bars at my funeral. I hate lemon bars. I thought everyone knew that."

"You hate a lot of foods."

"Yeah, but *especially* lemon bars."

Her parents had organized the service; they probably should've known. But they'd always been a mystery to me; a strange, aloof family that respected one another at a distance; never hugging or touching. Like human oil paintings. She'd confided in me once that she used to smoke as a teenager, in Birmingham, England, and it took her dear mom and dad two full years to notice. By then she'd kicked the habit but kept a reminder: a yellow Zippo lighter with Pac Man on the side. Always in her purse, just in case she decided to relapse. Or commit arson, I guess.

Our footsteps echoed up the grated stairs; a wobbling twang that rang up and down the tube-shaped building. It was almost musical, like a cat walking on piano keys. There was a handrail, but it was too loose and screechy to trust.

"So." She followed me closely. "You bought the cursed rifle in February."

"March."

"After I'd been dead for three months."

"Yep."

"What was your plan? Point cameras at the rifle until it did something scary? You didn't have live ammunition in the house, right?"

I smiled guiltily.

"*Jesus*, Dan."

"Don't be mad."

"You basically deserve this, you know."

Yes, I absolutely did, but assigning blame was unproductive now. I explained: "I kept one Mosin Nagant round and cannibalized the gunpowder from the others. So the one cartridge in the house was over-loaded. Explosive. So if somehow the rifle was actually haunted — which now seems to be the case—"

"Sure looks that way, huh?"

"Basically, I'd stop it. The gun would still kill me, but it wouldn't survive to kill anyone else. That was my backup plan."

Admittedly, most backup plans don't end with you blowing yourself up in your house, but I'd never really planned on being right about the Head-Scratching Rifle. It was probably time to start worrying.

We passed a porthole window; we were halfway up the spiral stairs. The reverberation of our footsteps grew tinny, hollow, the way a passing ambulance siren changes pitch. I hoped the Deer Cap Dude was still up there waiting for us on the balcony. What if he'd been just an illusion, to lure us up here?

"Dan . . . that was so, phenomenally stupid."

"It worked."

"Well done. You found a horrifying, demonic spirit—"

"No," I said. "I meant I found *you*."

She smiled, embarrassed, and we climbed up a few jangling steps in silence. "That's . . . very sweet, Dan. But you're somewhere, alone, with that rifle. With a round of live ammunition—"

"An exploding bullet," I corrected her.

"That won't change anything, except maybe the kind of mop the paramedics will use when they find your body—"

"I think I already fired it."

"You *what*?"

"Before the Gasman, right before time started running backwards. I saw my reflection in a mirror, holding the rifle to my chin like the other victims. I pulled the trigger, but it only clicked. The cartridge . . . well, it must've misfired. It made a weird underwater sound, like a burp. My exploding bullet was a dud."

She stared, aghast.

"Yeah. I forgot to mention that part. Sorry."

She was silent for another few steps, flicking her Maglite on and off absentmindedly. She kept building up to say something. It took her a few tries to get it out, her words a slow drip of icy dread: "What if . . . what if it *wasn't* a dud?"

All I could do was shrug.

"Dan, what if the rifle fired, and you already killed yourself? You saw it in the mirror, and you already blew your head off in your kitchen? And this, all this 'time-travel,' is really . . . I don't know . . ."

. . . The afterlife?

Limbo?

Hell?

What's that cliché about your life flashing before your eyes when you die? Maybe it's a slower process than that, more of a guided tour, like walking through your memories in reverse.

Or maybe this really was something darker. Maybe Hell isn't a literal place with fire and sulfur and pitchforks — maybe it's just the things we bring with us. Our negative feelings, our mistakes, our memories. Maybe Perdition is actually a black void, as inert and empty as the gulf of outer space, utterly removed from God, and we populate it ourselves. If so — man, I'd sure done my part.

Addie was still staring at me as we climbed, shaking her head. She looked utterly offended. "You *dumb shit*," she snarled, her cheeks red. "Maybe my dad was right about you. When he told me that—"

"You killed yourself driving drunk," I blurted out.

"I did not."

"Just throwing that out there—"

145

"I didn't do *anything*, Dan." She grabbed my shoulder and halted me on the stairs, her voice a wounded hiss, her English accent intensifying: "Everything was status quo for me. I woke up on the morning of December thirty-first, we toweled up a gallon of wort in the kitchen, and we went to LJ's party. I had wine with Jamie and Corey. You were upstairs, and someone said something about Kale lighting his face on fire, and then you came back down and *everything changed . . .*"

I don't know why I was so upset about the driving-buzzed thing. It had already happened (or maybe it hadn't) and it changed nothing. I had her back, somehow, and as previously stated, assigning blame is unproductive in a world where time runs backwards. I guess I just liked the narrative better when she was completely innocent, blind-sided by a white pickup, her head crushed by the whim of random, neutral chance. The truth is always so much more complicated.

We ascended the last few steps without speaking.

I checked the EMF meter, which held steady at fifty-six degrees, and peered back down the hypnosis-spiral stairs for any sign of the Gasman. So far, so good.

"I'm sorry," she said as we reached the summit.

"Me, too."

This is what we always did: Band-Aid up our fights with cheap apologies and move on. It feels nice, but the wound is infected underneath. It always resurfaces later. It reminded me that during this investigation — at the real Disappointment Bay Lighthouse in 2014 — I'd been sick of Adelaide. Grateful to be a state away from her. I hadn't even called her that weekend; I just appeared in the driveway afterward and found her in the dining room, quietly cutting celery. She can have a coldness, an icy prickle to her voice, an evolved response to being female in an industry dominated by neckbeards. And as for her side? Well, I'm awful with showing emotions. Mental Tupperware.

Were we doomed, long-term? I'd always feared it. Years ago, we'd been at a state fair and a grease-painted clown had noticed us holding hands, and said something that lingered in my memory like a curse: *Aw, how cute. But you'll never make it.*

"Let's not fight," Addie whispered. "Not now."

I climbed the final step. We were inside a greenhouse of paned glass now, and outside it looped a circular balcony. Slick and beaded with condensation. The sky was deep blue and the Fresnel lens was now blinding; a caged sun in a kaleidoscopic dome of mirrors. Up close, it looked a little like a spaceship's warp drive. I shielded my eyes and followed the rotating light as it swept along the outer handrail, a clockwise sweep . . . and splashed over the shoulders of the enigmatic Deer Cap Dude, standing by the edge. Still staring inland. Facing away from us.

I sighed. "Well . . . there he is."

She nudged me. "Go."

"Go what?"

"Go outside and talk to him."

"Just like that?"

"You're the pro." She glanced fretfully down the stairs. "You always bitch about not finding ghosts. Well, here you go."

I exhaled through my teeth. Adelaide can sometimes be abrasive (we've fought about that, too), but here and now, she was absolutely right. This needed to happen fast; whatever *this* was. Somewhere behind us, the Gasman was gaining on us. I approached the floor-to-ceiling windows — like standing in an aquarium — and tapped my fingertips twice against the dew-splattered glass to get the ghost's attention. He didn't turn.

I knocked. Hard. The window creaked in its old frame.

Another sweep of light revealed the Deer Cap Dude was still facing away, blithely unaware of us, staring out into the darkening Washington coastline like a sentry in a guard tower. A visual echo frozen in time.

"Go outside," Addie whispered in my ear. "Ghost hunter."

"You're enjoying this."

She grinned, all teeth. "Just a little."

I groped for the glass door built into the greenhouse wall — it had a cheap plastic latch, like the kind you'd find on a porta-potty. The entire pane swung outward, squeaking on hinges half-eaten by sea salt. Pacific air breathed over the lighthouse, flapping our clothes. I heard faraway waves pounding barnacled rocks. I took slow steps outside, my soles squealing on the wet grate. Slippery as oil. Through the gaps in it, I could see the cement walkway and mowed grass a hundred feet below. The mossy roof of the nautical museum.

I approached to within five feet of the apparition. I was about to tell Addie to stay back in the safety of the light room, but she was already behind me, one hand hooked to my elbow. The Beretta was in her other hand.

I cleared my throat. "Uh . . . hi."

The Deer Cap Dude didn't answer.

"Excuse me?"

Nothing.

I reached out and touched the phantom's left shoulder. Just a touch, not a tap. I half-expected my quaking fingertips to just sink right through like a hologram, but no such luck. Apparently you can touch ghosts. The red and burgundy flannel was cold, and underneath it the man's flesh was firm and solid. Like a block of ice.

The Deer Cap Dude still said nothing. A terrifying thought slipped into my mind — what if he turned around and revealed a bulgy gas mask?

Addie reconsidered: "Maybe we should go."

But now that we were all the way up here, I at least wanted to see the apparition's face. Maybe I was finally rediscovering my ghost-hunting courage. After all, we'd driven five hours and spent two days searching for the damn thing back in August, and all we had to show for it were a few EMF anomalies and Holden's three stupid thermal blobs—

Oh my God.

I froze there in another pulse of light. My mind shuttered.

Three figures.

We were it.

Me, Addie, and the Deer Cap Dude. Standing here on the lighthouse balcony, the three of us had combined like puzzle pieces to form Holden's ghost story. The thermal camera must have been recording us. His ever-hyped Exhibit A, which I'd always dismissed as warmed glass. I hoped I'd live long enough to hear him gloat about it.

I thought about freewill, predestination, the grandfather paradox (the one about going back in time and murdering your grandpa), and wondered what would happen if, right now, I raised a hand and waved. Would the universe rupture? Would I suddenly, magically, remember one of our captured orange blurs doing the same thing?

I lifted my arm to try—

But Addie hissed in my ear: "Okay, I was wrong. This was a bad idea—"

The Deer Cap Dude shuddered violently, head to toe, and made a squelching noise. I jolted backward, into Addie, nearly knocking her over. It was a wet, fleshy sound — instantly nauseating — like squeezing a fistful of cottage cheese and letting it spurt between your fingers. Suddenly my stomach was squirming, my skin crawling. Suddenly I didn't want to see his face anymore.

Something clicked to my right. Addie had the Beretta aimed with knuckled hands. If she fired, the muzzle blast beside my ear would deafen me.

"Sorry," I told the apparition, like I'd just bumped into him on the bus or something. "Sorry about that. We're going now—"

The man shuddered again, harder, as though a thousand volts were surging down his spine. A full-body seizure, rattling the metal balcony under our feet.

"Okay," Addie said. "He's doing that now."

"Yeah. Let's leave."

"Deal."

We were just turning to go down the staircase when the Deer Cap Dude spoke to us. The voice was thick, strangled, *inhuman*, like swamp gas bubbling up through heavy mud, pushing blisters of air. And with it, the apparition delivered a message that transcended time and space:

"Dan Rupley, you're a complete fuckin' idiot."

* * *

Addie stopped with her palm on the glass door. She'd heard it, too.

I turned. "What?"

For a long moment, the figure said nothing. The Fresnel lens rotated quietly behind us, throwing light and darkness in alternating waves.

I tried again: "What'd you say?"

Addie shrugged. "I heard him just fine."

I guess I'd heard him, too; I'd just been expecting a different message. Did we really climb ten stories for this? I'd already been getting an earful from Adelaide, and now the ghosts had to give me shit, too?

Silence.

"He's got a point," Addie muttered.

"Yeah, I know," I said. "I brought this upon myself when I bought a rifle that's famous for killing people. I practically stuck my neck in the guillotine and now—"

"—you're dead," the Deer Cap Dude finished my sentence.

Silence.

I nodded. "Yeah. I was afraid of that."

The ghost still didn't look at us. His voice sounded clotted. And I detected a subtle southern twang — the contagious kind — that didn't really fit the Pacific Northwest. He sounded like a guy who'd voice a bourbon ad on the radio.

I backpedaled. "Who . . . are you?"

"It doesn't matter."

"What day is it?" I asked. "Really, what day is it?"

"I don't know," the Deer Cap Dude said with a juicy, congested sigh. "It's every day ever, and it's the end of the world. If you're here, it doesn't matter."

"I'm here," Addie said. "And I never touched the stupid rifle—"

"She's dead, too."

"No." She lowered her Beretta. "I don't remember dying or anything. I went to a New Year's Party, and then Dan came down the stairs and told me—"

"She's dead, too, Dan."

She raised her voice: "Hey, hillbilly. I'm *right here*."

For some reason the Deer Cap Dude ignored her and spoke only to me, like I was the only one on that lighthouse. It was like buying a car. When we'd gotten her Mercedes, the hairy little salesman had talked over her and only to me, like Addie's delicate female brain couldn't comprehend the nuances of gas mileage. It had pissed me off.

BEEP. The EMF meter chimed.

"Why won't he talk to me?" Addie hissed.

"Dan, she's just in your head," the phantom in a deer hat told me. "A chunk of your memory that you uprooted and dragged along with you. Think of her like . . . a goldfish in a plastic bag. She may look like your fiancée, and sound like your fiancée, but she isn't real. She's dust. She's just your recreated memory of Adelaide Radnor, limited to the things you already know. And you'll discover that, in time, when you realize she can't offer any new information."

"Fuck this guy." She raised her pistol. "And his hat."

That was an Adelaide-comeback: blunt but effective. Still, I saw tears glimmering in her eyes in the next rotation of light.

"No." I stepped between them. "No, I *know* she's real. Because I've already learned new information from her. I learned that the night she died at that four-way stop, she actually drove drunk—"

"Buzzed," she corrected me.

The Deer Cap Dude's voice lowered. "You already knew that, Dan. You just couldn't admit it."

"Bullshit."

"She's *not real*, Dan. Let her go—"

BEEP. The EMF meter chirped again, urgently. The air was chilling; the Gasman was approaching. Time was running out, so I asked the big question, maybe the only one that mattered: "How do we stop the man in the gas mask?"

"You don't."

Addie threw up her hands. "Well, great. This was productive."

"You're already dead," the Deer Cap Dude told me. "You were dead the second you touched the rifle. But maybe you can disrupt its next meal—"

"Forget disrupting it," I said. "I want to *kill* it."

The ghost made that fleshy slapping noise again. This time, it sounded mocking, like a clucking tongue. A thick globule of something thudded to the grate at his feet. "You can't kill it, Dan. Any more than you can kill bad weather, or poverty. It's beyond your understanding. The best outcome — the absolute most you can hope for — is to maybe inconvenience it, piss it off, and save its next victim. Trust me. That's as good as it gets."

"What if we fight the Gasman?"

"Any weapon you can imagine would just be a three-dimensional solution to a five-dimensional problem."

"Yeah? He seems to have trouble with one-dimensional doors."

BEEP.

Now the EMF meter registered an ambient temperature of twenty degrees Fahrenheit. Nineteen. Eighteen. And under the breeze I heard a soft clicking downstairs, back on the lighthouse's ground level. Low but impatient, like a cane tapping a floor. I hadn't noticed it at first, but now I knew — it was that heavy door being stupidly jostled by the Gasman. He'd followed us, he'd caught up to us, and now, big door or not, he'd get in. He always did.

That was when I realized the depth of my mistake.

Addie gasped. "We're cornered up here."

Oh, shit.

The Deer Cap Dude made that squelchy tongue-slapping noise again. Amused laughter, maybe. Another dollop of something moist hit the grated floor.

Shit. Shit. Shit.

Yes, I'd forgotten — the Disappointment Bay Lighthouse had no exterior stairs or access ladder. Just that dew-glazed spiral staircase we'd climbed, and that arched Middle Earth door the Gasman was currently pounding. We'd combed every inch of this site during our *Haunted* investigation; LJ had even dug up old thirties-era blueprints. There was no other route down. No other way to the blurring edges of this memory and into the next. We were trapped up here.

So far, I was really living up to the Deer Cap Dude's assessment of me.

"What does it matter?" Addie whispered in a blaze of harsh light. "What does it matter, if we're both dead?"

I didn't have an answer for that.

BEEP. Ten degrees. I noticed the moisture on the handrails was hardening into pale veins of ice. Frost fractals crept up the glass panes encircling the light. They creaked and groaned.

"We'll get out of this," I said. I'm a horrible liar.

But that wasn't even the part that bothered her. She sniffed, checking her own reflection on the glass. "I'm real, right?"

"You're real."

"I'm not imaginary," she repeated to herself. "I have a soul. I'm *real*—"

I kissed her forehead. A window shattered, startling us, and dumped a shower of shards onto the grated floor. Some of them slipped through and seemed to fall forever, glinting in the blackness like stars. The Pacific surf below us sounded crunchy, and I knew the waves were freezing solid with the Gasman's arrival. Scales of sea ice, crackling and breaking on the shore.

The storm door splintered downstairs. Chunks of wood crashed down to the cement. The sound roared up the lighthouse and the handrails vibrated.

I looked back at the ghost, holding Addie under my shoulder. "Fine," I said. "How do I . . . how do I help the next victim?"

"Are you sure you're even committed to this?" The Deer Cap Dude burbled through what sounded like a mouthful of maple syrup, and another window broke above us, peppering him with chattering pieces. "You obviously wanted to die. Out of dozens of victims, you're the only one who *actually sought it out*—"

"Just tell me."

Downstairs, the door crashed down. In seconds I knew we'd hear those terrible footsteps, echoing up the spiral stairs . . .

"This *thing* is . . . well, on its own, it's deeply stupid," the Deer Cap Dude said. "I don't know exactly what it is. But it grows like fungus, like mildew. An infection that learns. And it needs a host. It can't create. It only knows how to eat and sustain itself . . . and put its long, dirty fingernails inside minds and dig up what it finds. Everything it knows is second-hand. It knows this lighthouse only because you do. It was never here in Seaflats, Washington. Only you were. What do you think would happen if you went to a part of the building that you hadn't visited? Do you think the parasite that lives in the Head-Scratching Rifle has the imagination . . . or even the intelligence . . . to fill in the blanks?"

CLANG. CLANG. The Gasman's footsteps, coming fast.

Addie squeezed my arm.

"Thanks," I said. "But I've seen every square inch of this lighthouse—"

Except—

There was, in fact, one part of the Disappointment Bay Lighthouse that the entire production crew had been prohibited from entering (insurance reasons, I think). One tiny space, up here atop the circular summit. A painted-over chain of ladder rungs led up the greenhouse of glass panes, up to a little crow's nest or something atop the domed roof. A slippery, suicidal climb. I didn't know exactly what was up there — and that meant the Head-Scratching Rifle didn't, either. We'd escape the tower.

They were my memories, after all. The Gasman was only a guest here, exploring them on the fly. A five-dimensional entity clumsily navigating my three-dimensional recollection of past events. It was a little empowering.

"Okay," I said as another window broke. "That'll work."

Addie looked at me. "What'll work?"

I circled the structure and found those ladder rungs with my Maglite — jutting L-shaped handholds, like the things electricians use to climb telephone poles. These were painted white and encrusted with bumpy ice, raised into hard blisters.

She rolled her eyes. "If we can climb it, so can he."

"Trust me, Addie."

CLANG. CLANG.

She stuffed her Beretta into her purse and went up first, her boots squealing on the slick surface. An arctic chill raced between us, whipping the edges of her dress taut. It slashed my face and my eyes, a scalding coldness. My ears ached. Instant frostbite.

The Deer Cap Dude clucked: "She's *not real*, Dan. Why let her climb first?"

"Shut up."

I followed my fiancée up the rungs, one handhold at a time. The bars clicked and wobbled on loose rivets. Another window blew out and peppered us with glass, and Addie yelped, covering her face.

The lighthouse's Fresnel lens made a hellish grinding sound — like a car out of oil — and stopped swiveling, as if the moisture in the gears had frozen it in place. It now spotlighted the ghostly Deer Cap Dude where he stood by the railing, still not turning to face us. He didn't seem bothered that the Gasman was coming up the stairs. Maybe they were old drinking buddies. Another gust of wind flapped his jacket and lifted his hat a few inches. I caught a teasing glance of bristled gray hair. And . . . something red and glistening.

"You didn't answer my question," I shouted down at the thing as I climbed. "How do I save the next victim?"

"I can't . . . tell you exactly how."

Addie sneered. "Of course he can't."

"It's listening. It's in your mind now. Learning what you know. Any conventional plan would be like trying to beat yourself at chess." The Deer Cap Dude paused thoughtfully, bubbles rising in his voice. "So instead . . . I left you a clue. So you'll recognize your chance when it comes, and seize it, before it can stop you—"

"What's the clue?"

"Remember your trunk? Coffee house parking lot. March."

My mind fluttered back to Jitters. I recalled leaving Holden at our table, venturing out into the random blizzard, popping the trunk of my Celica, picking up the Head-Scratching Rifle. The shock and disgust of discovering moist clumps of cat litter sticking to the wood and metal. The sharp odor. The . . . the Kitty Roca rattling in the barrel.

I paused. "Cat shit?"

"Good. You found it."

"The clue is *cat shit*?"

The Deer Cap Dude turned to face us just as the Fresnel lens fizzled out in a crackle of blue sparks, and the Disappointment Bay Lighthouse plunged into complete darkness. I glimpsed his face for a fraction of a second, but it was enough.

His cottage-cheese voice: "It's got all the time in the world. You *don't*, Dan."

His face was a concave, blown-out shell, as if a firework had gone off behind his sinuses. His scalp was peeled like the blossoming of an awful, meaty flower. No eye sockets, no forehead, maybe a hint of a nose, but crushed off to the side in a chunky-salsa-tangle of cartilage. No upper jaw remained. But his lower jaw was intact, his white teeth and chin protruding to form a Neanderthal underbite because there was no face to compare it with. I saw a pink tongue nestled in his half-ruined mouth, and recognized the slapping noises we'd heard. Another chunk dropped to the grate, and I realized—

Ben Dyson.

Ben "SO COLD IN HERE" Dyson. The rifle's second American victim after it had been imported stateside. The WordPress-blogging gunsmith from Georgia who, without warning, stuck the Mosin Nagant under his chin and blew his face all over his workshop on that scorching August afternoon.

The Deer Cap Dude was Ben Dyson. Or maybe Ben Dyson was the Deer Cap Dude. Time was a hairball. Had I seen a blood-soaked hunting hat on the floor in one of those fuzzy photos? When had the narrative even begun? The sheer weight of it came down on me like a rockslide.

It's listening.

"Dan," Addie urged above me. "Keep climbing—"

But I froze there, clinging to the rungs. Guts heaving. It made no sense at all.

It's in your mind.

CLANG. CLANG—

"*Dan.* The Gasman's coming—"

Somehow I forced myself to keep going. Up, up, up. One warty rung after another, so frigidly cold they felt searing hot. My hands froze to the metal, suctioning free of every bar with a dry, tearing Velcro sound. Like licking a frozen pole. I flinched at a flare of hot pain on my left palm, and then a sticky snap. I'd left a postage stamp of bloodied skin on that one. No time to stop.

It knows what I know.

My mind was racing. I don't think I really grasped the true malevolence of this *thing* — attached to this bolt-action rifle that came to me in an oily skin of plastic, reeking of centipede musk and yeast — until I personally witnessed what it had done to Ben Dyson's face. That made it real, somehow. No censor pixels here. Evil is just a word. But faces are personal. And this gun destroys them.

And it would be mine next. For maybe the first time since I'd lost Adelaide, I experienced true existential terror. I was utterly screwed. I was trapped in the orbit of a gangrenous evil that existed outside of time; it was already rooted in my past and future. I was already dead, and it would keep killing, passing from corpse to corpse on the American gun market like an invisible predator. An unstoppable cycle of violence.

Unless I could decode the riddle of Ben Dyson's secret message.

A goddamn cat turd.

Last rung. Addie grabbed my wrist and tugged. I kneed up onto the lighthouse roof, groping blindly in the freezing darkness. I expected rough tile, or coned roofing, or whatever the hell the Disappointment Bay Lighthouse roof was built of. Because I didn't know what this little crow's nest looked like, and neither did the Head-Scratching Rifle, and that meant we weren't on top of the lighthouse at all.

As we slipped into the next memory, the Deer Cap Dude's wormy voice rattled up from below: "Leave your imaginary Adelaide behind, Dan. Let her go, or *the Gasman will use her against you—*"

"Dan," she breathed, gripping my arm. "It worked."

Sent: 3/19 6:09PM
Sender: LJ@haunted
Subject: OMFG!

Hey Dan-O,

Holden tells me you found the ancient Soviet Head-Scratching Rifle of Infinite Sadness or whatever it's called. Nice detective work, man. So drop by Ferguson and we'll chat about maybe doing a segment on that haunted gun, maybe a B-story to run with the Old Briar Mine. Or just come by the office. Seriously.

Production isn't the same without you. I'm really worried about you. I'm so sorry for your loss. Take care, friend.

-LJ

PS: But seriously let me know if you're dropping by with that cursed gun. Too f'ing cool!!!

LJ Baxter
Unit Production Manager
Haunted (Sundays at 11pm and Wednesdays at 2am, only on KSPM)

2 Hours, 40 Minutes

I watched Adelaide closely after what Ben Dyson's corpse said to me. For some reason I was fine with being already doomed — I pretty much deserved it — but the idea of Addie being imaginary? That terrified me.

So I studied the way she moved as we hitchhiked through our past: her small hands fidgeting at her sides, her New Year's Eve dress gliding over her legs. The little things she did — the birdlike way she bobbed her head to throw her bangs from her eyes, the way her British accent intensified under stress and relaxed when she did, and always, that cautious flash of a smile. New or remembered? Real or imagined?

Disturbingly, I began to wonder: what's the difference, anymore?

"Aw, crap." Addie recognized the next memory. "The lobster disaster."

I grinned. "I like this one."

Yes, lobsters.

Twenty-six lobsters. The warty brown ones that sold for $12.99 a pound and skittered around the floor of a hundred-gallon aquarium. All knuckles, claws, and rubber-banded pincers. This was in a grocery store in Astoria, under the flamingo struts of a mile-long bridge joining Washington and Oregon over the mouth of the Columbia River. September or October, I think it was, when we'd driven out to help my parents move out of my childhood house. With an icepick-jab of fear, I realized — we'd already dropped from 2014 to 2013. Was the train of thoughts accelerating?

I'm going to save you, Addie had whispered with her nose squished to the glass. *I'm going to save every last one of you.*

I remember glancing up at the whiteboard and wishing we'd done this on Sunday, when the lobsters were $11.95 a pound. But it was her money, not mine.

The entire tank, she told the clerk. *I wish to purchase the entire tank.*

The tank isn't for sale.

No, not literally the tank. The lobsters in it. All of them.

Four hundred and fifty-one dollars. The cashier had to call in a fussy little manager to swipe a red override card. Normally, I guess they box them up for you, but we just bought a Rubbermaid bin and stuffed them in a writhing heap with six inches of tank water. From the grocery store it was a four-minute drive west, past a mothballed arcade and boarded-up VHS rental place, to a coastline of slippery black rocks.

In the rearview mirror I glimpsed the Gasman, stepping out into the road to follow us at a walking pace. We left him behind.

Addie was giggling in the passenger seat. *Is this crazy?*

I sighed. *Not by our standards.*

We reached the coastline with time to spare. From growing up in this seaside town, I'd learned there were basically two kinds of weather in Astoria: 'raining' and 'almost raining.' Cold drizzle pinpricked the air.

We carried the sloshing bin to the cliff's edge and Addie winced, rubbing a shiny sore on her palm. Mine ached too; a paradoxical blister from climbing the subzero rungs of the Disappointment Bay Lighthouse, where we'd learned that I was dead, the Gasman was un-killable, and that Addie didn't exist. Shitty revelations, all-around. But she didn't want to talk about it, and neither did I, so we just let this lobster memory play for a few minutes, like a television in a darkened room that we were too exhausted to switch off. This time and that one tangled together, like ribbons of mixing paint.

Twenty-six lobsters, I'd said. *I thought we'd just save one or two.*

What would the other twenty-four think?

Probably nothing. They're lobsters.

I knew I'd regret it, she told me atop that rock berm, looking out into the choppy water with her hair clumping and her cheeks rash-red. *I'd have an Oskar Schindler breakdown. I'd go home and look at the MacBook Air, and the pretentious bullshit on the walls, and I'd wonder how many lobsters I could've saved. The little glass fruit bowl on the table is, like, ten lobsters. I could've saved ten more.*

She'd just signed her soul over to the tech startup Cubek. Any chance of vet school was, of course, years in the rearview mirror, but this had been the point-of-no-return for her. The event horizon of her career. Who doesn't feel the pain of letting go of their dreams? I'd always wanted to be a screenwriter or film director, and instead I walked around on TV with a flashlight and a restaurant-issue thermometer gun. Life twists your dreams, but in subtle and painless ways, until one morning you wake up and you're out of time.

She picked up the first lobster. It blew furious bubbles and whipped its antennae, clicking in her fingers. *You're free*, she whispered. *You were going to be dropped into boiling water, cooked alive, but you're free now.*

This contrasted nicely with each clumsy splash. I held back laughter. Something about the way the little critters flailed in confused panic; it must've been like being liberated from a prison camp via circus canon.

Addie's frost-burnt hand had started to bleed and she rubbed a smear of red on her dress, her hair windswept, her eyes bloodshot. *I know, Dan. I know how stupid and pointless this is—*

It's fine, I said.

I just needed this—

It's fine, Addie.

She turned away. She had always been ashamed of these little outbursts. She never knew how to be vulnerable around me. I made it difficult, I think. Even after her savannah monitor had disintegrated in her arms, she'd been embarrassed to cry in front of me back at BullsEye's, like I would judge her or mock her for it.

She chewed her lip. *I know . . . I know this is stupid.*

Yeah, I thought so, too. And I didn't have the energy to pretend to disagree.

At this point, circa 2013, we kind of hated each other. The drive from Farwell to Astoria had been deeply tedious — you can only have the same argument so many times, in so many forms, before it turns into a recital, and then what? Hell, skip the recital. Silence is easier. The drive back was looking like six more hours of eggshell quiet, so Addie had decided to skim off the top of her embarrassingly disposable bank account and do something 'productive.' Not donating to a homeless shelter, or leukemia research, or paying it forward and picking up a stranger's grocery bill — nope. Twenty-six lobsters.

I hurled another one like a football, giving it backspin. He splashed down a hundred feet out, barely missing a red buoy.

Wait, Dan. She grabbed my elbow, her voice pitching with alarm. *These are Pacific lobsters, right?*

Yeah, I said. *Of course.*

You're sure?

Nope. That whiteboard had definitely said Maine lobsters. I'm not even sure lobsters are native to the Pacific at all — if they had been, they probably wouldn't have been so damn expensive. But I'd lied, because back then, I was sick of her stunts and hadn't wanted to drag this farce out any longer. There were just a few stragglers left, and then we could get back on the road. The horizon had darkened with clouds.

In silence, we threw the rest. But she studied the final one and turned it over, like there might be a product code on its belly. *Are you . . . are you really sure, Dan? Or are you just saying that?*

Addie. They're sea spiders—

She looked heartbroken. *You don't care.*

I threw the last one extra hard, and we listened to the distant splash. *I'm just saying, we can save twenty-six lobsters here in Oregon, and that's nice, but on the drive back home we'll straight-up murder four hundred bugs with our windshield.*

She winced. *You don't need to have a comeback to everything, Dan.*

But I always did, I guess.

For a moment we just stared out to sea together as salt water lapped barnacled rocks. The rain came in indecisive spurts, pattering the rocks and soaking our hair. We were going back to my Celica, crossing the crest of gravel and dandelions, when she sucked in a sharp breath, slapping a hand to her mouth.

I stopped. *What?*

She sat down on the shoulder, shaking her head. Disbelief.

What, Addie?

She pulled something from her pocket — a pair of yellow scissors — and let them drop. She looked up at me with big eyes. *The rubber bands,* she said. *We . . . we forgot to cut off the rubber bands.*

That's right. The blue rubber bands the grocery store had bundled the lobsters' pincers with, to keep them from attacking each other in captivity. Or injuring the cook. Or, you know, catching food.

I shouldn't have laughed, but I did.

Oh my God. She buried her face in her hands. *They're . . . . they're defenseless down there, handcuffed in the wild. They can't even pick up food—*

I sat beside her. *Yeah, they weren't Pacific lobsters, either.*

For a moment I thought she'd cry, but she laughed instead; one of those miserable barks that cuts your throat on the way up. Pitch-black chuckles. The wind blew in handfuls of gritty rain, stinging our eyes and forcing our faces down, and I realized she was pressing her head on my shoulder. Her jaw shivered with pained giggles, and I joined her, as natural as sneezing. It felt good to laugh together. For a few minutes, we could just be two people laughing together, and we could forget about the growing fault lines in our relationship, the cracks in the supports, all the stupid little things we couldn't fix that might someday doom us. We'd just accidentally murdered twenty-six lobsters, and it was hilarious. That was it.

The EMF meter beeped.

I looked at her now — in *this* now. "Tell me something I don't know."

"What?"

"Tell me something I don't already know. So I know you're not imaginary."

She shrugged. "I . . . I don't know—"

"Anything, Addie. The capital of Guam?"

"I don't know."

"The *location* of Guam?"

"Well, that's the problem." She shrugged bleakly, brushing damp hair from her eyes. "I could tell you anything, and it could just be your imagination making facts up. The real challenge is: how do you *prove* something I say is true?"

Since we were trapped within the finite horizons of my own memories, I guess that was the real problem. It was an awful feeling. A mix of claustrophobia and loneliness. Who knows — maybe Laika had imaginary friends, too, in her cramped aluminum tomb miles above the stratosphere.

"For what it's worth," she said with a small, sad smile, "I *think* I'm real."

I wish that was enough. It wasn't.

The EMF meter beeped again, so we took in one last glimpse of the gray ocean, now twenty-six Atlantic lobsters richer, and I helped her to her feet. We got the hell out of there, before the raindrops started to freeze in the air, the sun began to dim red, and the Gasman came to claim more of my soul.

"Wait," she said as we raced further back in time. "Do you seriously not know where *Guam* is?"

Sent: 3/20 10:32PM
Sender: jeffmckee89@webmail
Subject: Viewer Feedback (redirect)

Hi,

First off, BIG fan of the show. Bought the first two seasons on DVD. Was watching the WA Lighthouse episode with the Deer Cap Dude and I noticed something.

Fifth segment, pause at 32:53 on the wide shot of the lighthouse. Look at the far left corner. It's grainy and you'll have to increase the brightness, but you can see a tall guy standing by the door. He's wearing a gas mask.

WTF is this guy? HOW DID NO ONE NOTICE HIM?????
Jeff McKee

1 Hour, 55 Minutes

"A cat turd? We're up against an ancient, five-dimensional demonic entity, and the only clue Mr. Dyson left you was a *cat turd*?"

I shrugged. "Unfortunately, yes."

"Did you keep it?"

"Why would I *keep it*?"

"Is the Gasman's weakness cat turds or something?"

"I really doubt that."

"I hate cats." She crossed her arms. "Why couldn't Dyson just tell you upfront?"

"Because . . . because the Head-Scratching Rifle is already in my head," I said. "Following me through my memories. It's learning everything. Like he said, it would be like trying to beat yourself at chess."

She sighed. "And . . . I might be a figment of your imagination."

"Yep."

"Let's wait for the Gasman this time." She lowered her voice, like a quarterback in a huddle, her Beretta discreetly tucked in her lap. "Let's watch him. Study him. I want to know what we're up against."

We were seated on wobbly white furniture in the Timber Ridge Mall, a three-story shopping complex just north of Boise. Walled on three sides by ferns, footbridges and smelly koi ponds, the food court was a blinding ocean of sunlight, cast by a twenty-yard skylight cut into the shape of Idaho. Or at least that's what they'd intended, but they'd botched the panhandle's eastern border, creating a major PR headache that had plagued the mall for years. Between the shape of the silhouette, and the unfortunate sunbeam it traced at certain times of the year, local teenagers had come to know it as the *Sky-dick*.

Timber Ridge's owners would recut the skylight eventually — Holden told me that it's now a bigger chunk of the inland northwest, including Montana, Washington, and Oregon — but that hadn't happened yet. This was 2013, and the Sky-dick cast a proud, phallic sunbeam.

Summer. This had to be summer. The sunlight was too fierce; the crowd's clothing was too sparse. The red board over the theater ticket booth was thirty percent superhero movies and fifty percent superhero movie sequels. Near the Subway sandwich line, a toddler was crying over a dropped ice cream cone which was melting into the tile like a squished head. I knew where we were . . . but why were we back here?

Addie poked me. "Dan?"

"I'm just wondering why we're here at Timber Ridge," I thought aloud. "Why are we jumping back months at a time, skipping hundreds of memories?"

"Well, what happened here?"

"I told you I hated your dad," I said. "And we had a fight."

Calling it a fight was like calling *Star Wars: The Phantom Menace* a mild disappointment. She'd stormed out past the Japanese noodle place and taken her still-new Mercedes. I'd spent the next six hours in the mall, too stubborn to call a cab or Holden. I bought a movie ticket and theater-hopped until nightfall. We slept in separate houses for four days — Addie shacked with her Cubek friend Jamie, while I claimed Holden's couch — because each of us assumed the other would be taking the house. Tragically, Baby missed her weekly dead rat feeding.

I recognized a balled napkin on the table between us. During our milder tiffs, I used to puncture the tension by waving a napkin like a white flag. It only works so many times.

Our argument even lingered in the air, aching fragments: *Fuck you, Dan.*

You're so selfish.

But I realized I'd answered my own question.

"I think it's the big moments," I told her. "It's the big events, the ups and downs, the landmarks of the mental landscape."

She nodded slowly. "So . . . how does it end? We get chased through your high school prom, then you're playing tag in kindergarten, then you're in diapers and building sandcastles on the beach. We're out of memories. Then what?"

"The Gasman . . . kills me, I guess."

But my morbid imagination went a little further. I envisioned a bullet bursting out of someone as it punched through their other side. The entry wound is always so small and subtle — just a modest hole, like being jabbed with a nail — but the exit wound is the apocalyptic payoff. All that pressurized blood and flesh, blowing out the back like a balloon full of raw meat. Explosive, violent, irreversible.

Addie was staring at the ceiling. "The skylight looks like a dong."

"It does."

"Not related. Sorry."

"It's okay."

The EMF meter beeped on the tabletop between us. Sixty-six degrees.

We each agreed on a direction and watched it. We were waiting for the Gasman to catch up, because . . . well, I don't know. Studying our enemy was better than just fleeing him. I was sick of running. And there were only so many memories left.

The mall hummed with Saturday activity. Teenagers gathered in tight circles, heads hunched over phones. A swirl of fire leapt from one of the woks at the Japanese noodle place. The new *Captain America* movie was showing at 3:10 p.m. and looked ready to sell out. I whiffed an algae odor; the koi ponds hadn't been cleaned in a while. It smelled like the aquarium aisle of a pet store.

It was all fake, I knew. It was a dream, or a reenactment; something conjured up by the Head-Scratching Rifle digging through my brain and exploring my recollection of the Timber Ridge Mall. Just set design of stunning detail and depth. None of it was real, but I still brushed my palm over the wired tabletop and marveled at the subtleties I'd thought myself incapable of imagining — the warbling vibrations, the crooked leg, the dings and irregularities in the meshwork where the tables had been stacked together so the janitors could buff the floors. All convincing, but all synthetic.

And Addie, across the table from me. Most convincing of all.

BEEP. She checked the EMF meter. "He's getting closer."

I hoped to God she was real. She couldn't be a bagged goldfish, like Ben Dyson had claimed, as imaginary as the Timber Ridge table between us. I'd found her — I'd reached into the past and *found her*. She was the ghost of Adelaide Radnor, her spirit, her soul; whatever you wanted to call it. Yes, she was real.

BEEP. Sixty-five degrees.

Addie noticed a placemat. "Wow."

"What?"

She scooted it toward me. A child's dining mat with a colorized map of the world. The Mercator projection, so Greenland and Antarctica were bloated. The countries were sharply defined and labeled — but only the big, identifiable ones. The US, Canada, Mexico, Russia, Brazil, China. Most others were blurred out; their names smeared, their borders mushy and indistinct. Europe was a projectile-vomit splatter of primary colors. The Philippines didn't exist.

"It's like a parody map," Addie said, "of how Americans see the world."

"We're in my head."

"And you can't remember a *single* country in Africa?"

I glanced up at the eateries lining the food court. The restaurant titles were all there — Subway, Edo, A&W, Carl's Jr. — but the menu items were blurred. The generalities were there but not the specifics. Apparently the subtleties of my imagination had a limit, because there was no way of knowing the exact price of a Meatball Sub. I felt stranded, submerged deep inside my own head, like poor Laika.

BEEP. Fifty-nine degrees.

The Sears lights fizzled out, darkening the storefront.

I was worried about the Gasman. "We should see him by now."

"Where is he?"

We craned our necks and scanned all approaches to the food court. Throngs of people, coming and going, but no snouted gas mask. No tattered greatcoat. Seated there in the Timber Ridge food court with my fiancée, I felt like bait, staked to the ground, waiting for the predator. And the predator was running late.

I shivered. "Is he stuck in traffic?"

The seconds ticked by. No Gasman.

"Dan, something's been on my mind." She rubbed her arms. "About how you worded that exploding-bullet thing. The burp sound it made—"

"Doesn't matter. It was a dud."

"Exactly," she said, her breath fogging. "The gunpowder didn't burn. You contaminated it, maybe, when you were pouring it into the casing. Sweat from your fingers, or oil. Or maybe it was just crappy Nixon-era ammunition that spent too long on a warehouse shelf."

I nodded. All possible explanations.

"Right, Dan?"

"Right. What's your point?"

BEEP. Fifty degrees.

Addie's eyes darted busily, full of sunlight. "Okay, how's this for 'something you don't know?' Gun safety for dummies: if a round doesn't fire due to bad powder, there's still some explosive force from the primer. Just not enough to push the bullet down the barrel. So you get a malfunction called a squi—"

She froze.

Squi—

"What?"

Her eyes snapped down to the Dan Rupley edition placemat between us.

I leaned forward. ". . . A malfunction called a *what*?"

"I'm . . . I'm not sure I should tell you this." She looked up at me crookedly, a ghost of a smile on her face. "If the Head-Scratching Rifle is really . . . you know. Inside your brain. Learning what you know."

Like Ben Dyson said. I shrugged tiredly, neither agreeing or disagreeing. It gets old fast, having people tell you they have an important and possibly life-saving idea . . . but they can't actually tell you what it is.

She softened. "Sorry, Dan."

But I was too curious to let it go. Like a high-stakes Scrabble match, my mind kept hurling letters at her half-spoken squi- word, struggling to complete it. . . . Squiggle? . . . Squish? . . . .Squirt?

BEEP. Forty-seven degrees.

Still no Gasman.

Addie exhaled impatiently and scanned the koi pond perimeter again. "He should be here by now," she said. "Something's different."

"What changed?"

"I don't know."

I rose too, half-standing, searching the milling crowd for any sign of our gas-masked friend. Maybe he was stooping low, hunching his seven-foot frame to blend in and then ambush us up close. Maybe he was waiting around a corner. Or maybe he'd just grow out of the floor beneath us. Who knows? Physics didn't quite work here; we'd recently escaped a lighthouse by climbing up to its roof.

And still, my mind gnawed on Adelaide's mystery *squi*— word. What was the malfunction called? What'd she meant to say?

. . . Squid?

. . . Squirrel?

. . . Squire?

All unlikely names for firearm malfunctions.

"Maybe we should go," she said. "Maybe we—"

I'm not sure why I glanced up.

But I did, and my blood froze in my veins when I spotted the Gasman on the third-floor balcony above us. A hundred feet away, on the north end of the disastrously misconceived Idaho skylight. Standing by the upper entrance to JCPenney in a harsh band of sunlight; a moth-like, tattered shadow against white walls. Staring down at us. He'd been watching us the entire time.

He had something in his hands.

* * *

It was jolting, seeing the Head-Scratching Rifle again.

But I knew the antique Russian weapon intimately now. Its subtleties were burnt into my mind; its heft, its little clicks and rattles, its rancid odors. The yellow slug-slime that made it sticky to the touch. The coffin-nail bayonet, the weathered birch, the clunky analog feel of the Mosin Nagant's patent-dodging design. It had been *in my hands*.

Now it was in the Gasman's hands.

The tall man in the greatcoat turned it over, dutifully inspecting every inch with those rimmed glass eyes. Even up on that balcony, his motions were broad enough that I could discern exactly what he was doing. He checked the trigger, fiddled with the rear sights, unlatched the bolt, and peered down the barrel.

Addie tapped my arm. "What's he doing?"

"It's like a . . . a pre-firing safety check." I didn't know how else to put it. "According to the legend, everyone who shot themselves with the Head-Scratching Rifle did that first. Like a little ritual, to make sure the rifle was ready."

"To fire without damaging itself?"

"Exactly."

Addie looked disappointed.

"What?" I asked.

"Nothing."

The Gasman click-clacked the Mosin bolt back in place, shouldered the firearm, and aimed it down at the Idaho lunch crowd. Down at us. My stomach heaved against my ribs, but my mind knew better.

"Don't stand up," I whispered to her. "Or he'll see us."

"You think he's testing us?"

"Maybe."

No one noticed the Gasman up on the third-floor ledge. The summer-2013 Timber Ridge Mall scene continued around us obliviously, like the background activity of a film set. People sat and stood, chewing, slurping, crumpling sandwich bags and pocketing phones. A chair squealed. A woman guffawed sharply at something and the laugh thumped off the tall ceiling. The smell of koi, barbecue sauce, and baby wipes. All fake, I reminded myself. All bits of a shrinking universe.

"Just blend in," I whispered.

Addie studied the Gasman on the ledge, her fingers tightening on the rim of the table. She'd scooted her legs beneath her so she could spring upright when the first gunshot whip-cracked through the dull roar.

But it didn't.

Because the Gasman wasn't firing. Bafflingly, he just tracked the old Mosin Nagant over the churning crowd of summer shoppers. He inched the muzzle right to left. Left to right. Then up and down, from the AMC Cinemas ticket line, over the frozen yogurt stand, to the Starbucks and the first-floor entrance to Sears.

"He likes that spot," Addie murmured.

"No kidding."

"Why would he like that spot?"

Fragments of our 2013 argument echoed between us, like radio bleed-through: *I can't take it. You're a miserable person, Dan. And you make me miserable—*

The Gasman abruptly slung the Mosin Nagant back over his shoulder and backpedaled from the balcony handrail. In two seconds he was gone, vanished behind white pillars. Like a sniper scoping out enemy territory and then returning to base to make a report. Around us, 2013-era Timber Ridge kept humming with mundane life, like nothing had happened at all.

Addie looked at me.

I shrugged. "Playtime's over, I guess."

"This is different," she echoed.

Yes, it was. Maybe the Gasman was using my mind as a lens, combing the past for something. Maybe the Head-Scratching Rifle nurtured bigger goals than just blowing my head off. Without a human brain to play with, it was just a gun, just a dumb piece of wood and metal. It was deeply frightening — and a little empowering — to suppose that maybe the Head-Scratching Rifle *needed* me for something.

Again, the past whispered between us: *You're selfish, Dan.*

You're so self-absorbed. You obsess over things, and chase them to the gates of Hell. Like the stupid Nielsen ratings for your show. Holy Christ, Dan, I have never seen anyone punch a wall over a fifth of a decimal point. One dumbass viewer comment about the lighting and you mope for hours. You're miserable, because you make yourself miserable. I think, deep down, you're a sociopath.

"I forgot I called you a sociopath," Addie said. "Sorry."

I shrugged. "I deserved it."

And that's what hurts me most, Dan. Realizing that I . . . I kind of hate you. Realizing that sometimes I wish I could just move back to England. That sometimes when I'm driving home, I realize I'd rather stay at work, at a job I loathe, than spend an evening with you.

Addie winced at her own words. I think I remembered the fight better than she did. It went on and on. If we sat still at this little table and concentrated, we could relive every last second of our vicious back-and-forth here in the Timber Ridge food court . . . if we wanted to. If there wasn't a gas-masked predator coming for us.

I pointed. "He's back."

The Gasman entered the food court. He'd descended the staircase and now approached from the theater admission line. The crowd milled around the gas-masked figure like a school of dumb fish, not even noticing. One salesman in a charcoal business suit almost walked right into him, but hastily apologized and veered past. The Gasman didn't mind; he was coming for us. Only us. Maybe he'd learned to not get distracted with tearing the scalps off of bystanders; they were just extras populating my memories. The idea gave me a chill — this intruder was learning from his errors at the New Year's Eve party. He was adapting to my mental terrain. Hopefully I could, too.

Addie stood, squeaking her chair. "Well, shall we?"

"This memory blows. He can have it."

She tossed me the EMF meter. "Adios, Timber Ridge."

Onward, to the next memory on this finite train of thoughts. It was only a retreat, but it felt like surrender. Another time and place claimed by the Head-Scratching Rifle, like the geography of my mind was blown up on a Risk game board, and every memory we abandoned was marked with a growing sea of red tokens. I was land, and I was being conquered. Possessed. What would happen when there was nowhere left to run? One small silver lining — it probably wouldn't involve tedious dice-throwing.

I started to run but Addie held my shoulder. "Wait."

"What?"

"Just *wait*."

Excitement trembled her voice. I turned. The Gasman had halted at the outer perimeter of the food court, maybe ten feet from our white table. Right by the koi pond. Those eyeholes were still locked on us, buried in that snouted Soviet mask that revealed nothing of the face underneath — if a face even existed. But the entity wasn't coming any closer. He stood there, stymied, like he'd been boxed out by an invisible wall.

"See?"

"What's he waiting for?"

This was the closest I'd ever been to the Gasman in full daylight. The odor was predictably awful. Like decaying fruit, decaying meat, decaying *everything*. Back when *Haunted* was a basement-project webcast, I'd worked night shifts at Farwell's Quality Foods, and one of the more unglamorous responsibilities of an already unglamorous job was hurling trash down a twenty-foot chute crusted with food waste. The Gasman smelled like that chute, like the green-and-red shit that coated the duct walls. Rotten lettuce bits, hardened cow blood, salty oyster sludge.

His boots and double-flapped greatcoat were glazed with shards of ice. Snow stuck to the wool in cottony globs, like dryer lint. He looked like he'd just trudged through a frigid Siberian tundra, through miles of waist-deep snow, before arriving here in Idaho's Timber Ridge Mall, circa summer of 2013. Hell, maybe he had. Like the corpse of Ben Dyson had supposed, it didn't seem to experience time the way we did.

His proportions were wrong, too. I was now certain of it. The Gasman's forearms were longer than his biceps, hooking at the elbow like a praying mantis. His legs were too skinny and vaulted, stilt-like, while his midsection sagged like an insect abdomen. His belly could've been full of spider eggs. The mask's breathing hose dangled like a rubber proboscis. If all the wool, fabric, and rubber was just a human-shaped spacesuit, I was terrified of the four- or five-dimensional creature that shambled inside it.

"He can't cross water," Adelaide gasped.

"What?"

She pointed.

Sure enough, he had halted at the edge of the raised footbridge over the Timber Ridge koi pond. The toes of his snow-crusted boots were planted exactly where the fish tank began. Not an inch further. Something about his pose — the way he'd rigidly frozen mid-step at the very, *very* edge, told me Addie was correct. He'd stopped at the water. A blade of ice slid off his thigh and shattered on the phony wood.

"Like a vampire," she said. "He can't cross water."

I looked at her. "Vampires can cross water."

"No. *Really?*"

"Vampires can totally cross water."

"Well," she said, pointing with her Maglite. "This asshole can't."

My mind shuttered to what Holden had told me back in Jitters, under those warm paper lanterns, two years in the future: *Some mediums believe that unclean spirits can't cross bodies of—*

The Gasman abruptly pivoted, one boot squeaking, and paced along the koi pond. The water encircled our food court on three sides, and was just a few feet wide in spots — just a step across — but he didn't even try. For all the aesthetic failings of the Timber Ridge Mall (the three-edged koi pond had been ridiculed as 'C-World' by the Inland Voice), the layout was giving the Gasman at least as much trouble as a closed door. His anteater face tracked us as his angle changed.

"He can't cross water." I remembered Ben Dyson's clue. "Does that relate to cat litter somehow?"

She watched the thing circle us, chewing her lip thoughtfully. "Cat litter looks . . . like sand. A beach has sand. A beach has water."

"Nah. Too obtuse."

She rolled her eyes. "Right, Dan. Because a *cat turd* is so clear and literal—"

She was interrupted by a jagged scream. Someone — finally — had noticed the Mosin Nagant belted on the Gasman's back. Chairs scooted, drinks spilled, breaths gasped, and a panicked crowd heaved in all directions. The Gasman approached from the direction of the A&W burger stand; he'd taken the long way around to reach the one side of the food court that didn't bridge over pond water.

In the chaos, Addie snapped her fingers. "Ah! He hates water. Like a *cat.*"

That seemed pretty tangential, too, but it did give me an idea. The Gasman couldn't seem to cross bodies of water . . . but what about contact with it? You never know if you don't try, so I grabbed a cup of water from a table and hurled it at the advancing figure. It splashed harmlessly off his chest.

Addie slow-clapped. "Nice, Dan."

As we retreated through the thinning crowd, I scooped another cup off the next table and threw it, too. It thudded off his snout, splashing brown soda. "Crap. I think that was Dr. Pepper—"

"What's he supposed to do? Melt?"

"Worth a try." I grabbed a third and hurled it. By now I'd figured Holden's weird little demonology rule only applied to bodies of water, but I didn't like proving Addie right. Sometimes she's such a know-it-all. Like her constantly correcting me that contrary to common belief, Velociraptors were actually only two feet tall, like clawed chickens, and the six-foot Utahraptor is the species I'm really remembering from *Jurassic Park*. Her little smartass jabs had a way of turning me stubborn, of making me dig into an illogical position and defend it to the death—

The water cup struck the Gasman's forehead, and one eyehole exploded.

The gunshot exploded beside me, answered by a rising crescendo of screams. Addie stood to my right, that Beretta up and out in clenched hands, teeth bared, a brass casing pinging off tile somewhere. She brushed a strand of hair from her eyes.

The Gasman didn't even flinch. One eyehole was blown out, encircled with daggers of splintered glass, but I still saw nothing inside. Only blackness. With the accuracy of a brain surgeon, Addie had drilled a .40-caliber tunnel right into the creature's left eye socket — only it didn't have a left eye socket. It just kept walking toward us, flipping a chair.

I looked at her. "See? Told you that wouldn't work."

"Says the guy throwing *water*."

"Nice shot, though."

She beamed, stuffing the handgun back in her purse as we ran. "Thanks. I practiced every Monday for this."

That made me laugh, a hoarse rattle in the thinning air.

Dan, I think I hate you.

We kept running. Yes, we were doomed, running out of time and memories, but so what? We jumped the pond together — the surface now crystalizing into ice, orange koi trapped and dying underneath — and raced through the emptying mall, our fingers locked and our footsteps echoing. Past RadioShack, around a cluster of massage chairs, alongside a row of Jurassic-looking ferns. I'd visited this shopping center dozens of times and had most of the megacomplex committed to memory, so it would be awhile before the edges started to blur. Addie giggled beside me, breathless and rattled and somehow giddy.

"Most eventful mall trip," she said. "Ever."

"Way better than shopping."

We slowed near Yankee Candle to catch our breaths and suddenly she was holding my arm, looking at me dead-on, her eyes impossibly big and clear as quartz: "Dan, you traveled through time just for me. That's weirdly romantic."

"I'm a sucker for British accents."

"Yeah? Have I told you yours sounds stupid?"

"Many times."

"It's really drawly. Like . . . Yee-haw, let's go watch the NASCAR—"

"*The* NASCAR?" I laughed. "What the hell are you, an alien?"

I'm sorry, Dan, but I hate you. Everything about you. You're clever and funny and kind of brilliant, but you're also a deeply ugly, obsessive person—

I kissed her there. In front of a green GameStop poster for the not-yet-released Xbox One, in an evacuated shopping mall in 2013, with the Gasman pursuing us from the food court like a masked terminator. I touched her cheekbone, and it must've tickled because she turned sharply, her breath curling in the air like smoke. Jesus, she was so real. She couldn't just be my imagination.

You can't let things go, Dan, and it's killing us—

"Addie," I said. "Do you think we would've made it?"

"What do you mean?"

"If you hadn't died on New Year's Eve. You think we would've lasted to the next one in 2016? And after?"

"Who's to say?"

"I'm asking what you *think*."

She shrugged, her voice wavering through chattering teeth. "Maybe . . . maybe it's best that you just remember me like this. And we never find out."

I kissed her again. It felt rebellious, dancing on our own fault lines. Somehow, a fatalistic corner of my mind had always assumed we'd prove that stupid clown right (*How cute — but you'll never make it*). We'd end up fighting for child custody, maybe, or held hostage by a loveless yuppie marriage. We may have been born of the same atoms, sure, but our pieces were mismatched. Somewhere behind us, I heard the Gasman's black boots squeaking on tile, the very embodiment of our dwindling time.

She rubbed her eye. "Let's just . . . try to enjoy these memories. Okay?"

"Okay."

"Being together. That's all life is."

"Okay."

"*Okay?*"

I stroked her hair. "Alright."

Snow fluttered around us. It was shocking; it literally came from nowhere. A frigid arctic winter imported direct from Siberia, forming now in Idaho's Timber Ridge Mall as a surreal indoor blizzard. It was as cold as the vacuum of space; a godless void that blackens your fingertips and ruptures the blood vessels in your eyes. But it was also bizarrely, achingly beautiful to see snow drizzling from the ductwork of the ceiling, collecting on the red blocks of the GameStop sign, cresting the fronds of potted ferns, and swirling across the floor on breezes that shouldn't exist.

Addie smiled, catching snowflakes in her palm. She was three months from twenty-six but I saw her as a little girl stepping outdoors for the first time, marveling at the things the world is capable of. "I'll admit," she said, crunching crystals between her fingers. "It's . . . kinda cool."

"Kinda."

"You're sure vampires can't cross water?"

"Positive," I said. "You're thinking of being invited in. They can't come into your house without you first inviting them in."

"Ah." She glanced back at the Gasman, following twenty yards down the shopping corridor, silhouetted behind a screen of impossible snow. "Bummer that isn't his weakness. That would've been handy."

But I had an even better idea now. It had slipped into my mind like a daydream; a way the Gasman's inability to cross water could potentially save us both. But I'd be counting on a few things. A few big things.

"Dan, it's *snowing inside the mall*," she gasped aloud as we cut through the men's section of Macy's, past rows of posed mannequins collecting white on their shoulders. She scooped up a handful of fresh snow from the khaki pants display. "How often can you say that?"

"Hopefully never again."

As we passed the last mannequin — a dude-bro in denim — Addie beaned it in the face with her snowball.

So, yes, I had an idea. But also a pool of dread in my stomach, growing as my dead fiancée and I raced through the freezing memories of our summer of 2013, and into whatever came before. Fluorescent lights sparked and fizzled as storefronts bulldozed themselves around us; plate glass disintegrated and the floor writhed in rolling waves of shattered tile. Through this storm of snow and plaster, we kept running, barreling deeper into the past with the Gasman at our heels. If this new plan of mine failed, I couldn't stand to lose Addie a second time. I'd already lost her once on New Year's Eve, and it broke me.

I couldn't lose her again.

NEW TEXT MESSAGE
SENDER: "Holden" (509) 555-8727
SENT: 11:41 a.m. Mar 20 2015

I drove by ur house WTF are you? Ur car is gone.

NEW TEXT MESSAGE
SENDER: "LJ" (509) 555-5622
SENT: 12:01 p.m. Mar 20 2015

Holden says you're MIA. Last chance for Old Briar. We're at the park-n-ride, leaving at 1300. Call by then or don't call at all. Running outta time . . .

59 Minutes

"The dock," I said, "where we first met back in 2011. That'll be our Alamo."

"Our *Alamo*?"

"You know. Our Alamo. Our last stand. The place we stop running. The Gasman won't be able to cross the water. We'll be safe there."

"So . . . the exact opposite of the real Alamo?"

"Hopefully, yes."

It all seemed convenient, but yes, in theory, we'd be safe back there on that FrightFest boardwalk over lapping tidewater. The place I'd first found her, stumbling out the broken door of the Total Darkness Maze on October 24, 2011. The place our lives had collided. For weeks after she'd died, I'd struggled vainly to relive that moment. How ironic, then, that it might just save us.

Let her go, Dyson whispered in the back of my mind.

But I squeezed her fingers and led her further back in time. Timber Ridge led to the Hostess factory investigation. Those catacombs of rusted-out ovens and peeling paint led to the candy-colored beanbag chairs in the Cubek lobby, where Addie interned for a summer.

Man-children, energy drinks, and keyboards speckled with crumbs. Every memory folds into another; daytime in one room, midnight the next. A floor leads to a wall. Gravity bends ninety degrees in a nauseous twist.

And still I worried as we fled the gas-masked creature through time. Like Dyson had told us, the Head-Scratching Rifle was digging through my mind and memories, learning my secrets. Adapting to my mental architecture. What if it was only feigning an aversion to water? To trick us into going where it wanted us?

Let go of your imaginary Adelaide, or the Gasman will use her against you—

Abruptly she halted, a whiplash of blonde hair, yanking my wrist backward.

"Wait, wait, wait," she said. "Do you smell that?"

"Smell what?"

But I did, too. An ammonia odor, acrid and thick. Dyson's clue.

Cat litter.

* * *

"Where are we?"

My first thought was *landfill*, but I knew better. We were in the foyer of an early-century rancher, absolutely crammed with hoarded junk, reeking of stale cat urine. Tons of heaped debris packed into every square inch. The floor was crunchy with yellowed newspaper, soda bottles, and grocery bags. Sunbeams caught updrafts of frizzy cat hair. Boxes stacked to the ceiling, leaning precariously on mildewing cardboard.

"This is . . . Montana. Out by Butte," I told Addie. "I drove out here one weekend to help Holden clean out his grandmother's house after she croaked—"

I realized Holden was in the room.

"—Uh, died."

He clapped his hands together. "Thank you — both of you — for making the drive. I really appreciate it, more than you know—"

I elbowed past Holden mid-sentence, venturing deeper into the stagnant house, and Addie followed. Cats skittered underfoot, feral tabbies and torbies with matted fur.

"What are we looking for?"

"The litterbox," I guessed.

It wasn't hard to find. It was a giant bin, scooted to the center of the living room by a perimeter of looming trash. It was every bit as horrifying as I remembered; a damp mountain range of sand under a fuzzy carpet of black mold. The box looked like it hadn't been scooped since the Bush administration.

Addie gagged through a sleeve. "I hate cats."

Covering my nose, I looked around at the room of towering clutter — Aquafina bottles, paperbacks with bent spines, German porcelain figurines. 'Needle in a haystack' doesn't do it justice, because at least in that situation you know you're looking for a damn needle. What was the objective here? I tried to recall what Dyson told us atop that lighthouse: *I left you a clue. So you'll know your chance when it arises, and seize it.*

Before the Gasman realizes.

Realizes what?

And . . . what chance?

Addie sighed. "He couldn't have been more specific than a cat turd?"

"It had to be a clue."

"Well, he must suck at charades." She stared into the litterbox. "Think he . . . uh, buried a weapon for us in there?"

"God, I hope not."

She grabbed something white off a nearby trash pile, hit her knees, and started digging into the disgusting box. Chipping like an icepick.

"Wait—" Holden snatched the token away. I didn't see what it was.

I joined Addie on the floor; she'd rolled up the black sleeves of her *Haunted* hoodie and now dug with her bare hands, lifting and breaking bricks of cement-like sludge. No time to be repulsed. The Gasman was coming.

It's got all the time in the world. You don't, Dan.

"Could Dyson have left us a message?"

"Why?"

She pointed at a black turd. "That one is shaped like a P."

"Dump it out. Maybe they spell something."

They didn't. We tried. I'd started to suspect it was futile about halfway through, but once you start arranging cat shit on the floor, you kind of have to see it through. We found a P, six C's, two L's, and an S. Everything else was an I. For a long, bleak moment we scrutinized a floor full of Kitty Rocas, trying to decode an intelligent design where none existed. Like finding EVPs in audio slush, or incongruous shadows in photos. Stare hard enough into the random, and you might eventually find something, but is it worth it?

Holden watched us, mortified. "What the *hell*—"

"I can explain," Addie said, wiping her hands.

I didn't bother. This version of Holden was just a memory — like the extras populating the Timber Ridge Mall, or the partygoers at LJ's lake house — but still, I couldn't help but notice how *young* my best friend looked. This was 2012. Three full years in the past. You don't really notice aging in yourself or your family until you stumble across an old photo, and this Holden was a living, breathing photograph. His hair was thicker. His bald spot smaller. His face was rounder, newer. He was also sixty pounds heavier; he hadn't yet been exposed to the anonymous venom of *Haunted*'s viewer comment board.

And I realized, with an icy jolt — what if he's dead, too?

Like me?

For all I knew, the Head-Scratching Rifle could've already gotten him. This evil *thing*, whatever it is, spreads indiscriminately, quietly reaching in all directions, like exploratory fungus stalks. It grows on anything within touching distance. Whether you're a forklift driver or a transient — if you're breathing, you're potential food. I should have known this from the start, but I'd been convinced I could contain it; limit the risk to myself. I'd thought I could trick it with something so remedial as a bullet with too much gunpowder — hell, W. Louis's book even warned me that the Head-Scratching Rifle diligently remembers to perform a safety check before firing.

"Holden," I said. "I'm sorry."

He looked at me.

"I . . . I was selfish, Holden. I was incredibly selfish, and did something stupid. And I allowed you to drag yourself along with me, because I was lonely. And now you're in danger, too. You might already be dead. It . . . whatever *it* is, it doesn't seem to experience time the way we do."

My best friend stared, eyes wide.

God, I must've sounded like Dyson already. A ghost lost in time, speaking in grim riddles. And really, what did it matter anyway?

"I know . . . I know you're not real." I let out a breath, my shoulders sagging. "I know I'm just imagining you. You're not the real Holden — the real Holden is somewhere else — so it doesn't matter what I say."

Behind him I saw Addie looking at me, her eyes crystalline, pierced with heartbreak. She sensed that I was really speaking to her. And truthfully? I guess I kind of was. Like Laika, I was trapped in this tiny world, bottled up inside an echo chamber with my imaginary friends. It's a lonely feeling.

After a long silence, Holden asked, "Dan, are you . . . having a *stroke?*"

Under his voice, I heard something.

A . . . faint, dry scratching. A whisper of friction, of gently grinding wood. Something was in the room with us, and it wasn't a cat.

We all turned.

At first I only saw the white token — the thing Addie had used to dig cat litter before Holden snatched it from her. It was moving, by itself, as if tugged by invisible strings, atop a shelf of piled detritus.

"Oh my God—"

Then I recognized what it was — the pale plastic, the arrowhead shape, the dirty glass lens — because I'd seen it before. It was a Ouija planchette. On Holden's grandmother's Icelandic mirror board. Scraping over the aged wood before our eyes like a movie special effect, a slow, deliberate zigzag across the alphabet. Letter to letter.

Spelling a message.

* * *

IDENTIFYYOURSELF.

Addie read aloud. "Uh . . . identify ourselves?"

"That's wrong," Holden said.

"You *think*?"

"No, not just that." He stumbled closer to his grandmother's vintage board, tipping a heap of books. "See, on this kind of mirror board, 'identify yourself' is what we — the human operators — are supposed to ask the spirit. Not the other way around."

The planchette slid to the TURN tile and stopped.

We all stared at it again in another slow drip of bewilderment. I tried to remember what Holden had told me, in another time and place, about the significance of that special TURN spot on his grandmother's ancient board. *Like when you're on a walkie-talkie and you say 'over.' So you don't talk over each other, because this mirror board exists in two dimensions at once. It's both the input and the output.*

It was waiting for us to answer.

Addie huffed. "I wish we'd seen this *before* digging into the litterbox."

I grabbed the planchette — surprisingly light, like it was made of bird bones — and traced from letter to letter on the sticky surface, answering the spirit's question with another question. The ultimate question: WHATDAYISIT?

I pushed the token back to TURN and waited.

"Dan." Holden came up behind me. "This is dangerous."

"I know."

"You could be talking to a demon—"

"Believe me, buddy, *I know*."

The planchette darted, startling us both: MAR202015.

March 20, 2015. The day after I bought the Head-Scratching Rifle from Joe's Guns. Okay. I reached again for the token, but Holden grabbed my wrist with a big hand, his fingernails digging into my skin. "Stop, Dan. Stop—"

"Let go of me—"

"You don't know what evil you could be screwing with—"

"Actually, at this point, I could draw you a detailed picture."

"Holden," Addie said, "For what it's worth, I'm sorry I used your grandmother's magic Ouija board to dig up cat shit."

But somehow I suspected that was what set things in motion. She'd triggered the Ouija board, *awakened* it in some way, when she grabbed the planchette and plunged it into the litterbox. Had that been Dyson's plan all along?

Now she craned her neck and looked out the half-blocked window, over a heap of bubble-wrapped porcelain. "Uh . . . Dan?"

The planchette scraped: WHEREISDAN?

"*Dan*." Addie's voice pitched. "The Gasman is outside. He brought friends."

Holden turned. "Who's the Gasman?"

I ignored them both, answering: THISISDAN. Then I asked: WHOAMITALKINGTO?

"Dan!" Addie screamed from the window. "Come here now—"

But I couldn't. I stared at that antique mirror board, waiting for an answer. I needed to know who or what was on the other end of the supernatural channel, and why it wanted to speak to me. This was Ben Dyson's plan. This was my one fleeting chance to save the Head-Scratching Rifle's next victim, whoever it was.

Then I realized what Addie had said. "Wait . . . he brought *friends*?"

"Yeah," she said, her voice low with terror. "Come see."

I stumbled to the window.

I saw trash bins, spindly trees, and a yellow lawn scaled with snow. And of course, the Gasman, standing by my black Celica. His left eyehole was still shattered from Adelaide's bullet back at Timber Ridge. A thin stream of fluid — something pale and milky yellow — leaked from the broken aperture. It wasn't blood; I knew we hadn't really hurt it. It was just a utility fluid the creature stored inside itself, not unlike oil in a car.

And like Addie had said, our pursuer was now flanked by frozen corpses. Toothpick skeletons in baggy flaps of Red Army clothing. Like freeze-dried stick figures. I saw sunken cheeks, calcified teeth, eyeless faces with skin pulled taut and browned like dead climbers in old photos from Mount Everest, express-delivered from somewhere hopeless and frigid. Jesus, I saw dozens now, creeping in from the corners of the suburban Butte neighborhood like termites wriggling out of wood. Every face was a gory portrait of 7.62x54R destruction. Each was unique, in the way that every car accident is. They congregated around him; the Gasman's morbid, icy flock.

I sighed. "Well, this sucks."

"Look at that one." Addie pointed. "His head looks like a banana peel."

"Gross."

But I recognized the one by the mailbox, his skull an empty, exploded grape skin. He must've been Nikolai What's-His-Name, the Kalash worker who'd tried to destroy the Head-Scratching Rifle back in the nineties, but biffed the serial number, melted down the wrong rifle, and taken a vodka-soaked nap with his ear on a railroad rail. He'd been so close, I realized bitterly. Just one digit off. Just a letter.

"He's the closest anyone's ever gotten," I said. "To stopping it."

Addie squeezed my hand. "Until now. Until us."

"We'll see."

The Ouija board scraped again behind us — finally, a reply. An answer for my question of whom (or what) we were speaking to. I whirled away from the window, just in time to see the pale planchette trace:

THISISHOLDEN.

* * *

Holden saw it, too, and looked at me. "What did you ask it?"

"I asked it who I'm talking to."

"But it gave *my name*."

Yes, and the puzzle pieces were already snapping together. The mirror board was a two-way conduit, simultaneously the input and output, existing in two realities at once. "Because I'm talking to you, Holden," I told him. "You, in 2015."

His eyes widened. It would take hours to explain.

"Hurry up!" Addie shouted from the window. "The Gasman is coming up to the front door—"

"Wait." I grabbed the planchette again and traced:
TELLMEEVERYTHING.

This was too important. Never mind the icy phantoms surrounding us in Butte, Montana in 2012; I needed to know what was happening in Farwell, Idaho in 2015. In my world, in the real one, where Addie was dead, where I'd purchased the Head-Scratching Rifle from Joe's Guns, taken it home, and performed a fruitless paranormal investigation on it shortly before . . . before it possessed me, I guess? Was I possessed?

Somewhere, 2015 was happening without my consciousness. If my red-tipped bullet had really been a dud, then I guess I was still alive. Still somewhere with the cursed Mosin Nagant. Where? And doing what?

The front door squealed open.

We all turned.

The Gasman stood in the thin doorway, one gloved hand outstretched, head cocked in bewilderment, as if he hadn't expected it to work on his first try, either. The doorknob banged on the wall. The insectoid face swiveled to us.

"Okay, mental note," Addie whispered. "He's gotten better at doors."

"And . . . that's our cue to leave." I grabbed the Ouija board off the shelved debris — the conversation would have to wait.

I raced to the back exit and twisted the knob, but the door thudded against something outside. A green yard rake, wedged tightly between the outer doorknob and the siding. A 2.0-version of the recycling bin trick from New Year's Eve.

"Shit."

"He's learning," Addie said.

I grabbed her hand and tugged her to the stairs leading to the underground garage — the only exit we had left. The Gasman came trudging in through the front doorway, lifting his icy boots over a shallow sea of hoarded crap. I heard a crackle of claws in carpet, caught blurs of racing motion underfoot, and realized the old lady's half-dozen cats were running at the creature. They tripped over each other to clamor at his boots like feline groupies, pawing at the flaps of his greatcoat, rubbing and purring.

I opened the staircase door. "Of course . . . *of course* cats love him."

"See? Cats are evil."

"You called it."

The Gasman crashed through the small house after us, knocking over glassware and trash, all elbows and knees. The kitchen lights died behind us as we raced down the dark stairs. Like entering a coalmine; a tight funnel of creaking steps. I took two at a time, carrying the Ouija board, with Addie stomping behind me. Through claustrophobic breaths she asked: "What's happening in 2015?"

"I don't know. Holden hasn't answered."

"Are you still alive?"

That was a damn good question and I didn't know. All that mattered right now was the Ouija board. Ben Dyson's desperate gift, and our one chance to do . . . something. To save the rifle's next victim, hopefully. I didn't have a plan yet. Upstairs, a piercing scream rang through the cramped house as another version of Holden was murdered by the Gasman. At the moment I felt nothing, because I knew that past-copy of my best friend wasn't real. Right?

. . . Right?

We stumbled into the windowless basement garage. Our shoes squealed on smooth cement foundation. The sour odor of mold and mothballs, which was at least better than the upstairs odor of cat litter. It was too dark; I couldn't even see the mountains of half-excavated crap Holden's grandmother stored down here like a pharaoh's tomb. The only light was behind us; a wan glow from the top of the staircase.

I gripped the board. "Not good."

"Are we trapped?"

The glow behind us dimmed. It was blocked by the broad shoulders of the Gasman, his gloves slick with blood. An orange cat rubbed its chin against his ankle but he ignored it. He started to descend the narrow stairway to us, hunching his shoulders to barely fit like a circle peg down a square hole. A clumsy, scraping shuffle. The last light bulb popped behind him, a firework splash of sizzling sparks. The garage was suddenly in perfect darkness.

I heard urgent clicking beside me. "Addie?"

"My flashlight's out."

Heat, electricity, light — all energies absorbed by the Gasman. But I knew from my two-day project of cleaning out Holden's grandmother's house in 2012 — this garage had one exit, and it wasn't the garage doors (those were blocked with thousand-pound pallets of junk). I'd need light to find it — and I recalled a light bulb near the stairs with a scratchy pull string. Tucking the all-important Ouija board under one arm, I groped with the other, sweeping my palm through the cold blackness . . .

"Dan—"

"I'm trying the lights—"

"*Dan.*" Her voice heaved with panic. "Something just touched my arm."

It couldn't have been the Gasman; he was still behind us, squeezing his refrigerator-sized ass down the narrow 1920s stairs. But I heard something else in the garage, something down here with us already.

Something moving.

To my left, a whisper of motion. A breath of displaced air on my cheek. And a . . . crackling, crunching sound, like an ice tray being slowly twisted. The source of this brittle sound seemed to hover mid-air. I couldn't tell where it was coming from, but it was nearby. Too close.

My outstretched fingers found the light bulb string — a wisp in the darkness, like a strand of spider silk — and gave it a hard tug.

The string snapped.

"Oh, *come on.*"

"What? What happened?"

That clicking sound again. Closer. It was moving.

"Dan. Do you hear that?"

I fumbled for my own Maglite and clicked the spongy button. I hadn't expected it to turn on, since Adelaide's hadn't, but it did — barely — and burnt a dim yellow circle on the bare foundation at our feet. At that same moment, something cold stroked the back of my neck.

I dropped the flashlight.

"*Dan!*"

The Maglite banged off cement. I hit my knees, following the twirling beam, but something else swooped in from above me. Something big, reaching. It wasn't spectral or ghostlike; this was a physical *thing* with solid mass that pushed cold air as it moved, still crackle-crunching. I imagined beetle mandibles, hairy and chittering.

With unfurling arms, it grabbed the Ouija board. Ripping it up and away.

I reached, but it lifted further. "Oh, shit—"

"What?"

"*Shit.* I lost the board—"

I scooped up the dying Maglite and aimed the flickering yellow beam up into the darkness. At the floating, rising *thing* that had stolen the board.

Addie gasped.

It was a hanging body. Dangling bat-like, upside-down from the ceiling by a knot of barbed wire tangled cruelly around one ankle. At first I thought its upper body bristled with twenty-inch porcupine quills, but they were spiny dripstones of frozen blood, the dead color of rust, growing off his shoulders and face like inverted toadstools. The corpse clutched Holden's Ouija board with a tightening arm, bladed with bloodsicles. I couldn't see its face, and didn't want to. I hoped I'd live long enough to be traumatized by it.

Well, the Gasman has summoned me.

Addie screamed. "What *is* that?"

"The board!" My voice came in panicked tugs. "It stole the board. We need it—"

"The Gasman's coming—"

"We need the board, Addie. It's our only chance."

I jumped for the hanging creature, but it was too high. My fingertips swished empty air. Suddenly the basement ceiling had morphed thirty feet higher; a crisscross of beams I recognized from murky photos of the Kalash armory. The body contracted defensively, cocoon-like, and pulled higher and higher, squeezing its chest up to its knees with a crackle-pop of frozen vertebrae. Too high to reach, an inhuman shape curling away to vanish into the 1970s-Kalash ceiling with Holden's board, going, going—

CRACK. CRACK.

Two orange flashes, and the corpse's wrist exploded into crystals of icy red meat. A sprinkle of bloody chunks. The Ouija board dropped.

I caught it.

Addie stuffed her smoking Beretta back into her purse just as our second Maglite flickered and died. I left it clattering on the floor.

"Nice shot. Again."

"You're welcome," she said. "But we're still trapped."

On cue, the Gasman's footsteps hollowed on cement foundation. He'd squeezed down the stairs. I heard the swish of his wool greatcoat, the biomechanical creak of flexing leather, plastic, and rubber.

"He's down here with us." Her voice rattled. "And we're trapped—"

"No, we're not." I clasped the Ouija board to my chest, feeling a surge of shivery adrenaline. Reckless glee. We'd mightily pissed the entity off. The Head-Scratching Rifle and its vast backlog of murdered victims — all were after us now, zeroing in on Adelaide and I like antibodies. Hell, the barbed-wire hobo hanging from the ceiling like an inverted Venus flytrap had been *seventy years* in the making. And it failed. The Head-Scratching Rifle needed to stop us. It needed that Ouija board.

The fight might have been suicidal, the odds impossible, the battleground morphing beneath our feet, but at least it wanted to catch us and hadn't yet. I'm told I have a talent for disappointing people.

And I still had Addie.

Flicking her Pac Man lighter for illumination (appropriate, since we, too, were fleeing ghosts), I found drywall in the glow of orange light, and groped behind boxed clothing and hanging gowns to find a brass doorknob. The brass doorknob I only barely, *barely* remembered from the long weekend of unpacking this foul house with Holden, because I'd only seen it. And never actually touched it.

"Thank God for closets I never opened."

"Evil is unimaginative," Addie echoed.

"Damn straight."

The Gasman was just a step behind us, so I swung the door open and pushed Addie through first. As I followed, a gloved hand pawed at my back, dumb cigar fingers tightening, almost gripping a fistful of my sweatshirt. Almost.

"Too slow."

I have no idea what Holden's grandmother kept in her garage closet in real life, but it sure as hell wasn't the 2012 Basin State Fair.

NEW TEXT MESSAGE
SENDER: "Holden" (509) 555-8727
SENT: 12:21 p.m. Mar 20 2015

Dan my Ouija board was moving by itself in the box. Answered it, says its U?!

36 Minutes

"Yes!" Adelaide fist-pumped. "I *love* the Basin State Fair."

"Close call," I gasped.

We'd entered a world of halogen lights, carnival games, and drunk teenagers. Livestock barns to the north, creaky rides to the south, and food trailers up the middle. Straw, axle grease, and kettle corn. Hand-painted signs advertised scones, German dogs, and deep fried butter. Against a dusk sky pinpricked with stars stood the oily black trestlework of the "Widowmaker" roller coaster; a rattling behemoth built in 1932. It was perhaps one medium-sized gust of wind from fulfilling its name.

I still had the Ouija board and planchette. I elbowed past a throng of kids and slammed the thing onto a picnic table. It had a splintered chip on the edge where one of Addie's bullets had grazed it.

"Come on, Holden." I dropped the token on the board and repeated my question with quaking fingertips: WHEREISDAN?

"What if it's not Holden?" Addie asked again.

"Least of our worries."

A falling chorus of faraway screams — I flinched — but it was just the Panic Plunge dropping a cartload of riders.

"I'm just saying." She grabbed an unattended beer and took a swig. "The rifle — the Gasman, the demon, whatever — it's getting smarter. How can you be so certain that this isn't a trick?"

The planchette scraped:

YOURNOTHOMECARGONE.

"My car's gone," I said.

A pause.

Then, urgently: KALESAWYOUONMAIN—

"Too fast." Addie circled the table. "I can't—"

"Kale saw me downtown . . ."

The planchette darted again: SAIDYOUBOT—

"Said I bought . . ."

The token stopped. Circled once, then: BOUHGT.

"Bought. I get it."

BOUTGH.

"Jesus Christ, Holden."

BOUHGT.

Addie groaned. "He already tried that one."

BOUGHT.

"Yes!" I said. "Good job. What did I buy?"

But Addie glanced up sharply, whipping her hair in my face, looking toward the deep-fried butter trailer and gasping: "Oh, crap."

SAIDYOUBOUGHT—

I dug my fingernails into the dusty wood. "Hurry up, Holden—"

"Oh, crap," she hissed in my ear, rising panic: "Dan."

BOUGHTBOXESOFBULLETS—

"*Dan!*"

"Wait." I watched the planchette. "Just wait—"

DRIVING—

"Driving to—"

She grabbed my shoulder and wrenched me backwards, off the picnic bench. I saw a whirl of carnival lights, stars in a rotten purple sky, and then we both slammed into the grass. Like being tackled. Dirt clods in my teeth, the taste of yellow grass. Something metallic and heavy crashed down on the table behind us. A warbling BANG, like a deafening, five-foot gong.

My mind raced in the chaos: *I bought bullets, and I'm driving to—*

I tried to stand but Addie tugged me again, into a bruising sidewinder roll . . .

The thunderous splash came next; gallons and gallons of liquid. I heard sludgy raindrops plopping to the grass around us, sizzling and hissing, drawing curls of steam. Scorching hot droplets, peppering the air like shrapnel from a nail bomb. The unmistakable odor of tater tots, elephant ears, and fryer grease.

Fryer grease?

The aluminum deep-fryer tank tumbled past us, spraying more scalding droplets, and bounced off another picnic table. The first screams came, a crescendo of horror, as fairgoers scattered under a mist of acid rain. Most in terror, some in blistering pain.

Someone threw a *deep fryer* at us.

I blinked, my eyes watering in the hot air. The picnic table we'd occupied — and Holden's Ouija board — was now dripping sizzling brown oil. Four hundred degrees of artery-clogging deliciousness. Like it had been dipped in magma.

Addie blew hair from her face. "You're welcome. Again."

Stupidly, I dug my fingers into the patchy grass and scrambled back toward our table. Even drenched in smoking oil, the Ouija planchette was moving — Holden was transmitting critical details from the world of 2015 — but Addie grabbed my wrist and stopped me, her breath in my ear. "No—"

"I have to know—"

"Dan, stop."

At the funnel cake stand, the Gasman was stooping to pick up another deep-fryer vat, wrapping his arms around the ten-gallon tub in a bear hug. Frothy grease splashed on the counter and poured copper waterfalls over the DEEP FRIED TWINKIES sign.

And that scorched Ouija planchette kept moving, kept racing urgently from letter to letter, too far away to see—

"I have to know," I gasped.

"Too late," Addie screamed, digging her heels into the grass.

I tugged but she was right. Nothing to do.

The Gasman hefted the second vat to his chest and the cooking basket fell out, clattering to the ground like a birdcage full of limp French fries. His gloves and greatcoat smoked with spilled oil. He lowered his masked head, firmed up his stance, and whirled like an Olympic log thrower, hurling a lethal payload our way—

She gasped. "Go. Go. Go—"

We vaulted another picnic table and raced past the Mystizmo fortune-teller booth with the second fryer tank incoming. It crashed down somewhere close and we outran a shower of sizzling oil, droplets splashing down just moments behind us. All I could think about was that all-important Ouija board behind us, drenched in scalding grease. Our weapon. Our only chance, lost.

Everything. Lost.

By the scone trailer I halted and chanced a look over my shoulder — "Dan, don't stop!" — and for just a frozen half-second, I saw one of the Head-Scratching Rifle's mummified Red Army ghosts standing over Holden's four hundred degree Ouija board, lifting it from the table with nerveless brown hands. Raising it over a knee.

As we raced through the emptying Basin State Fair, I heard a single CRACK echo behind us. Like a wooden gunshot. So much for that.

And as for the real world?
My exploding bullet misfired.
So I drove into town.
I bought more bullets. And I'm driving to—
Where was I driving? And how close was I to getting there? The stakes had changed. It wasn't just a suicide anymore. Why hadn't I suspected it from the start? The Head-Scratching Rifle likes to kill. It's a dumb hunger, a spiritual disease. Why would it settle for just one meager suicide in my sad little house in rural Farwell, Idaho, when it could use my body like a vehicle and go on an indulgent murder spree? A house-to-house slaughter? How many people would die now, because of my recklessness?

And worst of all, Holden's Ouija board, our single tether to the real world of 2015, was out of action. Our lightning was out of the bottle. My spine chilled and I tasted stomach acid, climbing my throat like salty tidewater.

This was bad.

"You were almost a six-foot chicken nugget," Addie said.

"Thank you," I said weakly.

"Next time, can you save *me* for a change?"

I was barely listening. My stomach coiled, snakelike. This was so bad . . .

As we raced down the carnival game alley, holding hands under a blur of hot lights and colored tarp, I recognized that asshole clown stepping in from the right to cut us off. Red nose, green ponytail, yellow firefighter jacket with saucer buttons. An artificial smile slathered on with white greasepaint, and under it, a real one, gawking with adolescent scorn at our clasped hands.

"Oh, how cute," he said as we passed. "But you'll never—"

I punched him in the face.

Sent: 3/20 12:30PM
Sender: cservice@outdoorwarehouse.com
Subject: Thank You!

Dear DANIEL J. RUPLEY,

Thank you for shopping at Outdoor Warehouse today! For your records we've attached a copy of your receipt:

20PK 7.62x54R NC00292
$26.99
20PK 7.62x54R NC00292
$26.99
20PK 7.62x54R NC00292
$26.99
20PK 7.62x54R NC00292
$26.99
20PK 7.62x54R NC00292
$26.99
20PK 7.62x54R NC00292
$26.99
SUB $161.94
TAX 6.00% $9.72

Total: $171.66/DEBIT****

27 Minutes

Lurching from the Basin State fairgrounds to the sludgy soil of the Mount St. Helens blast zone was a shock, like a fifty-yard dash straight into quicksand. Addie hit her knees behind me and I pulled her upright. Even on the Spirit Lake hiking loop, the sloped ground was an ankle-breaking trellis of bleached logs, half-buried in volcanic soil turned gray and sludgy by recent rain showers. Recent, as of 2012.

"Oh, *no*. He's right behind us," she gasped, her shoes slurping in gritty mud. "He's still coming."

Fifty feet back, the Gasman scaled the crest of Johnston Ridge, silhouetted against a pewter sky. He missed a step, dumping a small landslide of rocks. Something about his stumbling pose, his gas mask, the scarred land around him — he looked like an astronaut on some barren planet. A space-suited, five-dimensional creature navigating the uncharted terrain of my mind. This came like an odd epiphany. Perhaps this was why he had so much difficulty opening doors — he'd come from some indescribable plane of existence where doors didn't exist.

More figures rose into view behind him. His icy flock. His unhallowed crowd of burlap flesh, shattered skulls, and empty eye sockets. Trench coats in gray, brown, and black. Fox fur hats and Waffen-SS helmets. I saw bright red, the wet glisten of freshly opened meat, and recognized the destroyed cavity of Ben Dyson's face, the gunsmith falling obediently into line with the older corpses. You can resist all you want, but sooner or later everyone joins the Gasman's frozen parade.

Including . . . that one orange tabby cat from Holden's grandmother's house, still affectionately mewing and pawing at the Gasman's boots. I don't think the cat was actually dead like the others; I think he was just a big fan.

I tugged Addie's hand as she sighed: "Man, *fuck* cats."

"Come on."

"I told you they're evil."

We kept running along the slanted trail, up and over rising waves of cracked trees, their bark scorched away decades ago by pyroclastic fire. Like running over a river of rolling logs. It was dreamlike in a futile way, a desperate pursuit over churning earth. A chunk of driftwood tumbled downhill and splashed into the gray stillness of pond water, thirty feet below.

"He's trying now," Addie panted. "He's really *trying* to catch us—"

"Good. It means we still have a chance to stop it."

"Stop what?"

I grabbed her wrist and helped her up a massive log, chapped and bone-white, like a dinosaur femur. "A mass shooting," I said. "That's what the Head-Scratching Rifle is going to use me for. Not a suicide — not yet, at least. First, a mass shooting. A horrific, nightmarish killing spree with that Mosin Nagant—"

Her jaw hung open.

"Yeah."

She nodded. "This . . . explains everything."

"How?"

Muddy ash shifted under my feet, like stepping on water. I crashed down hard on one kneecap but recovered and kept running. Over a shoulder, I glimpsed the Gasman and his friends trudging through the ash and crunchy underbrush. A grim march. Soldiers on the move. Thunder rolled behind them, a hollow rumble.

She grabbed my arm. "That explains why we're here, Dan. That's why we're traveling back in time. The rifle — the Gasman, whatever — it was going through your memories, flipping pages through your brain. Searching your mind for a location it likes. A place to stage its massacre in the real world. In March of 2015."

"So," I said, "what did it find?"

She looked at me, something on the edge of her tongue.

I had it, too.

The Gasman sure loved that third-floor balcony at Timber Ridge, hadn't he? Sweeping the Mosin Nagant up and over the crowd at the food court in a weird moment of childish play. Now we knew it wasn't play. It was a cold, witless mind assessing a target-rich environment. We'd witnessed a dry run. A rehearsal.

Oh, God.

"Timber Ridge," I said. "That's where I'm driving. Right now."

On Saturday, March 20, 2015. With the Head-Scratching Rifle in my trunk and a half-dozen boxes of 7.62x54R ammunition grocery-bagged in the back seat.

Another crash of thunder. She didn't flinch. "How do we stop it?"

"If we still had that Ouija board, I'd just tell Holden to call the police and tell them to come to Timber Ridge." I hesitated and let the next uncomfortable thought go unsaid — *so they can see me strolling in from the parking lot with a bolt-action Soviet rifle and shoot me on sight.* "But we . . . we lost it."

"So we'll find another one—"

"There aren't any Ouija boards left in my brain," I said. "That was the first one I'd ever seen in person, in

Holden's grandmother's house in Butte, spring of 2012, and it's gone now. That was our link to 2015. Our only link."

"We'll stop it."

"How?"

"I don't know."

"*How*, Addie?" I snapped, my voice a hoarse rattle.

A fork of purple lightning slithered across the sky, striking somewhere behind Mount St. Helens' destroyed caldera.

"Oh my God." She looked back at the pursuing Gasman and it seemed to fully hit her, her lip quivering in realized horror. "Oh my God. Oh my God . . ."

I imagined myself, thoughtless and glass-eyed, shouldering that slimy old Mosin Nagant on the third-floor balcony in front of JCPenney. Aligning the notched Russian sights, click-clacking the heavy bolt, and opening fire on a food court full of teenagers, baristas, book club members, young couples with babies in strollers. You always watch news coverage of the latest tragedy and wonder what goes through the insect-brain of a mass shooter; what disgusting force could pervert a human mind into willfully and carefully murdering strangers. It truly horrified me that maybe I'd find out.

I'd find out *very* soon.

"No. We'll stop it." She wiped a splatter of ash from her cheek under another double-flash of lightning. "How much time is left?"

19 Minutes

Behold: the ugliest Christmas tree in recorded history.

In December of 2011, Adelaide's parents cut down a juvenile Douglas fir by their front porch, and to be practical, elected to lop off the upper seven feet and drag it into their living room. Good idea, awful result. This was an emaciated mockery of a Christmas tree, its gangly branches sagging under only a few ornaments. The golden top star drooped against the wall, like a broken neck. My first mistake, on my very first holiday with Adelaide's family in Birmingham, had been commenting on it: *Your Christmas tree looks like a spider monkey.*

"Yes!" Addie raced past me. "This is perfect."

"What?"

"This is perfect, Dan." Her eyes gleamed. "My uncle Shaun gave my aunt a Ouija board for Christmas. You know, as a gag gift. What are the *odds*?"

"I don't remember it."

"You weren't here for the unwrapping."

There was a twinge of pain in her voice. Because here, on this Christmas Eve of 2011, I'd lost my temper and uttered a certain three-word sentence that she (and her

213

father) still haven't forgiven me for. Opinions vary on how justified I was, but everyone can agree — with three words, I basically ruined the Radnor family Christmas. Hell, it had taken the Grinch all night.

I still feel awful about it. But Addie's father, an oh-so-brilliant Bill Murray-lookalike who'd made a fortune designing Boeing 747 rivets or something, was one of those people who can insult you with such incredible subtlety and sniper-like precision, only you detect the barb. To everyone else, his words sound like small talk or even praise. But he knows what he meant, and so do you, and you find yourself locked in a staring match across the dinner table: *So, Dan, I watched your ghost show on YouTube. Are you hoping to eventually air it on TV?*

In 2011 it had been just a spare-time webcast with a shoestring budget, fuzzy audio, and a fan base in the low hundreds.

And Dan, you work at . . . Quality Foods? Is that right?

Yes, I did.

Her parents were seated in the dining room now, framed by the regal arches of a home that would've gotten them beheaded in the French Revolution. Addie's perfect mother and perfect father, with a perfectly-bred Yorkie napping by the fireplace, silently devastated that their perfect STEM-educated daughter had brought me, the starving artist, into their ivory palace. Everything was just so—

"Perfect," Addie said, kneeling at the base of that withered tree and shoving aside wrapped gifts. "It's . . . Shaun's present, the Ouija board, was one of these rectangular ones—"

"It won't work."

"Shut up." She threw a box aside.

I grabbed her arm. "Addie. It won't work."

Dan, you've heard of the Scientific Method, right? True evidence of ghosts should be reproducible, but all of your investigations are at nighttime. I mean, why not search during daylight hours? Shouldn't these alleged supernatural phenomena behave the same, regardless of lighting?

"Yes!" Adelaide slammed an appropriately sized present to the white carpet and tore away the wrapping paper. "Here it is."

I'm . . . I'm sorry for being so judgmental, Dan. I don't mean to rain on your hobby. I'm more curious about Quality Foods. How's that going? Are you a manager?

She ripped off the last layer of artsy wrapping paper, revealing her uncle Shaun's gag gift underneath — a featureless, generic cardboard box. No markings. No mailing tape. No flaps to open, even. Just cardboard.

"Wait." She turned it over. "Wait . . . what?"

I mean . . . you have real goals, right, Dan?

Of course.

He'd stirred his green beans. *Any that you've achieved thus far?*

Fucking your daughter is only three words. They take one second to say. Two seconds of petrified silence to sink in. And that, folks, is how you ruin a Christmas.

"What?" Addie turned the impossible box over and over. "I don't understand—"

"It's not a Ouija board," I said, "because I never *saw* it."

"But I saw it."

"We're in my mind, my memories, Addie. Not yours. We can't be in your memories because you're *dead*."

She hurled the generic cardboard box to the floor. "Goddamnit—"

I was pissed off too, exhausted, my thoughts slippery and churning. Right now (four years from now), I was driving to the Timber Ridge Mall with a vintage military rifle and over a hundred cigar-sized bullets. And I was helpless to stop it, trapped here in my replaying memories. Locked inside my own head, plunging deeper every second. So I lashed out and said something else I shouldn't have.

215

"You're *not real*, Addie. You're in my head. You're just my . . . my recollection of Adelaide Radnor. You're what Dyson said you are. A goldfish in a bag. A displaced dream, an imaginary friend that I've dragged along with me, and I *so badly* wish you were real, but you're not."

"Fuck you, Dan. I'm real."

"I wish you were," I said. "So much."

Her eyes welled with tears.

"But the real Adelaide is gone. Dead and gone—"

"You will be, too." Now her voice darkened and trembled, a wounded, bare-knuckle viciousness: "In maybe ten minutes, Dan, give or take, you'll go up to that Timber Ridge balcony and mow down a bunch of shoppers with that evil thing, and then you can find out for yourself if God exists—"

From the dining room came a series of wet, splashing thuds.

We turned.

Her parents, facing us at the long table, had abruptly stopped chewing. Their mouths hung open, paralyzed. Faces blank, eyes glossy, muscles slack. A stringy clump of half-chewed pork slid from her mother's mouth and jangled her plate.

Then Addie's father spoke, a thick echo, multiple voices bubbling up from his windpipe. Like ten people, speaking together in a dank cave:

"There . . . is . . . no . . . God."

The Gasman stood behind him, his Soviet greatcoat slick with congealing fryer oil, resting one gloved hand on the man's shoulder. His entourage of corpses were suddenly seated at the long table, too, like a mawkish reference to Christ's Last Supper, mummified figures of leathery skin, dried-out eye sockets, piano-white teeth. The chandelier dimmed, coloring everything orange.

Her father's voice burbled and a half-chewed mouthful of green beans plopped into his lap. A soggy, rotten voice: "There is . . . only . . . my tasty treats."

"Oh, *shut up*," Addie snarled. "You're not my dad."

"Only . . . my . . . yummy treats." The old man made an exaggerated chewing motion, grinding his canines together like a rodent. His reading glasses slid off his nose. "Only my . . . yummy, tasty treats . . . yes, please . . . to eat and pull apart and eat—"

"Come on." I tugged her shoulder. "Let's get out of here."

She sniffed. "What's the point?"

"I don't know. But we have to go."

"What's the point, Dan? If you're a mass shooter and I'm just a piece of your imagination, what's the *fucking point* to even trying?"

I pulled her past that godawful Christmas tree, to the arched front double-door, and the Red Army ghosts stood up in eerie unison, rattling glassware on the table. The Gasman just watched us through the circular holes of his aardvark-like breathing mask as we left, and Addie's father made another tooth-shattering chomp, as loud as a snapping branch: "I eat and I eat and I eat—"

Addie struggled, her eyeliner running with tears. "I just want to be dead, Dan. Just . . . please, let me go. Let me be dead—"

I kicked open the front door. "Come on—"

"Leave me. Please."

But I dragged her anyway.

We broke out through the Radnor's re-landscaped front lawn, beyond wheelbarrows and dirt piles, and into the frigid blackness of a deserted Edgbaston peppered with snow. The words of the Head-Scratching Rifle echoed out after us, dozens of crowing voices of the dead ringing off burnt-out streetlights and chapped brick, celebrating the Timber Ridge massacre to come:

"—And I eat and I eat and I eat and I'll *eat them all, Dan*—"

NEW TEXT MESSAGE
SENDER: "Holden" (509) 555-8727
SENT: 12:35 p.m. Mar 20 2015

Do u have the gun? WHERE R U???

11 Minutes

The Total Darkness Maze.

Halloween FrightFest. October, 2011.

I first saw Adelaide Radnor on the edge of an Anacortes dock, gagging over a handrail into the Puget Sound. Far away from the costumed monsters and giggling teenage crowds. Silence here; just the lap of the water. She'd been a hunched silhouette against harbor lights and a night sky pierced with stars. Following her out of the maze, I'd watched her for a good ten seconds — just clearing her throat and spitting into the black water — before I spoke.

You okay?

She raised a hand. *I'm fine.*

You sure?

Yeah. I'm just having a panic attack.

"This is it," I said to her now. "Our Alamo."

She nodded grimly. "Our Alamo."

Not that it mattered. Even if the seawater underfoot magically protected us from the Gasman's oddly specific weakness, we were still trapped in a tiny corner of my mind. Cut off, stranded. Helpless to stop the coming slaughter.

A panic attack? I hadn't believed her. *You're barfing from a panic attack?*

I get these sometimes.

Barfing panic attacks?

Claustrophobia from the stupid maze. Dark, confined spaces make me really anxious and my stomach gets weird. Either way, I'm fine. Stop looking at me. She raised her hand again. *You can go now.*

Addie sighed. "I can't believe the first thing you ever saw me do was vomit an entire funnel cake off a dock."

I grinned. "I wish I could put that on a Hallmark card."

The doorframe (NOT AN EXIT DOOR) hung in bright yellow splinters where twenty-one-year-old Adelaide had shouldered right through it on her way out of the Total Darkness Maze. Just demolished it. She'd demonstrated better offense than the Dallas Cowboys that year. Hell, I still don't know how she'd done it.

The off-limits area I'd unwittingly followed this strange girl into seemed to be a staging area for FrightFest, packed with deflated ghoul costumes and rows of neatly stacked synthetic gore. Four gutted torsos, six severed legs, and a dozen bloodied hands. Cigarette butts on the dock where the werewolves and tree monsters had their smoke breaks. Addie lowered her head and spat again into the tidewater, clenching her hair back in a fist. Back then her hair had a crimson streak in it. Called a feather, I think.

When I still hadn't left, she waved again, harder, like she was swatting a gnat: *I said I'm fine. What are you staring at?*

I . . . I don't know. I remember smiling shyly by the broken door, cheap vodka still warm in my throat. *It's just weird hearing a posh British accent from a girl power-puking into the ocean.*

Oh, shut up.

We were just college kids. Our courtship dialogue hadn't been penned by Shakespeare. Here and now, Addie looked at me in a glow of remembered starlight. "It was . . . it was really decent of you, that you didn't leave."

"I was concerned."

"You didn't know me."

"I wanted to."

She smiled, in this time and then, a bashful grin.

This is so embarrassing, she'd said, gripping the thin handrail and wiping her mouth. *I don't even want to know what I look like right now—*

An angel.

Oh my God, shut up—

A vomiting angel.

That was the first time I'd ever heard her laugh, on that FrightFest dock in 2011. That sound was now gone from the real world, I realized. It existed only here, in my memory. Only in my thoughts, a deteriorating shadow of the real thing.

"We failed," she said flatly. "The Gasman, the Head-Scratching Rifle, whatever you want to call the thing. It's won already."

"I know."

"Jeez, Dan, I *really* wish you'd seen more Ouija boards."

"Yeah, me too." Funny how it comes down to the stupidest things. Icelandic mirror boards, doors that open inward, and cell phone chargers.

"I think I'm real," she said. "I know you think you're just imagining me, Dan, but for whatever it's worth . . . I'm certain I'm the real Adelaide."

I didn't believe her, but I shrugged. "I was . . . I was just trying to hurt you because I was angry. I'm sorry."

"Story of us."

I noticed the Gasman on the shoreline. Standing on another boardwalk, in the fogged glow of the street lamps between the saltwater taffy shop and the Louisiana Blood haunted house. Watching us from a hundred feet. As the current of pedestrians and costumed ghouls fanned around him, he almost looked like he belonged here. Like he was a particularly well-designed FrightFest monster, flecked in Siberian ice and glistening with slimy fryer grease from the Basin State Fair. His boots were muddied with Mount St. Helens ash. We'd led him on quite a chase through remembered times and places. But it was over now.

As I'd anticipated, he couldn't come any closer, because the Puget Sound water lapped at the dirty sandbanks between us. Waves pushed big knots of kelp in and out, like floating bodies. True enough, this off-limits dock behind the Total Darkness Maze was our Alamo. We were finally safe. I imagined the rest of my mind withering away under the Gasman's influence, while we'd remain here in this tiny, intact pocket of memory, shivering together in Anacortes circa 2011, wondering how many innocent shoppers died at Timber Ridge by my own possessed hands.

"He can't get us here," Addie said. "But he doesn't need to."

I hated the Gasman — of course — but really I hated myself. It was my stupidity, my recklessness and arrogance, that had brought the Head-Scratching Rifle into Idaho. I could've taken Holden's advice and moved on after Addie's death. I could've sucked it up, packed her things, and enlisted for the Briar Mine investigation out in Bozeman, chasing shadows and anecdotes with a directional thermometer. Chasing fake spirits, instead of being chased by this very real one. I'd chosen to live in the past, and this was my sentence. I'd be stranded here in this pickled memory, with the too-good-to-be-true shade of my lost fiancée, while unspeakable tragedy unfolded in the Timber Ridge food court. Because of me, people would die. *Lots* of people.

"Goddamnit."

I kicked a row of FrightFest's severed leg props. One flopped under the railing and splashed into the water.

"God-fucking-damnit—"

I took a running start and punted one of the eviscerated torsos. It thudded against the wall of the Total Darkness Maze, coiled intestines slapping.

Addie watched grimly.

It's hard to throw a tantrum when all you have available to break is rubbery B-movie gore. I hurled a dismembered hand into the ocean, and then another, and then I sat down across from her, catching my breath through my teeth.

"There are more body parts to kick around." She pointed. "Over there."

"All those people."

She winced. "I know."

"It's my fault, Addie."

"I know."

A furry shadow darted between us on pattering feet. I recognized one of Holden's grandmother's cats. The orange one. The Gasman's number one fan. At first I didn't think much of it — just an itinerant memory — but then I noticed the napkin crudely tied around its matted collar.

A white napkin.

Our white napkin, from the Timber Ridge fight.

"A truce," I said.

Addie nodded. "He's done chasing us. He's got a mall to shoot up."

I glanced over at the Gasman. He watched us expectantly from the adjacent boardwalk, like he was awaiting our response. I'm no good at negotiation, so instead I just flipped him the most hateful middle finger I've ever wielded in my entire life.

He just stared back, unbothered.

I closed my eyes and wondered what was happening in the real world of 2015. If I'd reached the Timber Ridge parking lot yet. Maybe I was up on the JCPenney balcony right now, performing the Head-Scratching Rifle's tedious little pre-firing safety ritual. Checking the barrel for obstructions, scrutinizing the bolt, thumbing in the cartridges. Maybe the killing had already started. Maybe it was already over. Maybe I was in a police holding cell right now, splattered with drying, coppery blood and dead-eyed, while the Mosin Nagant was tagged and filed.

Maybe I'd never find out, I realized.

The orange tabby perked an ear and darted away on soft feet, and we watched it disappear into the coal-black guts of the maze. "I hate cats," Addie said, for what must've been the third or fourth time.

She'd always joked about housecats being servants of evil (granted, this one pretty much was) but I knew the real reason she disliked them so viscerally. One birthday, when she was five or six, her parents had bought her a kitten she named Penny. Late that night, she woke up to go to the bathroom and didn't see Penny follow her inside. She shut the door on its head. An hour later, they'd all piled into the car and driven to the emergency vet, and she watched her kitten die on a white table.

I guess hating cats was just how Adelaide coped with that.

The Gasman abruptly turned — peace talks concluded, apparently — and walked back into the darkness, vanishing into the fog machine-mist behind Louisiana Blood. Not so much obscured as evaporated. Leaving us alone on our dock.

"There he goes," I said.

She sagged against the wall beside me, deflating with a hopeless sigh. "Maybe we'll be here forever. You and me, Dan, at FrightFest 2011 forever. This'd be our Limbo, for all of God's eternity."

That used to be all I wanted. Be careful what you wish for, right?

"I don't really believe in it anyway," she added quickly.

"Really?"

"The rifle said so. No God."

"Doesn't the existence of a demonic rifle sort of . . . *imply* a God?"

"Not really," she said, her eyes glimmering with orange harbor lights, staring out at where the Gasman had disappeared. "It's just an extra-dimensional carnivore. Like a . . . a pitcher plant with tendrils that grow out into five dimensions, I guess. We can't even comprehend the shape of it, and it seemed pretty certain that there's no God. And I'm inclined to believe it."

"So what, then?"

"I don't know." She sniffed, resting her forehead on my shoulder. "Let's just . . . I don't know. Enjoy the moment. Enjoy meeting each other for the first time."

What's your name?

Dan.

Okay, Dan, for the record, the Total Darkness Maze is the stupidest Halloween attraction ever. It would have been cheaper to lock yourself in a coat closet while groping for a light switch. I'm not going back in there.

One by one, the Victorian streetlights on the shore fizzled out. Then the boardwalk's electricity cut out and the swamp-netted Louisiana Blood house went dark. The sky seemed to collapse in on us, a lowering ceiling, and I noticed the stars were dimming, graying out. Like sinking into deep water. My own shrinking universe.

I'm not going back into that maze. I'll puke again.

We have to. It's the only way back.

"I missed you," I said. "After New Year's, I mean."

She winced. "Sorry I drove drunk."

"It's okay."

The tidewater crackled below us and through the gaps in the floorboards I saw shingles of growing ice, thickening the waves into scales. They crunched and broke against the boardwalk piers, vibrating the wood under our feet.

"Dan?" She chewed her lip, watching the stars die above us. "You . . . mentioned that the little house in Butte was the first time you'd seen Holden's magic, multi-dimensional Ouija board. Right?"

"It sounds stupid when you say it like that, but yes."

"When did you see it next?"

"Only once."

"When?"

"2015. Our house. After you died. Holden brought it for my ghost hunt."

"So . . . it's a memory?"

I froze. Had it been?

I tried to recall my very first encounter with the Gasman, where reality and recollection first diverged, where the Head-Scratching Rifle first invaded my thoughts and wormed into my nervous system. I'd put the rifle to my chin and the insidious rifle made me pull the trigger, but my red-tipped round had misfired, ironically sparing us both. The front door opening itself. The footsteps into my dark living room. Flicking on the dining-room lights. And . . . seeing Holden's Ouija board on the table.

"It was the very first memory," I said. "I just didn't realize it."

"Not that it matters," she shrugged. "We can't go back."

I'm not going back into that maze.

It's the only way back. I'll lead you through. We'll retrace our steps through the stupid-ass Total Darkness Maze, feel our way back to the entrance, and we'll get you some water. Backward is forward.

I looked at her now. "Backward is forward."

"What?"

A slow, revelatory grin crept over my face. "We'll retrace our steps, Addie, because backward is forward."

Agreed. This maze blows.

She looked at me quizzically. "How?"

"We've been going backward in time, because we've been moving away from the Gasman. This entire chase, we've been retreating, avoiding him. Running the opposite way. So, to go forward in time, maybe all we need to do is retrace our steps."

"Toward the Gasman?"

I don't know if I can go back in, Dan.

We'll make it. Take my hand.

"Backward is forward," I said, holding out a hand. For a second, present and past achieved a strange synchronicity:

Backward is forward.

She took my hand, then and now. Forcing a weak smile.

In the dying starlight, I noticed something down on the floorboards, by her ankle. It was just an object, an object with no special powers or real significance, but seeing it froze the air in my lungs. Addie glanced down, too.

A bundle of FrightFest glow sticks. Green glow sticks.

She looked back at me, breathless.

Yes, we were doomed. I know. But we had to try.

"We'll return to that first memory in 2015." I knelt, scooped up the glow sticks and tore off their crinkling plastic wrappers. "We'll grab that Ouija board. We'll contact Holden, tell him to call the police and evacuate Timber Ridge. And we'll stop the mass shooting. We'll *stop it*, Addie. We'll save them."

"Dan, I don't know if—"

"We have to try."

"You're making a lot of assumptions—"

"We have to try, Addie."

We have to try.

Okay. Let's do it.

With the glow sticks in hand, I reopened the busted access door to the Total Darkness Maze. A splinter of wood labeled NOT AN EXIT DOOR clattered to the floor at our feet. A sprinkle of paint chips. Inky darkness within. In my original memory, the maze had been crowded with groping people and the firefly glow of cell phone lights — Holden was back there somewhere, and so was the sorority group Addie had come with — but now it was empty and silent. Like an airlock into the vacuum of space. An icy coldness exhaled through the doorway, and I shivered.

"Retrace our steps," I echoed.

"Alright, Dan." She shrugged. "Let's . . . save Timber Ridge."

We shared a smile — a knowing one. Even if there was still time, even if another copy of that spirit board was still back there, we didn't stand a chance. Our fates were already written. We were already a ghost story. We'd even been immortalized in W. Louis' book; we were the famous glow stick-carrying wraiths spotted by a Russian watchman in the Kalash armory—

We have to try.

"The Gasman," Addie fretted behind me. "He knows what you know. He'll backtrack. He'll destroy the Ouija board."

"So we'll hurry."

"Or he'll lay a trap—"

"We'll outsmart him."

"He lives in five dimensions."

"And he just recently figured out how to operate a *door*." I took the first tentative steps into the Total Darkness Maze, into the vicious coldness, with her fingers gripping my back. "Come on, Addie. Let's stop the shooting. And for Dyson, let's give the Head-Scratching Rifle something it's never had before."

"An easy meal?"

I kissed her, my teeth chattering. "A fight."

She smiled wearily.

Just hold my hand. Don't let go.

Okay.

I led us back into the stupid maze. Like before, I felt with one outstretched palm, touching the dangling rubber snakes and fake eyeballs, the patchwork of dollar-store Halloween nostalgia, and she followed with her hand on my back. Squeezing a fistful of my *Haunted* hoodie. I reminded her again not to let go, but I knew she wouldn't.

Keep breathing.

Walls, edges, and corners became indistinct, and the temperature plunged into something otherworldly, excruciating, hardening the moisture to scales on our eyes and lips. I could already tell it was working — backward was indeed forward — but there wasn't much time left. Minutes, maybe seconds. Maybe not enough.

What did you say your name was?

Dan.

Nice to meet you, Dan. I'm Adelaide.

Part III

THE BLOOD GUN

. . . Was it a ghost? A demon? A djinn or pagan deity? The real question isn't what kind of supernatural force was attached to the M91/30 Mosin Nagant known in some circles as the "Head-Scratching Rifle." Some, this author included, speculate that such answers exist beyond the edge of human comprehension.

The real question we should ask is this: what were its goals? Had it achieved them? What if its victims killed themselves willingly, out of selflessness, to render themselves useless to the machinations of this vicious and hateful entity? To spare the world from something much worse?

Excerpt from "Cursed Objects of the New Century" (W. Louis), published by Haunted Inn Press in 2002.

5 Minutes, 38 Seconds

I snapped the first glow stick, a hollow pop.

Addie gasped. "Oh my God."

My memories didn't all link up neatly like coupled cars on a train anymore. The Gasman must have terraformed them as he chased us, crushing times and places together to his liking. It was a claustrophobic mental meat grinder, a tunnel in perfect blackness and only now illuminated by the green glow I'd brought with us. A sickly whisper of light.

"Oh, God, oh, God . . ."

"Keep going."

The tunnel's floor was a flash-frozen stew of mismatched locales. I recognized the slippery bones of Mount St. Helens logs sealed in gray ash. Rumpled Basin State Fair stands, glazed and crunchy with ice. That spider monkey Christmas tree touched us with prickly fingers as we passed. Every memory was compressed into a landslide of jagged debris, and that debris formed walls and a descending ceiling, shrinking deeper and deeper into a cramped nightmare. A corridor of knife-edges. This was no environment for humans. Even the air was thin and hostile. I whiffed an alien sourness, like formaldehyde.

Addie clenched up behind me and gagged.

I pulled her along, holding the green stick forward like a lantern. "Don't stop. We can't stop."

"I can't do this, Dan."

"Yes, you can," I said. "If it makes you feel better, you're already dead."

"That does *not* help."

A deep-fryer vat banged at my feet, startling us. It was the one the Gasman had hurled at us, but it wasn't boiling hot anymore. Corndog grease congealed to the sides in brown warts. The cold had transformed everything. It pierced our clothes. Every inch of exposed skin stung. When I opened my mouth, my tongue froze to the back of my teeth.

"Dan," Addie said. "The light—"

The glow stick was already dimming in my hand. Absorbed by the frigid darkness enclosing from all sides—

I dropped it and snapped another. A fresh burst of green illuminated a narrowing passage, lined with crooked teeth of shattered wood. Hanging roof tiles, drenched in glittering icicles. A blocky GameStop sign from the mall, crumpled like an accordion.

"You always take me to the nicest places, Dan."

"You're welcome."

Boards creaked and popped underfoot. We stooped under the lowering ceiling, really an unnatural amalgamation of ceilings, leaking handfuls of gravel and plaster. A fluorescent light dangled by a veined cord. A Disappointment Bay Lighthouse pane warped somewhere like a big drum, and glass shards sprinkled on bathroom tile. Darkness ahead and darkness behind us, like we were carrying a weak lantern down a mine tunnel.

I glanced back to ensure we weren't being followed and realized with a sour tequila-shot of fear — we were on the wall, somehow. The mangled pathway had gradually corkscrewed, and the floor was now a wall, and still rotating up to the ceiling. Gravity was distorting. We followed this downward spiral the way captured matter encircles a black hole.

You've heard of the Scientific Method, right, Dan?

Echoes whispered in the darkness, cobwebs of memory. Like walking through rainclouds of half-remembered dialogue: *Oh my God. They're defenseless down there, handcuffed in the wild. They can't even pick up food—*

Cruelty is its language—

"I'm scared." Addie tightened her grip on my back, a hard squeeze. Her breath fogged the glow stick, diffusing the green light. Her whisper in my ear. "I guess . . . I guess I'm just afraid to be dead. I'm afraid of what it'll be like."

"Me, too," I admitted.

"How much time do we have?"

"Minutes. Maybe less."

We clambered over a glass retail counter, exploded by the temperature change, bristling with tagged pistols and revolvers. A bent jail-bar door hanging to the left, still holding a few crooked signs. I recognized that bumper sticker with the ghillie-suited sniper: REACH OUT AND TAPP SOMEONE. This was good. Joe's Guns was close to where it all began.

It's a blood gun. It's killed someone.

"I hope we die at the same time," Addie said. "Like, I hope it gets us at the same time. I don't want to die alone."

"You won't."

"It's just . . . dying always looked so *lonely* to me." She sniffed in the dimming green light, and I remembered her limp body in the crushed Mercedes, her skull deflated, the tubes hooked under her skin, the glimmering blue-white cubes of safety glass in her hair. "Because . . . because I know there's no God."

I snapped another glow stick. "Addie, there's a God."

"Stop, Dan. You heard it, too—"

"You believe that thing? Really?"

"Got a better source?"

"Addie, it's a bottom feeder." I ducked under a smashed car door sparkling with crystals. "It's bacteria. Growing on an antique rifle. For all we know, it's just one of the roaches that skittered under the fridge when God said *let there be light*. There's nothing to learn from it. It's a stupid, mindless piece of shit that only knows how to eat, and together, we're going to stop it."

She smiled as we went through the Gasman's playground, groping and pushing through a collage of destroyed memories. To our right, I glimpsed coffin-like forms in the darkness. Bathtubs of gun parts submerged in oil. A yellow flashlight strobed at us, and I saw the terrified eyes of a Soviet guard. Watching us detour right through his patrol at the Kalash armory in 1981.

I waved at the poor Russian. "Don't mind us. We're just passing through."

"You're doing a great job," Adelaide added.

Now the tunnel tightened into a crawlspace and I recognized wooden chairs thudding at my feet, white coffee mugs from Jitters. Dropped paper lanterns. Paul Bunyan's grinning, severed head, caged by two-by-fours. We were almost there. Almost.

I hoped there was still time.

I hate you, Dan. I'm sorry, but I hate you.

"Whatever happens, we'll go together," I told her. "You won't die alone. And afterward, I'll meet you at New Year's Eve. Okay?"

She nodded rapidly in the green light. "Okay."

"I'll see you there, Addie. In 2014."

"Deal."

Maybe I was lying, but it sounded right. If Hell was the past, maybe Heaven could be, too. I had no idea what we were in for. I didn't know if we could possibly halt the Timber Ridge shooting, or if it was already written into our tangled fates — but all you can do is try. I hoped to God we could save them.

"And Addie?"

"Yeah?"

"First, we're going to kick its ass."

NEW TEXT MESSAGE
SENDER: Unknown
SENT: 12:39 p.m. Mar 20 2015

TASTYTASTYTREATSFORMETASTYYESTHANK
YOUTASTYTASTYTASTYYESYUMTHANKYOU

3 Minutes, 49 Seconds

The tunnel opened on all sides into a vast emptiness. The ground panned and flattened under our feet, morphing into snow. Knee-deep snow, whipped into rolling permafrost waves. I couldn't see anything beyond our small radius of green light, but I could tell from how our voices thinned and carried; we'd entered a massive expanse of open ground. I heard distant winds, a throaty howl, but felt no breeze.

My mind scrambled — where was our house on the night of March 19, 2015? With the Ouija board? Had we missed that very first memory?

Addie shivered. "What is this place?"

"I don't know."

"The edge of the world?"

"I don't know."

I snapped another glow stick — my second-to-last — and hurled it high into the darkness. It arced a hundred feet, piercing the black like tracer fire, and . . . unexpectedly thudded off something.

Something huge.

Addie gasped.

As the glow stick dropped straight down, it threw green shadows, drawing contours of some hellish industrial machine, of struts, truss beams, and rigging cables, of rivets and plated joints pitted with rust. A towering metal creature that lived in this dark tundra. In the plunging green light I glimpsed the thing's long, railroad-trestle neck, and at the end, its 'head' — a massive, circular saw blade. Like a forty-foot band saw, lined with clawed steel buckets.

The glow stick landed in the snow with a soft plop.

It revealed a building at the foot of the eight-story industrial monster; a modest blue house frosted with ice. It was our home. Uprooted and carefully displaced here in a bleak arctic winter. And, if we stood the barest chance of contacting Holden before the Timber Ridge shooting, that Ouija board would still be inside. On the dining table.

"Trap," I said.

She nodded wearily. "*Totally* a trap."

But we kept going. No time for fear. There was enough space out here to run, but the snow was glazed with a thin skin of glittering ice, like an eggshell, and underneath it was strangely thick and sludgy. Molasses-like. Our shoes sank and slurped, as if jogging through a tar pit. My toes were numb, my calves burning. Every step was a heave.

"That's an excavating machine." Addie pointed up at the skeletal structure. "They used them at quarries, to dig tunnels for mines. I've seen photos of them."

I had, too. Most of it was cloaked in darkness; the surreal thing could've stretched on forever for all I knew. I had one final glow stick in my pocket, but I knew we'd need it inside the black memory of our house, coming closer with every step.

"Maybe . . . maybe the Soviets dug the demon up accidentally," Addie supposed. "In a gulag, a work-camp mine. It crawled out of the frozen earth and attached itself to a guard's Mosin Nagant—"

"Maybe."

"That explains the gas mask. Miners wear gas masks to—"

"Maybe," I said again. At this point, I didn't give a crap about the origin story. This thing was an asshole, and it wanted to murder a lot of people at Timber Ridge very soon. That was all I could be bothered to know.

Addie fell silent.

We came up to the memory of our house, a shadow lurking in the grim light of my half-buried glow stick. It was a blown-out wreck of the real thing; the roof sunken, the windows shattered, the siding peeling off like burnt skin. The front door hung ajar from a frost-warped doorframe, half-obscured by churned waves of snow. To our right, I spotted two lumped masses. My Celica and beside it, Holden's car. Dora the Explorer.

"Home, sweet home."

This was it. Our house, circa March 2015. The moment the Head-Scratching Rifle first dug its icy claws into my brain. The entry wound, you could call it.

"Wow." Addie touched the gutter, hanging like a chewed fingernail. "You really let the house go to hell after I died."

"You should see the dishes."

I pushed the front door, glazed with white bumps. It croaked open on squealing hinges, shedding flecks of ice. A claws-on-chalkboard squeal of audio static made us jump, and then the familiar home security system gasped through phlegm-clogged speakers: "Front . . . door . . . is . . . . ajar."

She looked at me now, steeling herself before entering our own haunted house, taking in a shivering breath. "Murdered by an extra-dimensional monster. Better than a drunk driver, I guess."

"It's no Velociraptor-mauling, but it'll do."

"*Utahraptor*, Dan."

"Whatever."

We went inside.

What's left to lose, right? I snapped my final glow stick there in our doorway. The doorway where we'd kissed goodbye every weekday before work, where I'd dented a wall moving a TV stand, where she'd told me with tears in her eyes that her grandfather had pneumonia. As we ventured into this alien mockery of that place, our footsteps creaking on deformed hardwood, my mind wandered back to Adelaide's half-spoken word back at Timber Ridge. Her mysterious little idea — something about my red-tipped cartridge — that she couldn't tell me, lest the Gasman find out.

An ammunition malfunction called a squi—

"Addie . . . you have a backup plan, don't you?"

She smiled guiltily in the green light. "A girl's got to have her secrets."

2 Minutes, 5 Seconds

"There it is."

The Ouija board was frozen to the dining table. The darkness inside the house was overpowering; a siphoning absence of light, like crawling through a shipwreck on the ocean floor. I held the glow stick out over the table like a lantern, weakly illuminating the debris of our ghost hunt — Holden's frosted laptop, the EMF meter, the audio recorder, the full-spectrum camera, scattered playing cards and two half-drunk homebrews. And centered on the table, in a rodent nest of oily shipping plastic, the Head-Scratching Rifle.

I touched the Ouija surface. Scorched letters under scaled ice.

Why had the Gasman left it intact? I'd expected to find the mirror board punched into splintered halves. Or to not find it at all. Hell, he'd *known* we were coming. He knew everything in my mind — like playing chess against yourself — and yet he'd politely left the all-important item untouched for us, right where it should be, out in the open. Why?

"Too easy," Addie said.

"No kidding."

"The tunnel, too. Like it led us here on purpose—"

I set the glow stick on the table and the dim light revealed a piggish face floating in the darkness. Rubber cheekbones and a snout. The Gasman was seated across the table. He'd been waiting for us. I recoiled with shock, and the goggled head swiveled to look at us. For a dumb moment, I half-expected the thing to speak.

Instead, the glow stick died.

"Oh, *shit.*"

A chair scooted. The Gasman was standing up.

In the pitch-blackness I slapped a hand to my pocket, but I already knew that'd been the last one. I was out of glow sticks. Beside me, I heard frantic jingling. Addie was rummaging through her purse.

I flinched, bracing for the roar of close-range gunshots, but instead heard . . . a soft threading sound. Like a plastic cap, unscrewing urgently in the darkness.

"Addie?"

She threw something. I heard a splash — it sounded like a water bottle thudding off the Gasman's big chest. The patter of droplets hitting the walls, drenching his wool greatcoat, clicking on his boots, pooling on the frozen floor—

"Addie, we tried that already. Water *doesn't work*— "

She flicked her Pac Man lighter. "That wasn't water."

* * *

A supernova of light.

I shielded my eyes, looking down, and recognized the plastic bottle rolling on the warped floor — Kale's bottle of tiki torch fuel (LJ's bottle, technically) from the New Year's Eve party. She must've found it back in the tunnel.

"Dan!" she screamed. "Grab the board—"

Her voice vanished under a whooshing roar. The dining room flashed over, a billowing tower of blue-orange flames, of liquid fire splashed onto walls, chairs, the counters and table. The Gasman was somewhere inside it, burning like the nuclear core of the sun, throwing waves of blinding, eye-watering heat. Our entire dining room looked like Kale Wong's face.

I pried the Ouija board off the tabletop, which was now soaked with burning fuel. "Nice trick. Got any more?"

"Just one."

"Hope it's a good one."

She smiled grimly in the orange light, as if to say: *It is.*

Then the Gasman came stomping through the firestorm at us, a charred shadow wearing a coat of flames. Sheets of frantic orange whipped off him. His breathing mask blistered with boiling paint, sizzling away, revealing cracks of white.

Addie aimed her Beretta, but I tugged her arm. "No. Outside—"

We raced through the kitchen, swinging left around the fridge and down the hallway, now roiling with smoke. The Ouija board clasped tight in my knuckles. My mind was already hurtling to the next phase of this crazy-stupid plan: we'd bolt back outside into the tundra, gain some distance between us and the Gasman, and use the board to contact Holden, to urge him to call 911 before—

Addie screamed.

A figure blocked our front doorway, a tall man in blue warehouse coveralls. The lye-drinking forklift driver. His lips and lower jaw were rotted down to a white mandible bone. His guts drooped out of his exposed ribs, his soured flesh sloughing like molten cheese, a hanging, sloppy mess of loose intestines and soaked fabric.

She slammed the door in its face. "Getting *real tired* of this shit."

The Gasman rounded the kitchen corner behind us, his ghoulish mask and shoulders still furiously ablaze. His boots were melting; his footprints were pools of bright fire. Although I don't think the fire really injured him, it at least made him easier to track. Like being chased by a lighthouse.

"Upstairs," I said.

"Okay."

She fired a shot over her shoulder as we raced up the distorted staircase. We took a hard right, coughing on smoke, and crashed into our bedroom. I slammed the door behind us. No lock, so I tipped our oak dresser. It banged on the doorknob.

Addie passed me the lighter. "Hurry."

We'd bought a few precious seconds. I slammed Holden's mirror board down to the frozen carpet and flipped it right-side-up. The lighter flame wavered in my fingers, barely illuminating the etched alphabet. I fumbled for the all-important planchette, our last hope to contact Holden, to evacuate Timber Ridge and mobilize the police to—

It wasn't there.

"Oh, no."

Addie turned. "What?"

"No, *no, no*—"

The Ouija planchette was missing. It had been missing all along. I hadn't noticed this back when I'd grabbed the board, but the Gasman must've taken it, or destroyed it, long before we'd arrived here. That was the trick. The trap. The Gasman's insurance plan. It had all seemed too easy *because it was*—

THUD. THUD. He climbed the stairs, coming for us.

Addie looked at me, clasping her hands to her mouth. "Oh, God, really?"

I punched a wall, hard as granite.

"Really? After *all that*?"

Yes, it was all lost, because the Gasman had reached the Ouija board first. Because he was inside my mind, and the *instant* I'd devised this plan with Addie, he had it, too. You can't beat yourself at chess. Just like that, in a single chancy instant, our hope had evaporated. I was a murderer, evil had prevailed, and everyone in the Timber Ridge food court was now doomed. About to die by my trigger finger, down the oily sights of that cursed Mosin Nagant.

Just . . . like . . . that.

I remembered her mystery *squi-* word and looked at her. "Please. Tell me your backup plan will—"

"It won't."

"*What?*"

"It won't work."

"You told me it was a good one—"

"And I'm telling you now it *won't work*, Dan." Her voice broke. "We had to save Timber Ridge first."

And we'd failed.

I imagined the Saturday afternoon murder spree. High-caliber bullets punching through bodies, eye sockets and upraised hands, cracking bone and ripping skin, splattering sandwiches and noodle bowls off tables, kicking up jets of koi water. My own thoughtless hands, cranking the Mosin bolt through wisps of smoke — up, back, forward, down — ejecting hot brass and thumbing fresh rounds by the handful, a grim rhythm of five-round salvos. Fire, load. Fire, load.

Something rattled in the bedroom closet.

Addie raised her Beretta. "Did you hear that?"

The closet door chattered again, urgently. Something thumped inside it like a sack of meat, jangling plastic hangers.

She backed away, her finger on the trigger. "What now?"

I had no idea. But honestly, what did it matter now? I slumped against our bed and watched the bi-fold doors scrape open. First the right, then the left. Then a broken figure slid out of the darkness and came for me, slouching closer in the firelight. I saw blood-drenched denim, sloped shoulders, skin withered to beef jerky. The face was deflated, like an empty Halloween mask. I recognized it from earlier. Yes, Addie's comparison had been apt; the flaps of unfurled skin definitely did resemble an opened banana peel.

It reached for me with crunchy fingers.

51 Seconds

The corpse turned its hand over. A planchette in its palm.

A Ouija planchette, sludgy with congealed deep-fryer grease from the Basin State Fair. Recovered in secret, perhaps, when the Gasman hadn't been looking. Offered now on outstretched fingers, held toward me in the wavering orange light. For a stunned half-breath I just stared at it.

Addie poked me. "Grab it, dumbass."

So I did.

Thank you.

Because this was the ghost of Nikolai What's-His-Name, the worker from the nineties who'd come within a single serial digit of smelting the Head-Scratching Rifle into a molten puddle. He'd been *so* achingly close, and his reward had been a vodka-soaked nap on railroad tracks. He'd been the closest anyone had ever come to interfering with the Head-Scratching Rifle's dark plans. Until now, as Addie had said.

Until us.

Thank you, Nikolai. And . . . I'm sorry I never remember your last name.

The Gasman's gloved fist punched through the bedroom door, showering us with wood chips, and I hit my knees and placed the planchette on the board. As Addie stood up, throwing the hair from her eyes and aiming her Beretta at the door in a bladed shooting stance, I traced a grinding pattern on the Ouija surface, over and over. Just us, just Adelaide and me, two ghosts relaying a final, desperate message to Holden, spelled one frustrating letter at a time:

TIMBERRIDGE
MASSSHOOTING
CALL911—

The lighter flame flickered out in my hands. Darkness again. But as the Gasman's other hand broke through the door, Addie's Beretta barked, and like navigating by lightning, I used her muzzle flashes:

EVACUATETIMBERRIDGE
THIRDFLOORBALCONY
EVACUA—

30 Seconds

Pain.

Blinding pain.

I hit my knees, slapping a hand to my throat, pierced by a burning javelin. Blood, boiling hot, squirting between my fingers and drenching my shirt. The Mosin Nagant dropped and clattered on bone-white tile, bouncing once. Twice.

Timber Ridge.

This was Timber Ridge.

This was the real world. March of 2015, present day, just north of Boise, Idaho. Being back in it was like climbing out of a swimming pool after hours of weightless floating. My eardrums pressurized. I recognized the bass echo of a gunshot. It raced a hundred feet from wall to wall of the food court, rattling off plate glass and marble, shivering department store mannequins.

Then came the screams. A rising chorus of terror. Chair legs scraping, shoes squeaking, soft drinks dropping and splashing.

As I fell away from the glass balcony railing (the third floor, near the entrance to JCPenney, just as we'd expected) I caught a blinking freeze-frame of the dispersing crowd below. At least a hundred shoppers, parents, teens, toddlers, employees with nametags, all ducking and panicking, scattering like pigeons. And one cop — standing by the koi pond — with his Glock in two knuckled hands, looking back up at me. It was almost fifty yards between us, a hell of an iffy distance for a pistol shot, but I knew he'd been the one. He'd been the one who spotted me shouldering the Mosin Nagant, drawn his own sidearm, and plugged me in the neck. Only one shot had been fired here today, and it was his. Not mine.

Good job, I managed to think. *Damn good shot.*

I hope they give you a medal—

I landed on top of the Head-Scratching Rifle and my forehead banged on tile. My skull made a jarring, rattling thud, like a cabinet full of glassware. A concussion of flashbulbs behind my eyes. It didn't hurt, though. My pain threshold was already occupied. All I felt was that fiery javelin pole under my chin, and a rising swell of blood in my throat.

The cop shouted something downstairs. It sounded vaguely familiar, like dialogue from an action movie.

Okay.

Coppery blood swished between my teeth. I tried to inhale but coughed out a furious red splash. My heartbeat jackhammered in my neck. And more blood raced between my clamped fingers, spurting in rhythmic beats, like hot water. I was draining out, leaking, dying, and that was perfectly fine.

Okay, okay.

I reached for the Head-Scratching Rifle.

Just one last thing.

I lifted the weapon into my lap. Leaving bloody fingerprints, I unlatched the bolt and an intact, store-bought 7.62x54R round twirled out. Plus five in the magazine. All six bullets, unfired. Jesus Christ, we'd really done it. We'd saved them all. The only casualty of 2015's

251

attempted Timber Ridge shooting would be me, Dan Rupley, local TV ghost hunter, and that was just fine.

Because before I died here on this balcony, I'd take the Head-Scratching Rifle with me. I'd press the barrel to the floor, yank the trigger, and let it explode in my arms. Turn it to shrapnel. Even if yesterday's red-tipped bullet had been a misfire due to contaminated gunpowder, by God, I wouldn't fail this time. I'd send it to Hell. I'd be the curse's final victim.

More voices below. More first-responders flooding into the food court. This was good — Holden had received my Ouija message and called the authorities to Timber Ridge, averting disaster by seconds — but also very, very bad. The cops were closing in and I had to finish this before I died. I had to fire the Mosin into the tile floor, to end this now. Or else the weapon would just be carried away and tagged, and hibernate in a police evidence room somewhere, and grow another lucid tendril to infect someone else's mind, and continue the decades-long cycle of ruined lives—

"Gun! He's still got it!"

More shots whip-cracked from downstairs and the balcony railing exploded into kernels of blue-white glass. I rolled over, peppered by shards and gouged plaster. A bullet pinged off the metal handrail by my cheek. A vivid flash of sparks stung my eyes.

"Drop the gun. Drop it!"

Nope.

I closed the Head-Scratching Rifle's bolt, chambering the next round. The downstairs gunshots sounded so weak and faraway now, like someone down the street was hammering nails. I braced the weapon under my arm, pressing the muzzle flat to create a seal against the crunchy floor, and groped for the trigger. My thoughts almost fell out of my brain but I held on, for just a second or two more. That was all I'd need.

We stopped it, Addie.

For a terrifying moment, I couldn't find the trigger guard. Then my rubber fingers thudded against it, all pins and needles, and I found the bladed trigger, and pulled it with my thumb, my head lolling back to face Timber Ridge's Idaho skylight. An indifferent little glimpse of blue sky. My nervous system thickened, my brain depressurized like an airlock emptying its contents into space . . .

We did it.

Pull . . . pull . . . the ancient Russian trigger felt miles long. My joints were spaghetti but I kept pulling, kept outrunning my own failing body, feeling the aged metal creak and contract, less than a millimeter now, just fractions of fractions, a shrinking sliver of a second away from firing a bullet into the floor and exploding the hateful thing in my arms . . .

I'll find you again, Addie.

At New Year's Eve.

Because we share the same atoms. I'll always find you. We'll always feel that tug that pulls us together—

But I noticed something.

The skylight.

Blinking away sweat, blood, and plaster dust, I squinted up into the cavernous ceiling, wracked my darkening thoughts, and realized . . . yes, that was it . . . the Idaho-shaped skylight was incorrect. It had only been shaped as Idaho (the *Sky-dick*) up until the summer of 2014. That was when, Holden once told me, the mall's owner finally caved in to public ridicule and redesigned it to include four or five states, the greater inland northwest. I knew this. I was absolutely certain. The skylight was wrong. As the headshot corpse of Ben Dyson once told me atop a freezing lighthouse, everything this entity knows is taken secondhand, because *evil is unimaginative.*

I realized what this meant, and my heart plunged.

Oh, God, no.

This wasn't real.

This wasn't the real Timber Ridge. This was just a dream, another car on the train of thoughts, an artificial one assembled from fragments of my memories. A distraction.

The Head-Scratching Rifle had tricked me.

(?) Minutes, (?) Seconds

In reality, I never even reached the Timber Ridge Mall.

I don't remember doing this, but based on the mileage on my Celica, I'd driven most — if not all — of the way there, with the Mosin Nagant and over a hundred bullets boxed in my passenger seat. Perhaps I'd even made it to within eyeshot of Timber Ridge's three-floor cement parking garage, where a cop flashed his lightbar and parked sideways to block the entrance ramp. On the east and south sides of the complex, by the Chili's and Red Robin, an exodus of confused shoppers funneled out through the double doors. Black Friday played in reverse.

So yes, Addie and I did it.

We'd still prevented the mass shooting and saved scores of lives. We'll never know how many seconds it came down to. But after the Ouija message and Holden's active-shooter 911 call, we'd rendered the Timber Ridge Mall an inaccessible target, locked down tight and swarming with AR-15's and radios. I guess the entity still had options — I could've rolled down a window and taken pot shots at the evacuating masses, or strolled next door into an Olive Garden and opened fire on the lunch rush.

But the Head-Scratching Rifle is petulant and vengeful. Hit it, and it hits back. Like a child throwing a tantrum in a Toys"R"Us, a furious spasm of blind, inarticulate rage. And it never forgets those who inconvenience it, or dare to stand against it. Like poor Nikolai What's-His-Face, pressing his ear to the railroad tracks in 1996. We'd ruined the demon's masterpiece, and now it needed to punish us.

So somewhere on Interstate 7, my hands twisted the wheel and flipped my Celica into a one-eighty. A squeal of rubber. I turned around, putting Timber Ridge in my rearview mirror, and raced back northbound.

Back to Farwell.

* * *

Somewhere real and unreal, existing outside of time, our house burned. Tumbleweeds of fire raced up the walls — blistering wallpaper, igniting framed photos, blackening our smiling faces at Reno, Maui, and Mount St. Helens. Erasing our life together, turning memories to ash. Scorching away all of her belongings I'd been too weak to box up.

We huddled now in our bedroom, backed into a corner, choking on mouthfuls of hot smoke. Our dresser, nightstand, and bedframe were tipped against the broken door, and the Gasman huffed and paced outside, an enraged shadow backlit by a corridor of flames. He reared back and kicked the barricade again, showering us with wood chips.

Addie brushed a splinter from her hair. "He's pissed."

"Good."

"I think we did it, Dan."

But had we really? I didn't think so. I was still alive somewhere in the real world of 2015, still possessed and armed with the Head-Scratching Rifle. The entity had been trying to distract me with that false victory at the counterfeit Timber Ridge. To keep me from doing something. But *what?*

"No," I said. "It's not over."

She smiled grimly. "Just . . . trust me, okay?"

"You're not real."

"I keep telling you I am." She glanced down at her Beretta, slide-locked and empty on the frozen carpet, a mischievous smile flickering on her face. "And now . . . now I think I have a way to prove it—"

The Ouija board scraped between us. The planchette darted from letter to letter, spelling my best friend's panicked message:

DANYOURCARISINMYDRIVEWAY.

* * *

Holden's front doorknob is broken off. I must've tried bashing the door with the Head-Scratching Rifle's butt stock before noticing the living room window.

It's shattered. That's how I got inside his house. A puddle of glimmering shards on the green carpet, crunched to smaller fragments by my footsteps. As I mantled through, I must've slashed my palm on the jagged frame, leaving a warm handprint of DNA evidence on the murder scene.

Inside the little house, details are harder to reconstruct. I know Holden had spotted my Celica in his driveway, and likely watched me break in. Maybe he briefly attempted to reason with me. Some of his roommates' hardbound law textbooks were off the shelf; perhaps he'd hurled them at me before fleeing through his kitchen, out the laundry-room door, and into the backyard.

Not fast enough.

I followed with the oily Head-Scratching Rifle in my hands. Thumbing cartridges into the breech, passing the Ouija board on Holden's coffee table while the planchette frantically skittered: RUNRUNRUN—

* * *

—RUNRUN, I traced, but Addie grabbed my wrist. "It's fine."

"I'm going to kill him—"

"It's fine."

"Addie, I'm going to *fucking kill him*—"

"Holden is fine," she hissed. "Trust me."

I looked at her.

Because Adelaide Lynne Radnor, the girl I shared atoms with, was suddenly a stranger again. And now, under a ceiling of rolling flames, she fought tears, reached forward, and squeezed both of my hands. Her forehead pressed to mine. The crackle of charcoal and fire, the Gasman snarling and tearing pieces off the barricade, all the chaos bled away and I only heard her shaky voice, floating on shallow breaths: "I have . . . I have a confession to make. It was never about the shopping mall."

"*What?*"

"You were fighting for Timber Ridge. But I was fighting for you, Dan. For the rest of your life." She smiled, her eyes brimming with firelight. "And now . . ."

The Gasman punched through the stacked furniture behind us. A dresser drawer banged to the carpet. I glimpsed his big hand gripping the bedframe and hurling it aside, his boneless fingers jellylike, squelching and leaking through charred gloves. Like five slugs sizzling in a campfire.

I looked back at her. "And now what?"

Her jaw curled, pinching, her face turning red.

"And now *what*, Addie?"

"Remember your exploding bullet?"

"Yeah?"

"Let's just say . . . it worked."

"But it didn't," I said. "It misfired—"

She shook her head, still smiling that strange, heartbroken smile, her tears mixing with ash to blacken her cheeks, and as the furious Gasman threw our nightstand against the wall and came stomping toward us, she reached for the Ouija board. With a trembling fingernail, she tapped a letter.

"Great job," she told me. "You did it."

The letter was B.

* * *

Holden ran into his backyard but barely made it past the woodpile. He wasn't a runner. He'd fumbled his keychain inhaler somewhere in the weeds. No time to grab it. The two acres were forested but the paper birch trees were too thin for cover. I must've halted in the house's back doorway — half inside the laundry room, half out — when I shouldered the Mosin Nagant and aligned the iron sights on my best friend's back.

I squeezed the trigger.

The hammer released.

The firing pin struck the primer.

And the Head-Scratching Rifle exploded in my hands like a nail bomb.

(?) Minutes, (?) Seconds

Addie's mystery word?

S-Q-U-I-B.

Apparently the full term is 'squib-fire.' It's an extremely dangerous malfunction caused when a round misfires without enough force to launch the projectile all the way down the barrel. So it gets halfway through and wedges there. I didn't know this, but Addie did — that yesterday's red-tipped bullet hadn't quite failed. It had misfired, yes, but in doing so, it became an airtight blockage inside the Mosin Nagant, as silent and lethal as a blood clot.

Like Dyson said, our battle with the Head-Scratching Rifle was really a chess game against myself. Only Adelaide knew there was a landmine hidden on the board. I should've figured — back in my dining room, when I'd watched my reflection raise the rifle and unsuccessfully pull the trigger, I'd feared that the bullet was in my brain. It was actually just a few inches down the rifle's barrel.

Guess what happens if you fire another bullet?

The blast sprawled me back into Holden's laundry room, pierced the door with jagged shards, and blew out a window. An abrasive storm of splintered wood and bladed metal. Gritty fragments sprinkled around me and suddenly I was staring dumbly upward through wisps of smoke, half-inside, half-out. Half of a watery, white sky, half of a stucco ceiling. Half-alive, half-dead, slipping under the rhythm of deepening waves.

We did it.

We saved Timber Ridge.

We pissed it off. And in its rage, it forgot its pre-firing safety check.

And it blew itself up, just like my original plan.

Well, almost like my original plan.

Holden came running, his footsteps soundless. His eyes widened when he saw my injuries. Not good news. But not a surprise, either. He fell to a crouch in the smoky doorway, hands closing into trembling fists, and his lips moved soundlessly. He was saying something to me. I guess whoever said hearing is the last to go is wrong.

Oh my God, Addie, we actually did it.

He grabbed my shoulders and propped me up against the washing machine. My head lolled and I saw my jeans were blackened with shiny blood. A warm pool spread beneath me, steaming in the crisp air. He mashed 911 on his phone, but his battery was dead. I tried to work my lungs and tell him it was fine, that I was fine, that everything had (accidentally) gone according to plan. That my red-tipped exploding cartridge had worked beautifully — but in an unexpected way. That the infamous, decades-old Head-Scratching Rifle had crossed oceans, picked human minds apart like delicacies, witnessed the Second World War and the fall of the Soviet Union . . . only to get distracted by us, forget its little safety ritual, and blow itself up in a backyard in Farwell, Idaho—

We got you, you son of a bitch—

—And in doing so, it must have released something akin to an electromagnetic pulse. The way the Gasman absorbed warmth and electricity in my memories demanded an equal and opposite reaction, I guess, so a bizarre surge of stored energy was violently discharged when the Head-Scratching Rifle exploded. Holden's phone was instantly bricked. So was mine. His neighbor's home theater system was fried, as was a power transformer and the AT&T cellular tower up the hill.

But we didn't know any of that yet. Holden dropped his phone and looked at me, eyes wide and glassy blue. I read his lips: "Stay, Dan."

Apparently I was leaking quarts of blood through my stomach. Bummer. He clasped my hands to the wound but my fingers slid right off. Why bother? Mission accomplished. The curse was over. I was done here.

I'll meet you there, Addie.

Holden was screaming silently into my face: "Dan. Stay with me. Stay with me—"

I tried to shake my head but I was sinking deeper into my own skull. My retinas bloomed. I felt my last breaths depressurizing through my teeth, a peaceful release. Falling away, back to her.

"Stay, Dan—"

But I was going.

"Please don't go—"

I was gone.

* * *

I reached the staircase just as the first firework launched over the glassy surface of Lake Paiute and ignited. A burst of violet filled LJ's lake house with racing shadows. On the landing below, I heard the muffled chatter of friends, Snow Patrol, and boozy laughter from the card game in the kitchen.

Down the stairs.

To the living room, where I'd found her before by a fireplace of flickering candles. Where she'd be waiting for me now, in the final moments of our last year together. And I couldn't wait to see her again. I imagined her fidgeting with that yellow dress, nursing the wine glass that killed her, stressing about the birthmark on her collarbone.

Another flash of blue-white, and I stepped out into the living room, searching the kaleidoscopic darkness, scanning faces to find her. She wasn't there.

"Addie?"

The foyer was nearby so I went there. I wasn't worried yet; I'd taken some weird detours through time and memory. But I'd found her here, at New Year's Eve, and now we could be together forever in this lake house built atop a shelf of limestone, because *we share the same atoms, and we'll always feel that pull—*

She wasn't in the foyer, either.

I checked everywhere. The dining room. The balcony. Even the upper bedrooms. Panic rising now.

"Addie!"

I was knocking on the bathroom door when a hand touched my shoulder. I turned and recognized one of her work friends from Cubek — a tall, spectacled girl named Jamie. Another fireburst of red colored her chipmunk smile, and then Jamie leaned in close, her lips to my ear as the music kicked up, and said something utterly devastating:

"She'll be right back, Dan. She just drove home to get her charger."

* * *

I woke up in the passenger seat of Dora, Holden's stupidly-named Ford Explorer, halfway to Sacred Family Hospital. He'd stuffed me into it, the seatbelt gripping my neck, the upholstery clammy with blood. I glanced around the vehicle in groggy horror, certain this was another dreamscape; another conjured hallucination, like Timber Ridge. I hadn't expected this. I'd assumed my shrapnel injuries were fatal, that I'd finally be joining Adelaide in death.

They weren't.

For a long time, we drove in silence.

Holden eyed Farwell's clock tower as we crossed the intersection on Main. "You beat it," he said, pointing.

"What?"

"You beat it."

"Beat what?"

"The rifle's curse. You know . . . the twenty-four hour record."

"Oh." I leaned my forehead against glass and watched coffee stands and discount stores blur past. "I had help."

We didn't speak at all for the rest of the drive.

They were stapling my stomach shut in the ED with a gadget that looked like a handheld sewing machine when it finally hit me; that I was still alive and she wasn't. That this was real, she was gone, she was really gone, and when tomorrow came, she would still be gone. I cried for three hours, a pressurized outpour of raw hurt. Like being electrocuted, raking every muscle in my body. It went on and on. Because Adelaide Lynne Radnor, the beautiful, superstitious girl who hated cats and lemon bars, who loved *Dirty Dancing*, who wrote software code but always wished to be a veterinarian instead, who accidentally murdered twenty-six lobsters with me on the Oregon coast in 2013, was really, truly gone.

I had to lose her twice, I think, to really *lose* her.

Northern Idaho

March 25, 2015

We scoured Holden's backyard for pieces of the Head-Scratching Rifle, collecting every last shard and splinter in a plastic bucket, and then we drove fifteen miles north to the White River. There, we descended a bank of slippery rocks and hurled every last fragment into the moving gray water. Five or six big splashes and sprinkling handfuls of little ones. The current carried away the ripples. In thirty seconds it was all done.

Kind of poetic, I supposed. This cursed weapon had infiltrated minds and crafted seven decades of grisly suicides.

And we'd tricked it into committing suicide, itself.

My mind was still thick with codeine, so maybe I was seeing poetry where none existed. Forty-six stitches, nine staples, and a concussion. But I hadn't lost any fingers or eyes to the explosion. It would take three full weeks for cellular service to return to the local area, and our phones were still bricked. This was actually a very good thing, since Holden had made a false-alarm 911 call with his.

On our way back up the moss-covered rocks, he smacked my back and asked if I finally believed in ghosts now. It was just a joke, and the extra-dimensional entity attached to the Head-Scratching Rifle wasn't really a ghost anyway.

But Addie had given me no choice. By supplying the first few letters of a word I only learned afterward via Google (*squi-*), she'd proven herself to be more than just my imagination. Ben Dyson had been right about a lot of things, but he'd been wrong about her. She wasn't a goldfish in a bag. She was real. She'd really been there with me, in my memories, embarking on one more adventure with me. Our last night. The squib-fire was just another card she'd held in her hand, concealed even from me, and this ramification was the beautiful final reveal. Say what you will about abrasive, know-it-all Adelaide — she's a planner. She's a thinker. She saved me.

She's my ghost.

Maybe I was her unfinished business.

I shrugged, hands in my pockets, as we crossed the gravel road and returned to his Explorer. "Ghosts, yes."

"Great." He unlocked the passenger door for me. "Let's talk about Bigfoot."

"You did *not* see Bigfoot."

"I did."

"Ghosts are real. Bigfoot is not."

He stomped the gas, skidding southbound. "Baby steps, Dan."

Speaking of, Addie's parents came and went from Birmingham and I still have custody of the savannah monitor. I can't say I've emotionally bonded with Baby — she's not exactly a golden retriever — but our pet/owner relationship has improved. She's a living, breathing headstone for Adelaide, waddling around the house on crocodile feet, and I've accepted it. You can't give it away, but you can't build a shrine around it, either. You just have to share your space with it, and feed it a dead mouse every two days.

Use tongs.

And yes, I'm back on *Haunted*, because motion is life. As of this writing, we're up for a regional Emmy and scored a new timeslot in what the TV station calls "weekday prime access" (also known as 7 p.m.). Darby is an on-air investigator now. Two new HD cameras grace our fleet, plus sturdier boom microphones and a revamped website. This year's season finale, we investigate the hotel they filmed *The Shining* in. Check it out.

And in exchange for my renewed loyalty, LJ enlisted the technical wizardry of Kale (whose burnt face is fully healed now) to perform a special favor for me. He accomplished what the teenagers at the Apple Store couldn't — he extracted the data from my EMP-fried phone and accessed the text messages I'd received over those strange, dark hours between March 19 and 20. Naturally, I used them as little timecodes in the writing of this memoir; my best guesses at chronological landmarks.

And, as we discovered, I'd received one more text.

It was from her.

NEW TEXT MESSAGE
SENDER: Unknown
SENT: 1:06 p.m. Mar 20 2015

Hey Dan.

I'm sorry I had to leave the party without saying goodbye. I wish I could have stayed.

But I can't do anything more. It's all you now. I wish I could fix you, make you happy again, but only you can do that.

I don't know how to say this, but here it goes: I love you. I've loved you since before we ever met. Every day, I thank God that I was brave enough to venture back into that lame-ass Total Darkness Maze with you. Maybe someday we'll get to be those kids again.

But, for now . . .

Just, well, do me this last favor: please stop trying to live in the past.

I'm not there anymore.

A

THE END

Thank you for reading this book. If you enjoyed it please leave feedback on Amazon, and if there is anything we missed or you have a question about then please get in touch. The author and publishing team appreciate your feedback and time reading this book.

Our email is jasper@joffebooks.com

www.joffebooks.com

Taylor Adams directed the acclaimed short film *And I Feel Fine* in 2008 and graduated from Eastern Washington University with the Excellence in Screenwriting Award and the prestigious Edmund G. Yarwood Award. His directorial work has screened at the Seattle True Independent Film Festival and his writing has been featured on KAYU-TV's Fox Life blog. He has worked in the film/television industry for several years and lives in Washington state.

Also available by Taylor Adams:
EYESHOT

Follow him on Twitter @tadamsauthor, find him on Facebook at www.facebook.com/tayloradamsauthor, and check out his author page at www.tayloradamsauthor.com

Made in the USA
Middletown, DE
28 May 2023